BANGSHIFT

SKID ROW KINGS
BOOK 3

WINTER TRAVERS

Copyright © 2016 Winter Travers
ISBN-13: 978-1539377054
ISBN-10: 1539377059
BangShift: Skid Row Kings, Book 3
Editor: Jennifer Severino @ Twitching Pen Editing
Cover Designer: Melissa Gill @ MGBookCoverDesigns
Cover Photographer: Reggie Deanching
Cover Model: Adrian Boomer Michalewicz

For questions or comments about this book, please contact the author at
wintertravers84@gmail.com

The Devil's Knights Series:
Loving Lo
Finding Cyn
Gravel's Road
Battling Troy
Gambler's Longshot
Keeping Meg
Fighting Demon

Skid Row Kings Series:
DownShift
PowerShift
BangShift

TABLE OF CONTENTS

<u>Coming Soon</u>
<u>About the Author</u>

DEDICATION

It's not the speed you go, rather the fact you went.

This is for everyone who went, and didn't look back.

Acknowledgments

My boys. With each book, the more I realize how much I love you both. Thanks for putting up with my crazy ways.

My family. Looooove you all!

Lizette. #RideOrDie We can't stop, we won't stop. (Yes, I just quoted Miley Cyrus. LMAO)

Nikki, Natalie, Kendra, and Alicia. Thanks for being my cheering squad. Much love! #BodaciousBetas

BangShift

Skid Row Kings
Book 3

CHAPTER 1

Leelee

"Ma'am, I'm going to have to ask you again to put your phone away. We're about to take off." Flight attendant Barbie glared at me as she motioned for me to turn it off. I could tell her patience was all but non-existent, but I didn't give a fuck right now.

"I just need to try one more time to—" I gasped as the ballsy flight attendant grabbed my phone from me and crossed her arms over her chest.

"I know you might not care about the safety of everyone on this plane, but I do. If you continue to use your phone, I'm going to have to notify the air marshal."

"Well, seeing as you just snatched my phone from me, it appears that won't be a problem anymore," I snapped. I was at my wit's end trying to figure out what the hell was going on. I couldn't get a hold of Luke or Mitch and Violet and Scarlett both had their phones turned off. "Can I please have my phone back? I promise not to crash the plane by sending a text message."

She thrust my phone back at me and flounced down the aisle back to the area where they served their little drinks from. I quickly hit send on my last message to Luke then powered down my phone.

It was six A.M., and I was on a plane about to take off for California to help the man who had saved my life not so many months ago, but who now hated me. To say my life was complicated was a bit of an understatement.

"First time to California?" the guy seated next to me asked. His dark blue pinstripe suit was rumpled, and he looked like he had been awake for six hours.

"Um, yeah. That obvious?" It was my first time flying, but I didn't want to admit that. There weren't too many people who had reached the age of twenty-six and hadn't flown before.

"Nah, I just like to make conversation. Helps the flight go by faster." He pulled his laptop out of his slim briefcase and set it on his lap. "Visiting family?"

Jesus Christ, wouldn't you know the last ticket to California was seated next to Motormouth Marty. "Um, yeah." I could technically say Kurt was family, although I'm sure he would argue 'til he was blue in the face that just because we were married didn't make us family. But that didn't apply to the state of Illinois, though.

"Man, I wish I could remember what it's like to travel for fun. Nowadays, I'm on a plane as much as I'm on the ground."

"Yeah, that must be rough." I wished like hell I could bury my nose in my phone and not have to talk to this guy. I had a three-hour flight ahead of me that I was already dreading. Add in this tool, and I would be amazed if I were sane by the time I landed.

"I can still remember the first time I went to California. I was amazed how green everything was, but when I got in the big city, I couldn't believe how much concrete there was everywhere. Although, you'll have that no matter what big city you go to."

Suit kept droning on and on, not waiting for me to answer or reply. I closed my eyes and leaned my head against the headrest, willing myself to fall into a coma for at least three hours.

"Ladies and gentlemen, this is your Captain speaking. I'd like to welcome you aboard flight 5462. Non-stop to Burbank California. At this time, we will be putting on the seat belt light, and we ask you not to move about the cabin until we are at cruising altitude. Sit back and relax. We should be in sunny California in three hours."

I leaned over, rummaged through my purse, and pulled out my headphones I had thankfully remembered to grab.

As I popped them onto my ears, a flight attendant stood at the front of the plane demonstrating the seat belts and what to do if we crashed. My stomach was in knots, worried about Kurt but also because this was my first time flying and I had no idea what to expect. I was anxious on top of concerned. A winning combination for a first-time flyer.

I snapped my belt into place, making sure it was extra tight and took a deep breath. I was headed to California to help a man who hated me. This was exactly how I had seen my day going. Not.

The flight attendant scurried off to what I assumed was her seat up by the captain, and the plane started to move. I gripped the armrest and glanced out the window. I had been lucky enough to get a window seat, although I was rethinking my luck as the plane made a wide U-turn and then started down the runway. The plane picked up speed fast, and before I knew it, the nose of the plane lifted, and my stomach went to my knees as we climbed into the sky. It took everything I had not to start hyperventilating and clutch onto Suit's hand.

The seat belt light went off, and the pilot's voice came over the speaker again telling us it was safe to move about the cabin.

Move? Hell no. I stabbed at my phone, trying to find a song that would distract me. I scrolled through my huge playlist and settled on Stone Sour to keep me company during the long flight. I glanced over at Suit, saw he was typing away on his laptop and was thankful he had gotten the hint I wasn't up to talking. He seemed like a nice guy, but I just didn't have time for small talk. At least, not today.

The last time I had seen Kurt played through my head and I couldn't help but wince remembering his face when his eyes had fallen on the date I had brought. Why the hell I had thought bringing Greg to the barbecue was a good idea? Kurt and I were already at each other's throats; me bringing Greg was the final straw that had driven Kurt away.

I closed my eyes and rested my head on the window. I didn't know what the hell to do anymore. What I had told Violet and Scarlett that night was the most truthful I had ever been about Kurt. I had messed up things between the two of us before we ever actually began. Things had happened so fast between us, and they were over even faster.

Kurt had become my knight in shining armor eleven months ago, and now, he couldn't even stand to look at me without a sneer on his face and making me feel like everything between us was a mistake.

I just wished I could go back to that night and change everything. If I could, Kurt would still be working in the garage with his brothers where he belonged.

Instead, Kurt had stormed off two weeks ago, leaving behind his family all because the only thing I could think about was myself. A tear leaked from my tightly clenched eyes, and I quickly wiped it away. I was an idiot thinking Kurt and I could work together, and everything would be fine.

I was a fool back then, and I still was. But now, I had a chance to fix everything. Kurt for once needed me, and I had every intention of being there for him even though I knew he was going to fight me tooth and nail the whole way.

I was ready for every punch that Kurt was going to throw my way. After all, I owed it to him to fix everything. He had saved me not too long ago, and it was only right to repay the favor.

Kurt Jensen didn't know what he was in for. He had wanted a wife all those months ago, and now, I was going to give him what he desired.

I only hope I wasn't too late.

****

CHAPTER 2

Kurt

Well, that fucking hurt. Note to self: Do not flip your car going seventy miles an hour. It does not end well.

I had yet to open my eyes, partly because my right eye was swollen shut, but I knew by the constant beeping and hum of machines around me, I was in the hospital. What a fucking way to end my night.

Everything had been going fine until I had hit that final ninety-degree turn and my two right tires left the pavement, and I knew I was fucked.

My arm was hurting like hell. I tried to move it, but it felt like a fucking Mac truck was sitting on it. Hell, my whole body felt like it had been run over by a Mac truck. I cracked my left eye open and looked at my arm, surprised as hell to see it wrapped up at a ninety-degree angle and resting at my side. "Fuck." My right arm busted up meant there wouldn't be any shifting for me for a while. Shit, who the hell was I kidding? It wasn't like I had a car left to drive anyway. My Camaro was probably crushed like a tin can.

I closed my eye and leaned my head back against the pillow. Just opening my eye and turning my head a bit had drained all my energy. I had no idea what the hell time it was. All I knew was I needed to sleep.

The sound of the door opening didn't even make me open my eyes. I didn't know anyone in California, so it had to be a nurse or doctor coming into the room. I listened to them move into the room, figuring there were two sets of footsteps, but no one spoke. I tried to speak, but all that came out was a weak grunt. Fatigue hit me and I sunk into the darkness calling to me.

I didn't care who the hell was in the room. Fuck, I didn't care if I ever woke up again.

I was fucking done.

****

Leelee

"You can sit in the chair, sweetie. He hasn't woken up yet. I know he looks rough, but he'll be fine." The nurse pointed to the chair next to the bed, but I couldn't get my feet to move. Kurt was lying in the hospital bed, machines surrounding him.

"Um, are you sure he's okay?" Kurt looked anything but good. His right arm was in a sling and wrapped in layers of white gauze while his right leg was elevated off the bed, also wrapped and in a sling. His swollen face had tiny, little cuts all over, and it looked like his right eye was so swollen that it would be a miracle if he could open it.

"Yeah. You thankfully missed all the waiting for tests to come back. His spine looks good and no internal bleeding. Just a broken arm and leg." The nurse grabbed the chart from the end of the bed and began scribbling in it at as she looked at all the machines. "If you plan on standing 'til he wakes up, you'll be standing for a while. He's heavily medicated right now."

"His leg and arm?" I gasped. I knew as soon as Kurt woke up and saw that, he was going to be pissed. No driving. Although, that probably wouldn't stop Kurt. He would probably figure out a way. Hell, he'd probably get a foreign car where the driver sat on the right side so he could still drive.

19

"Yeah. Two breaks in the leg, and one break in the arm. He was lucky nothing else broke." She flipped the clipboard shut and looked me up and down. "How long have you two been married?"

Huh, a question I thought I would never get asked because no one was supposed to know we were married. "Thirteen months," I replied numbly.

"Oh, newlyweds. Still in the honeymoon stage, although I think this might be slowing you two down for a bit." The nurse winked at me and slipped out of the room.

Honeymoon stage? Ha, she couldn't have been any further from the truth.

Kurt hated me, and I, well, I wasn't sure what I felt for Kurt. I knew I hated seeing him lying there, not moving and beat to hell. Fuck, I was confused as hell how I felt about him when he wasn't in the hospital. This just threw a massive wrench into everything.

He had grunted when we walked into the room but hadn't woken up. Now, I was left all alone with him, and I had no idea what the hell to do.

I dropped my bag in the corner of the room and ran my fingers through my hair. I was still in my pajamas and had barely stuffed my feet into my sneakers on the way to the airport. Everything had been a whirlwind these past six hours, and now, here I was. Now, what?

I had tried calling Luke again when I was in the cab headed to the hospital, but he had yet to answer the phone. I had left enough messages and figured it was up to him to call me now. I was beyond exhausted and didn't feel like picking up my phone and trying once more.

"What the hell do we do now, Lee?" I asked myself out loud. "How about we stop talking to yourself," I answered. Hell, I was losing my mind. My mom had always told me growing up that it was normal to talk to yourself, it was when you started answering yourself that you were bordering on crazy. Well, call me crazy.

I eyed up the chair next to the bed and wondered if that would be the best spot to be when Kurt woke up. I didn't think I would be the first person he would like to see after a near-death experience. The ugly salmon color chair looked semi-comfortable and had a handle on the side which I assumed popped open the footrest.

My feet and back ached as I stood there, deciding if sleeping that close to Kurt was a good idea, but my fatigue won out, and I collapsed into the chair. "Welcome to California, Lee," I mumbled. I had to admit; I had imagined the first time leaving the state of Illinois would be better than sitting in a hospital with a man who hated me.

My eyes wandered over Kurt, wondering how in the hell we got here.

Eighteen months ago, if you had seen Kurt and me together, you never would have thought we would end up hating each other and Kurt moving across the country to get away from me.

Eighteen months ago, things were so different.

Eighteen months ago, I fell in love with Kurt Jensen because he was my knight in shining armor who saved me.

Eighteen Months Ago...

"Two shots of whiskey and keep 'em coming," I mumbled to the bartender as I plopped down on the stool and opened my wallet. "Or at least, keep 'em coming until this is gone." I set a twenty-dollar bill on the bar, and I knew my plan of getting rip-roaring drunk was not going to go exactly how I had imagined.

I planted my elbows on the bar and rested my head in my hands. What in the hell was I going to do? Things were going so well. Well, as good as they can be when your parents are both drug addicts, and you're left to take care of your fourteen-year-old brother while they take off and chase after their next high.

Jay knew not to tell anyone about Mom and Dad. I had repeatedly said that if the school found out Mom and Dad had left, they would try to take him away and put him in foster care. And I should have known it wouldn't have been Jay who spilled the beans, but one of his fucking friends who couldn't keep their mouth shut.

I had just come from the school after getting a scathing message on my answering machine from the school telling me to get there now.

When I had walked into the school office, I was greeted by the principal and child protective services. But the thing that surprised the hell out of me was when they told me my aunt who lived three states away had said she would take Jay if there weren't a place for him to stay here.

"No!" I had screamed. Jay was all I had left of my family, and there was no way in hell he was going to move away to live with Aunt Jill. Hell, I had only met the woman once in my life, and Jay had never met her, but for some reason, CPS thought Jay living with a woman he didn't even know better than living with me, his sister.

"What's shaking, Lee?"

I didn't raise my head but knew exactly who had just sat next to me.

Kurt Jensen.

The bartender set my shots in front of me then grabbed a beer for Kurt. I tossed back both glasses of whiskey and motioned for the bartender to refill them.

"Whoa. Double-fisting it tonight, I see. Your parents finally roll back into town? I've only seen you drink like that when they're causing fucking problems."

22

I pivoted on my chair and turned to look at Kurt. And as always, my first thought was how hot he was. It was truly a miracle my panties didn't instantly combust when he turned his head and smirked at me. "I wish that was my problem. At least then, the state didn't try to take Jay away."

"What?" Kurt asked.

"It's nothing, Kurt. At least, nothing you can help me with. Although, this might be the last time you see me before I have to move to Tennessee." Ugh, just thinking of moving put me in an even shitter mood. I liked where we lived. Well, I mean, I liked the state we lived in. My neighborhood was less than desirable, but at least in Illinois, we had all four seasons. The further south you went, you had two or three seasons. Winter was non-existent, at least a snowy winter.

"You're talking crazy, woman. Why don't you start from the beginning and then maybe, I can follow." Kurt picked up his bottle and pressed it to his lips. I couldn't help but become mesmerized by watching the muscles in his arms twist and bulge. "Yo, Earth to Lee," he called.

I turned forward and shook my head. Jesus, my life was falling around me, but here I was, daydreaming about Kurt Jensen. Focus, Lee. Kurt Jensen wasn't interested in me before, and he certainly wouldn't be interested in me when I moved away. "You know my parents took off, right?"

"Not hard to miss, Lee."

"Well, the school finally figured it out, and now CPS is going to take Jay away from me because I don't have a stable environment to raise him in."

"I highly doubt that. Hell, he's been living with you for the past two years."

"I know that, but CPS just sees the fact he's fourteen with no parents."

"Lee, you're what, twenty-three? There are fifteen-year-olds having kids, and no one is taking them away. Why in the hell won't they let you take care of Jay?"

"I'm twenty-five," I mumbled. "And, I'm not his legal guardian, I live in a hell hole, and according to them, I'm not the stable environment that a fourteen-year-old needs."

"Utter bullshit. What the hell do they want?"

"Apparently, a picket fence, me to be married, and probably age ten years and then maybe, they might let Jay stay with me." I grabbed the refilled shot the bartender set in front of me and downed it. "So, if you could point me in the direction of the perfect life, that'd be great." I winced at the burn of the whiskey and grabbed the other shot.

"They let Luke take care of Frankie."

"They let Luke take care of Frankie because Luke is stable and makes a ton of money. Well, I am not Luke. I work at Tire & Lube making eight bucks an hour and last night, I'm sure I watched a family of mice make a home in my front hall closet. If that doesn't scream stable, then I don't know what does." I said, laughing. Jesus, when I said that out loud, I realized how shitty my life was. I thought when I had left my parents' house at the age of eighteen that I was going to take on the world and have it at my feet by dinnertime, begging for mercy. I was wrong. So wrong.

"I could talk to Luke about maybe getting you some hours at the shop."

I shook my head and tossed back the shot. "That only solves half of the job problem. I doubt Luke would give me a six-month advance to show CPS I have money now."

Kurt grunted and shook his head. "I can barely get him to give me my paycheck a day early. I think a six-month advance might be asking a bit much." Kurt set his beer on the bar and turned his stool toward me. "I can give you the money, Lee."

I shook my head and couldn't help but let out a manic laugh. "I think this is the one time money is not going to solve my problem. Unless, you think I can bribe the social worker and principal." At this point, I was not above greasing the hands of whoever might let Jay stay with me.

"Um, I think you might want to rethink that idea. Might get you into more trouble than you are in right now," Kurt replied with a laugh.

"Good idea." I grabbed the next refilled shot and held it in my hand. "I have to talk to the social worker again. Maybe if she sees that I'm the best thing for Jay, she'll back off or help me legally become Jay's guardian." I needed to be positive, no matter how much I wanted to throw in the towel and bury my head in the sand.

I set my glass on the bar, wishing I had more money, but I knew I was about to be cut off after only five shots. I barely felt buzzed, and I knew by the time I got home, I would be stone-cold sober. "Well, I'm going to head home and pray that my apartment magically turned into a two-bedroom house." I grabbed my wallet off the bar and tucked it under my arm. "You racing this week?"

"Every Friday."

"Maybe I'll see you there. I have to work the late shift for the suits who get off work late but still think they can get their oil changed at seven o'clock on a Friday."

Kurt opened his mouth but instantly closed it, changing his mind about what he was going to say. He nodded and took a swig of his beer.

"Nothing more to say?" I smirked.

"We'll talk Friday. I might have a solution to your problem."

I shook my head and knew Kurt was just trying to be nice. There was no way anyone was going to be able to help me. "Whatever, Kurt."

"Just come find me, Lee. Promise."

I waved my hand at him and headed out the door. The only way Kurt was going to help me with my problem would be to give me a shit ton of money and marry me.

A laugh bubbled out at the ridiculous thought, and I pulled my coat tight around me.

I was going to be the only one to save me. Now, I just had to figure out how the hell to do that.

I leaned my head back against the hard hospital chair and closed my eyes. That was where this all started eighteen months ago, and little did I know back then, Kurt was going to be the one who saved me.

Now, it was my turn to save him.

****

CHAPTER 3

Kurt

I jerked awake with a start, regretting it immediately. My leg and arm felt like they weighed 500 pounds and everything ached. I tried to pry my eyelids open but only managed to let a sliver of light in before I closed them. I could add my eyes to the list of things that hurt.

"Shh…" Someone hushed me, but I couldn't place whose voice it was. "The nurse is coming with more pain medicine. They didn't come when I told them before that you were getting restless."

Huh? I assumed the person talking was the nurse. "What?" I croaked out. I barely recognized my voice, and each time I swallowed, it felt like sandpaper.

"Here we go. Let's just pop this into his IV, and he'll be good to go for a little while." Someone had walked into the room, and I could hear them messing with something by my head. "Good to go. Holler if you need anything else."

"Thank you," the first voice mumbled. The door clicked shut, and then, I felt a hand brush the hair from my forehead. "Stupid woman. She acts like I'm some stupid girl that can't tell when someone is in pain." Her voice was heated, but she still spoke quietly. "Thankfully, there should be a shift change soon, and Judy will be back."

Judy? I had no idea what this person was talking about. I wanted desperately to open my eyes and see who was standing next to me, but I couldn't get my damn eyes to cooperate.

"The medicine should start kicking in. Sleeping and resting is the best thing for you right now." She continued to run her fingers through my hair, and the soothing touch lulled me back to the darkness where I had spent so much time. "Sleep, Kurt," she whispered softly.

I tried one last time to open my eyes, but I knew it was pointless. I drifted back to sleep, wondering who the angel beside was when my family wasn't even here.

****

Leelee

It had been six days since I landed in California and Kurt had yet to open his eyes or mumble more than the one word he just had.

The doctor reassured me daily that with every day that passed, Kurt was healing and getting better. I wanted to scream at him each time he said that. Then, why in the hell wasn't he awake for more than a minute at a time.

Luke called me daily, asking for an update on Kurt and spoke to the doctor personally. Both Mitch and Luke insisted on flying out, but I told them that until Kurt woke up, all they were going to do was sit by his bed and stare at the walls. Lord knew that was what I had been doing.

Even though the doctor said this was just the way Kurt's body was dealing with the trauma, I was still worried something more was wrong with him. He wasn't exactly in a coma, but it was damn close. When he would wake up, he would grunt and groan while he tried to lift and move his arms and legs. Each time, I would try to calm him down and talk to him.

I was told the more I spoke to him, the more likely he would wake up fully. I didn't have the heart to tell the nurses and doctor that my voice was probably not the best motivation for waking him up. Kurt and I were husband and wife on paper only. Although there had been about a week where it felt like there was more than a piece of paper between us.

"Just, please wake up, Kurt," I whispered. I would give anything to have him wake up, sneer at me like he always did, and ask me what the hell I was doing here. But what I really wanted, was for him to open his eyes and not hate me anymore. I scoffed at the thought and knew my lack of sleep was starting to catch up with me. It would be a cold day in Hell before Kurt Jensen would look at like I wasn't gum on the bottom of his shoe.

"Knock, knock. Shift change." Judy, the nurse I loved, peeked her head in and I couldn't help but smile. "How's he doing?"

"No change. At least, that's what they tell me." I leaned back in my chair and stretched my legs out. My butt had molded to the shape of the chair, and I wouldn't be surprised if after Kurt got out of here, I wouldn't sit for a week.

"No change is good. Flipping a car nine times going over eighty miles an hour tends to shock the system," Judy commented, laughing. "I just need to check in with the night nurse, and then I'll be back around." She slipped out of the door, and I wished she would have been able to stay. Judy had been my only form of human contact these past six days, and I was becoming dependent on her to help break up staring at the wall all day. And it also kept me from beating myself up for making all the mistakes I did with Kurt in the past.

God knew there was a list of them.

Seventeen months and two weeks ago

"Lee. Just listen."

"No, Kurt. I'm not going to listen to this. I can't even believe that you think that this is going to solve all of my problems." I paced the short length of my living room, my hands propped on my hips

and wondered if Kurt Jensen was a crack addict and he was on an ultimate high right now.

"Lee, it's a good fucking idea that is going to solve all of the problems you have right now."

"You're talking like marrying me isn't a life-changing decision!" I threw my hands up in the air and stopped in front of Kurt, who was sprawled out on the couch.

"It doesn't have to be. No one needs to know about it if you don't want them to."

"Marriage isn't something you easily hide under your bed, Kurt. You have a family, and, well, I have Jay."

"Lee, we get married, you tell CPS you got a husband with a steady and healthy income, and they lay the fuck off."

I shook my head and turned my back to him. "It isn't that easy, Kurt. I can't keep something like this from Jay. He's going to have to talk to them, tell them that I'm married. He's going to have to lie and act like our marriage isn't out of left fucking field, and Jay lying is the last fucking thing I want him to do."

"He won't be lying. We'll be legally married."

I ran my fingers through my hair and plopped down on the couch next to him. "You're high right now, aren't you?"

"What?" Kurt laughed. "I don't do that shit, Lee. I've seen too many lose themselves doing that."

Ha, wasn't that the truth. I saw first-hand both of my parents self-destruct because of drugs. "If you don't do drugs, I don't know what to think about the fact that you think this is a good idea."

"I'm trying to help, Lee, and you know that this is the only thing that has come close to fixing the problem."

God dammit, he was right. It was a fucking insane idea, but it was at least an idea. In the past two weeks, the only idea I had come up with was running away to Austria and joining the circus.

"Why? Why do you want to help me? As you can see, there isn't a line around the block filled with people wanting to help Leelee Perez fix her fucked-up life."

"You don't need a line of people; you just need me. I've known you for a while, Lee, and I know that you are trying your hardest to give Jay the life he deserves. Just let me do this to help you out."

"It's not going to work, Kurt. They are going to want to do a home visit, and as soon as they step one foot into this apartment, they are going to take Jay away from me quicker than Twinkies at a Jenny Craig meeting."

"Then, you need to move to a better place."

He was killing me. Seriously killing me. "Don't you think if I had money to live in a place better than this, I would be? I can barely afford this roach-infested hell hole."

"Then, I help you get into a better place, we get married, CPS sees that we're one big, happy family and then, they leave you alone." He said it so easily that I believed it could work.

"This is insanity. Why are you doing this, Kurt? Knowing me for a while doesn't mean shit. I've known lots of people for years, and none of them would help me out like this."

Kurt shrugged and stood. "I'm going to check on apartments, see what I can find."

"No! Kurt, I can't live in a fantasy land thinking that this is going to work. Even if you find a nicer apartment for me, I have no way to afford it."

"That's all details, Lee. We'll just get you a better job. Hell, everyone knows you're better than working for that shitty chain store." Kurt twirled his keys around his finger and headed to the door. "Just don't worry about it, Lee. Let me see what I can pull *together, and I'll talk to you on Friday." He breezed out the door, pulling it closed behind him without another word.*

I leaned my head back and looked up at the water-stained ceiling. "Fucking madness," I mumbled. Kurt Jensen was out apartment shopping for me, and there was a very good chance I could become Leelee Jensen. Well, Lily Jensen. When Jay was younger, he couldn't quite figure out how to say Lily, so I had been dubbed Leelee since.

Jay strode in the front door and tossed his backpack on the coffee table. "I hate school. I don't know why they think they need to give so much homework."

"Because you need to learn, kiddo."

Jay walked into the kitchen and opened the fridge. I cringed when I heard him moving everything around, trying to find something to eat. I didn't get paid for another day, so the slim pickings we had in the fridge were all that we had. "Was that Kurt I saw getting into his car?" he asked as he slammed the fridge door and started looking in the cabinets.

I hated to break it to him, but he wasn't going to find much more in there. "Um, yeah."

"You see the car he drives?" Jay whistled and shook his head. "That thing just looks fast sitting at the curb. I'd kill to see what he has under the hood."

I knew what he had under the hood. At the last race, Kurt had popped his hood, and my jaw had dropped. Kurt drove a 2016 Chevy Camaro 2.0T that, out of the box, pushed two hundred and seventy-five horsepower and scrambled from zero to sixty in 5.4 seconds. Fast wasn't even the right word to describe Kurt's car. I could spend hours under the hood, learning all her secrets. Although all the Jensen boys drove cars I would kill to get my hands on, Kurt's was the one that piqued my interest the most.

32

"Earth to Lee," Jay called, waving his hand in my face. "Zone out over engines again?" he asked, laughing.

"Um, yeah," I mumbled. What could I say? I was a girl who liked cars.

"So, what was he doing here?"

"Oh, he just wanted to run something by me."

"For the next race?"

"No."

"You two dating?" Jay reached back into the fridge and grabbed the last soda. He popped the top and drained half of the can in seconds. It was no wonder my grocery bill was massive. Jay could eat me out of house and home and still be hungry.

"Um, no." More like engaged. "He was just over trying to help me figure something out."

"I didn't know you two hung out."

We didn't. Well, not really. We talked when we would see each other at the track, races or bar, but other than that, we didn't see each other much. "Just friends."

"Cool. I'm going to head over to Mick's to work on some homework." Jay picked up his backpack and headed to the door.

"Homework or watch TV?" I asked.

"Probably a little bit of both." He smirked.

"Try to do more homework."

Jay nodded and was out the door, slamming it behind him.

I looked around the tiny apartment and didn't know what to do next. I had been racking my brain for the past two weeks, trying to figure out what to do and I was beyond exhausted.

Kurt's idea was sounding better and better.

Fuck me. I think I was going to agree to marry Kurt Jensen.

That day was the beginning of the biggest mistake I've ever made.

I was three days away from falling in love with Kurt Jensen.

****

CHAPTER 4

Leelee

"Why in the hell are you in California, Leelee?"

"I'm helping Kurt."

"Kurt? You mean the guy who has been a huge dick to you?" Jay sneered over the phone.

I was standing outside the hospital entrance, my phone pressed to my ear and trying to calm down Jay. I had been in California over a week, and this was the first time I had told Jay I wasn't home. "You don't know everything that happened, Jay."

"Because you won't fucking tell me what happened."

"Knock off the cussing, Jay. You're seventeen years old, not twenty-seven." I ran my hand through my hair and tried to figure out what I should tell Jay. "He was in a bad car accident, Jay, and I'm here to make sure he's okay."

"*Is* he going to be okay?" No matter what front Jay put on, acting like he hated Kurt, I knew he cared about him.

"The doctors say he should be fine. We're just waiting for him to wake up."

"How long have you been there?"

Shit. I was hoping he wouldn't ask me that question. "I, um, got the phone call a few hours after you left."

"Lee!" he boomed. "I left eight days ago."

"I know. I just didn't want to tell you and have you worry or possibly want to come home."

"I could have come with you to California so you wouldn't have been alone."

"I'm not alone. I have Kurt."

35

"Lee! Kurt is the same guy who has been treating you like a disease for the past ten months."

Ugh, I didn't need to be reminded how long Kurt had hated me for. "Things change, Jay. I couldn't leave him here with no one."

"He has a family, Lee."

"But they called me. Just don't worry, okay? I have everything figured out."

"Yeah, that's what you said before when you married him. It was all fine until something happened that you won't tell me. Kurt used to come over all the time and then it stopped. The last time I saw him at the store, he acted like he didn't even know me."

"Because Kurt and I both decided that was for the best."

"You're married, Lee! Don't you think you should have some relationship with the guy? I understand you got married so I wouldn't be shipped off to Aunt Judy's, but damn. I thought things were going to be different."

I now felt like shit, even more, knowing Jay thought there was going to be something between Kurt and me. "Don't say damn." I needed to have some control in this conversation. "How's the camp going?"

"It's fine, Leelee."

"Just fine?"

"Yes, fine."

Ugh, I knew that tone in his voice. I wasn't going to get any more information out of him today. "Call me if you need me. Otherwise, I'll call you in a couple of days."

"Let me know if you go home." He hung the phone up, and I couldn't help but roll my eyes. The older Jay got, the more I felt like he was the adult and I was the child.

I shoved my phone in my pocket and sat down on the bench next to the entrance. I needed a break from sitting in that tiny room, but I didn't want to go too far in case Kurt woke up.

Luke had called me this morning, saying if there wasn't any change in Kurt by Saturday, he would be flying in so I could go home. I was relieved at his words, but I also didn't want to go home. At least, I didn't want to go not knowing if Kurt was okay.

My phone buzzed in my pocket, and I pulled it out, seeing Violet had texted me.

Whatcha doing?
Sitting outside.
Hmm. Going stir crazy?
Stir crazy didn't even begin to describe it. *Eh, I'm good right now.*

So, Luke just talked to the DR.
And?
He told Luke that Kurt's wife is taking good care of him.
Fuck. Shit. Fuck. I had been able to get around telling Luke that Kurt and I were married by the doctor referring to me by name and not by relationship with Kurt. *Oh.*

Is there something you need to tell us, Leelee?
Not fucking really. *I have a bad connection, Vi.*
You're texting, Leelee. Knock it off and spill.
I wasn't going to be able to dodge this any longer. *Kurt has a wife.*

And I am assuming you are that wife?
Damn, Violet. *Yes, Vi. That would be me.*

It had taken five minutes before my phone dinged with her next message. *Luke changed three shades of red and went upstairs to book plane tickets to California.*

37

Fuck. That was exactly what I didn't want to happen. *You gotta stop him, Vi. Tell him to give me three more days; I need that.* I knew as soon as Luke showed up, things were going to get crazy. He was going to want answers, and I wasn't ready to give them yet.

I'm worried about you, Leelee. So is Luke. I'll try to hold him off, but just know, it won't be for long.

Thank God for Violet. *Thanks, Vi. I'm sorry I didn't tell you. I just couldn't.*

I get it, Leelee. But just know, as soon as I see you, your ass is telling me everything.

I didn't respond because I had no idea what to say. Did I want to tell her everything? No. Would I? Yes.

Violet had become one of my best friends, and I would have killed to have known her before Kurt and I got married. She might have been able to come up with a different plan, or at least have been a person to talk to.

Instead, I married Kurt.

Holy hell. Holy fuck. Holy shit.

I looked down at my hand and shook my head. I was married I was married to Kurt Jensen.

Holy hell.

"You gonna stare at your hand the whole way home?" Kurt asked, a smirk on his lips as he glanced over at me. We were headed back to my apartment in his Camaro, and we were married.

"I can't believe we just did that."

It had only been four days since Kurt had suggested his crazy idea of getting married, and now, it was done. That day, Kurt had found a better apartment for Jay and me, filed for a marriage license, and had somehow talked Jay into going along with this whole charade. "You didn't have to buy me a ring." I was still staring down at my hand, unable to process the fact Kurt had picked out a ring. It was a white gold band with small diamonds embedded into the band. I had never been into the bling of diamonds, but I had to admit that it was pretty.

Kurt shrugged and turned down the road to my new apartment. "You needed a ring to sell it to those CPS asses. I saw that one, and figured that it would do the job."

He talked like it wasn't a big deal he had not only saved Jay and me, he had also bought me a ring just to keep up appearances. "I love it," I whispered. I had no idea how to react. Kurt acted like this was like any other day, but to me, this was going to be a day I would never forget.

On the surface, I was tough as nails, and normally that was how I felt, but now, I had feelings for Kurt I knew wasn't what I should be feeling right now. "Good, Lee."

I had no idea what was happening, but I liked it.

Two Weeks Later

"Is Kurt coming over for dinner?" Jay was setting the small table in the dining room, and I was pulling the meatloaf out of the oven.

"Um, I'm not sure. It's racing night tonight."

"The race doesn't start until after eight. I bet he'll be here."

I set the massive meatloaf on the counter and closed my eyes. I secretly hoped he was coming tonight too, but I didn't know. He had been over every night since we had gotten married and it was like I was living an entirely different life. I still worked at my shitty job that paid pennies, but we lived in a much better apartment, and Kurt was always over if he wasn't working. Things were good, but I was getting worried. Rent would be due soon, and I had no idea how I was going to be able to pay it.

I had asked Kurt if he could see about getting me a job with him, but he had talked over what I had asked and changed the subject. That happened twice, and I wasn't sure how to handle it. I didn't want Kurt to have to support Jay and me. He had helped enough by agreeing to get married to throw off CPS, even though they were still sniffing around and hadn't closed Jay's case yet. It was getting better, but I was still worried.

There was a knock on the door and Jay's face lit up as he opened it and Kurt strode in, high-fiving Jay. "Sup, man. How was school today?" he asked.

"Good. Math blows, but shop was a blast. We have free reign to do any project we want."

"Nice. I remember when that was our assignment, I had Luke and Kurt help me rebuild an old engine." Kurt shrugged off his sweatshirt and tossed it over the couch.

"Really? That would be awesome. I'd love to do something like that."

Kurt and Jay glided to the table, and both sat down. "I can see what we have around the shop. I think we have an old Buick in the back that we could make your project."

"Hell yes," Jay beamed. "You hear that, Lee?"

I picked up the meatloaf and set it down on the table. Kurt's gaze traveled over me, and I felt my cheeks heat under his appraisal. I was still in my work clothes which consisted of dark blue slacks that were too tight on my hips and a light blue button-down shirt. I wasn't much of a girly girl, but I typically liked my clothes to at least make me look like a woman. "Sounds good, Jay. I bet you'll get an A easily."

"Are you racing tonight, Kurt?" Jay asked as he grabbed a roll and ripped into it.

"I planned on it. There are only a couple races left before the finals, so I better get in as many races as I can."

I pulled up a chair next to Jay and dished out the meatloaf and corn while Jay and Kurt talked about Kurt's chances of winning. I normally would be right in the middle of talk about cars and racing, but I just sat there, pushing my food around on my plate.

"Why don't you head to your room and get your homework done?" Kurt suggested, snapping me out of the pity party I was having in my head.

Jay grabbed another roll and headed to his room without one word of protest. It was amazing the way Jay listened to Kurt. If I had suggested that to Jay, he would have sat at the kitchen table for hours just to spite me.

"What's wrong, Lee?" Kurt asked as he grabbed Jay's plate and stacked it on top of his.

"Um, nothing," I lied. I didn't want to go into this with Kurt. He was so wonderful, and all I wanted to do was yell, scream, and ask him what the hell he was doing to me.

"You coming with me to the race?"

I shook my head no, grabbed my plate, and headed into the kitchen. I wanted to go, but I knew I shouldn't. Things were changing between Kurt and me, and I thought the less time I spent with him, the better. "I've got some things to finish unpacking." Lame excuse, Lee.

Kurt followed me into the kitchen and dropped his plates into the sink. "Really? I thought we could grab a drink after the race."

"I have Jay to think of, Kurt."

"I always used to see you out at the bar after races."

I shook my head and turned on the faucet. "That was before," I mumbled.

"Before what?"

41

I turned to look at Kurt, who was leaning a hip against the counter. "This. Whatever the hell this is."

"I don't follow you, Lee."

"I can't go out with you, Kurt. I don't know what the hell I can do anymore. I'm so fucking confused and scared, I don't know which way is up."

Kurt crossed his arms over his chest. "I thought things were going pretty well between us."

"But that's the thing, Kurt. There is no us. At least to the world, there is no us. You waltz in here, play family with Jay and me, and then you leave. You leave, confusing the hell out of Jay and me, thinking that this is more than a nice guy helping the poor half-Puerto Rican girl and her brother. I appreciate everything you've done for us, but I think it's time to stop playing this charade." Fuck, it felt good to say that finally, but I could tell Kurt had no idea where I was coming from.

"I'm just trying to help you and get to know Jay better."

"But why? You don't have to do that. We never agreed that this was going to happen."

"What do you think is happening, Lee?" he asked.

"What's going on is that you are here now, Kurt, but for how long? How long until you get sick of saving me and want to go back to your life where you don't have a wife with a brother that you have to support? Jay is getting attached to you." He was. God dammit was Jay getting attached to Kurt. And I really couldn't blame Jay. He never had anyone who was like a father, and genuinely talked to him. Kurt was giving us both things that we had never had before. Jay was getting a father, and I was getting someone to share my life with, but it was all fake. It was fake, and it was only a matter of time before it all ended.

42

"What does it matter if Jay gets attached to me? He's a good kid who deserves a better turn at life than the shitty past he's had."

"But who are you to give that to him? This wasn't part of our agreement. I'm already stressing trying to figure out how the hell I'm going to pay the rent and now I'm worried how Jay is going to be after you leave."

"Who said I'm going to leave? We did this whole thing backward, but I thought we could, at least, get to know each other, Lee."

I shook my head. There wouldn't be any getting to know each other because there wasn't going to be an us. "This is over, Kurt. I can't set myself and Jay up for the kind of heartbreak that is headed our way. He's already lost both of his parents; he doesn't need to lose you too after you get bored of hanging out."

"I don't fucking accept this, Lee. This is all bullshit."

"It's not, Kurt. This is me recognizing that this isn't going to work."

"I'm not going to divorce you. We get a divorce; they are going to take Jay away."

I didn't know what to say. He was right, but I couldn't expect him to stay married to me any longer. "I'll figure it out, Kurt. That's what I should have done all along. It was wrong of me to put this all on you."

"Where in the hell is this coming from, Leelee?" He growled. His fists were now balled at his sides, and there was a small vein bulging in his neck. Apparently, Kurt was as excited as I thought he would be learning he was off the hook.

"It's coming from the fact that I need to figure out my life on my own and I don't need you butting in, trying to fix everything."

"You can't afford a divorce or this apartment, Leelee."

He was right. God dammit, he was right. "I'll figure something out. You can file papers for a divorce, and I won't contest it, and then Jay and I will move back to our old apartment."

"No. Hell no. You want me gone, fine, but I'm not filing for divorce, and you stay here."

"Kurt, no. I'm not taking anything more from you."

Kurt took a step toward me and his eyes bore into me. "Don't fight me on this, Lee. You agree to what I want, and I'll back off."

"I don't want you to have to support us."

"You aren't making me do anything that I don't want to do. Agree to it, Lee, and tell me that you don't want me." His hand reached up and cupped my cheek. His thumb stroked my skin, and I leaned into his touch for a second. I could have this, Kurt and the life I wanted, but deep down, I would know I was just a burden to him. No one wanted a person who didn't have anything to bring to the relationship. All I had was Jay and a shit job.

"I agree, and I don't want you. I've never wanted you." My words broke my heart, knowing they couldn't be further from the truth, but this was the way it had to be. Kurt Jensen was meant for someone better than me.

Kurt looked at me one last time, and for one split second, I saw something I had never seen before. I saw a man who wanted the same thing I wanted, but I had just told him I would never want him.

He nodded, dropped his hand from my face, and prowled out the door.

That, ladies and gentlemen was the night I broke my own heart and made the biggest mistake of my life.

And he went away.

Kurt still paid the rent and didn't divorce me, but he wasn't there anymore. In fact, any time he saw me, he treated me like I wasn't there.

One time, he came over to the house a month after I told him whatever the hell we were doing wasn't going to work. CPS came over for a house inspection and Kurt played the part of new husband, but I knew he hated every second of it. The second the social worker left, so did Kurt.

Jay was mad at me, too. He didn't understand why I made Kurt go away, but then, he got mad at Kurt when he saw how Kurt was treating me.

I was trying to do what was best for everyone, but it seemed like everyone was miserable, including me.

I didn't think it was possible, but things got worse. I had been trying to save money by not paying rent so I could get a nice size nest egg built up, so Kurt didn't have to support us anymore, but then my hours got cut at work. I was barely able to buy groceries, let alone pay any bills.

I was stuck. I had no idea what to do, and like before, Kurt held the solution to my problem, but he refused to help. A job at Skid Row was the exact thing I needed to get back on track. He promised to talk to Luke for me, but he never did. Just like when we were actually talking, he didn't help.

Thank God I had wandered over to Luke and Violet that night at the track. He finally gave me the job I needed even though it had pissed Kurt off to no end. Then, I had made the stupid mistake of bringing Greg to the barbecue. I was pissed off at Kurt. I had tried talking to him more at work to try to get to a neutral ground where we could work together better, but he stormed off, not wanting to hear anything I had to say.

Then, he was actually gone.

And now, I was here, praying for him to wake up.

Things had changed, all because of that one night where I was too terrified to trust in Kurt and just see where things would lead.

Now, Kurt needed to wake up so I could try to fix everything. I just hoped he would let me.

****

CHAPTER 5

Kurt

"It's been over a week; don't you think that he should be awake right now? Is it good for him to be sleeping all this time?"

"All of his vital signs are good. There's no reason for us to believe that there is something wrong. Like I have been telling you all week, Mrs. Jensen, this is how his body is reacting to the trauma to his body."

The voices surrounded me, the voice of the woman angry and desperate. "Can't you give him something to wake him up? Just for a little bit."

"Mrs. Jensen, no. I know this is a hard time for your family, but you have to trust us. He is in the best hospital right now for the amount of injuries he has sustained."

"I'm sorry, I just don't know what to do." She sounded exhausted now, defeated.

"Just keep doing what you are doing, Mrs. Jensen. He'll wake up soon." Footsteps moved away and then a door closed.

"God damn, Kurt. Why won't you just wake up?"

"I am," I croaked out. Son of a bitch that hurt to talk.

"Holy shit!" she screamed. "Kurt, you can hear me?"

I tried nodding, but I had no idea if the damn thing actually moved. "Yeah," I gasped. I felt hands run over my body and touch my face.

"Can you open your eyes?" she asked. I had no idea who was talking to me. Her voice was familiar, but I couldn't figure out who she was.

My eyes felt like they were taped shut and I struggled even to open them a crack. My mouth was dry as shit, and it felt like a brick wall had fallen on my body.

"Are you still awake?" she asked urgently.

I tried nodding again, and I figure that I must be moving it since she breathed a sigh of relief. "God damn, Kurt. You scared the living shit out of me."

Her? Hell, I thought for sure when my car turned over that first time I was a goner. I could remember every second of the crash. "Ugh," I grunted.

"I should go get the nurse or doctor, but I don't want to leave you in case you fall back asleep." She felt around the bed, tugging on some of the wires that were connected to me and then I heard the static sound of a voice talking over an intercom.

"What can I get for you, dear?"

"He's awake," she sobbed out. Who was this and why was she crying that I was awake? I was in California, where I knew absolutely no one. Before she released her finger from the call button, someone on the other side said it was about damn time. How long had I been out for?

"Kurt, can you open your eyes?" she asked again.

I tried like hell and managed to crack them open a sliver. The overhead light was blinding, and I shut them immediately. I groaned and tried to move my arm to my head.

"No, Kurt. Be careful." A weight pressed on my arm, but it wasn't touching my skin. "I'll turn the lights down." A chair scraped against the floor. "There, now try opening them." I didn't have to try to open them hard this time and was thankful the lights were off. I looked down at my arm, wondering why I hadn't felt her touch me and saw my arm was wrapped up in a splint and bandages.

"They were going to put your arm in a cast tomorrow."

"It's broke?" I croaked out. Motherfucker, it was my right arm that was broke. How in the hell was I going to be able to shift?

"Um, yeah. So is your left ankle."

"My clutch foot."

I heard a light laugh. "I should have known that would be your first thought." The woman stepped into my line of view, and my breath caught.

"Lee?" What in the hell was Leelee Perez doing here? If you were to have asked me who would be at my bedside, Leelee's name would be at the bottom of the list. She had told me in so many words that she wanted nothing to do with me.

"Yeah. You, um, had my phone number in your wallet and the hospital called me. I'm as shocked as you are that I'm here." She crossed her arms over her chest. "I'm really—"

Her words were cut off as two nurses bustled into the room and turned back up the lights. I groaned and closed my eyes as they started rapidly firing off questions to Leelee and me.

"How long has he been awake?" one asked.

"Only about five minutes," Leelee mumbled. "I'll just wait outside."

"How are you feeling, Kurt? Are you able to talk?" a nurse asked as the blood pressure cuff on my leg went off and squeezed the hell out of my calf.

"Yeah." It felt like I had been chewing on gravel, but I was able to get a couple of words out.

"How about opening your eyes?"

"Lights," I mumbled.

"Jane, get the lights." I waited 'til I heard footsteps toward the doors, and the room dimmed behind my eyelids. I cracked open my eyes, wider than I had been able to before and saw two middle-aged women looking down at me.

"Told ya he was a looker, Jane. Even under all those bruises and cuts, you can see how this one managed to snag the wife he has."

"Stop hitting on the patient, Judy." The one I assumed was Jane laughed. "His wife is a sweetheart, but I think she's the jealous sort." Jane winked at me and turned to look at all the machines I was hooked up to.

"True, Jane. You don't sit by someone's bedside for eight days if you don't love them something fierce." Now, Judy winked at me. "You're a lucky man to have someone like her."

What in the fuck was going on? Leelee had told them she was married to me? She never wanted to tell anyone; now she was telling two nurses she didn't know. I closed my eyes and tried to wrap my head around what was going on. Not only had I been out of it for eight days, but Leelee had also been by my side the whole time.

"We've let the doctor know that you're awake. He should be here within the hour to check you over and let you know if and when you'll be able to go home."

The nurses flitted around the room, changed some of the bedding, making me more comfortable and then left the room with the promise they would be back soon.

Leelee peeked her head into the room. "Is it okay if I come in?"

"From what I understand, you've been here all week. What's stopping you now from coming in?"

She slipped into the room and shut the door behind her. "I was here for eight days because you scared the living hell out of me, Kurt, and I didn't know if you were going to live."

"Well, I'm awake. You can go." My words were harsh, but I didn't know what else to say. She didn't want me months ago, and now, I didn't want her. All I wanted to do was help her before, and all she did was throw it back in my face.

"Luke and Mitch have been worried about you," she said, ignoring what I had told her.

"Yeah?" I looked around the room, slowly moving my head and then closed my eyes. "Could have fooled me. You think if they cared that they would be here."

"I've been telling them what's going on and there wasn't much for them to do. We have all been waiting for you to wake up. Luke and Mitch had the garage to run too."

"Ah, Skid Row Kings. The one thing that Luke cares about."

"That's not true, Kurt. He cares about you, too."

"See, that is where you're wrong, Leelee. He doesn't care, at least not about me. All I've been is a fucking burden to him." I didn't want to have this conversation right now. Hell, I never wanted to have this conversation. I had moved to California to get away from Luke and Mitch. "You can leave. I'm alive, and I'll try not to die again. Report back to Luke and leave."

"Kurt, just sto—"

"No!" I bellowed. "I don't want this, Lee. I don't want you, waltzing in here acting like you fucking care about me, and I sure as shit don't need Luke and Mitch, either." My throat burned and ached from all the talking. "Just. Fucking. Leave," I bit out.

"Just let me—"

"LEAVE!"

Leelee jumped at my words, but she finally got the picture that I didn't want her here. She grabbed her purse and phone that were next to the bed and scurried out of the room.

I closed my eyes and slammed my fist down on the bed.

I didn't need anyone.

Especially Leelee Perez.

****

CHAPTER 6

Leelee

I knew that as soon as Kurt woke up, he wasn't going to want me there, but I hadn't expected his words to hurt so much.

I had run past the nurse's station, tears streaming down my face, and both Judy and Jane looked surprised as hell to see me. I heard Judy call my name right before I ducked into the bathroom, but I didn't turn around to see what she wanted. No one was going to say anything to make me feel better.

I knew I should call Luke and let him know that Kurt was awake, but I couldn't, not yet. Everything I should do, I didn't want to do.

The bathroom door opened, and I slipped into the nearest stall, not wanting to have to talk or act polite to anyone.

"You hear that 405 is awake?" a nasal voice asked.

"Yeah. It's about time. I swear his wife was about to go crazy," another voice replied. The door of the stall next to me shut. I peeked under and saw a pair of pink crocs and scrubs on the other side. These nurses didn't sound like anyone I had dealt with the past days.

"Hell, I think this whole floor knew about 405. It was hard not to feel bad for her. Especially now. I heard Judy and Jane whispering about the wife running from his room just now. I wonder what that is all about."

"Oh really?" The other voice asked, their interest piqued. "You would think after him being passed out for more than a week they would be having a happy reunion right now."

Gah. How in the hell did people know? Kurt had only told me to get lost five minutes ago.

"Who knows, maybe it's all too much." The toilet flushed next to me and then I heard the faucet run. Thank God, they were almost done.

"I guess we'll have to wait and see. It's always fun when the patients are entertaining," the nasal voice said with a laugh.

The bathroom door opened and then banged closed. Their voices faded, and I thanked God they were gone. They hadn't said anything bad, but it was just too much for me to deal with right now. I had gone from no one knowing Kurt and I were married to not only the hospital staff knowing but Luke and Violet too. And you could bet if Luke and Violet knew, Mitch, Scarlett, and Frankie would know.

My phone buzzed in my pocket, and I pulled it out to see that Violet was calling. "Well, speak of the devil," I joked as I put the phone to my ear. "I was just thinking about you."

"I don't know if that's a good thing or not," she giggled.

"It's good. At least, this time." I leaned against the counter and peered into the mirror, taking in the dark bags under my eyes and my hair that was tossed up in a messy knot on the top of my head. I looked like a damn train wreck. "Kurt finally woke up."

"Oh my God!" Violet screeched. "That's the kind of news you normally lead with, Lee," Violet shouted to Luke and told him about Kurt. I heard Luke mumble and then I heard Violet swoon. Yes, I swear to God I heard her swoon. I'm sure Luke had said something sweet, crude, romantic, or all the above.

"Um, Luke wants to know when they'll be releasing him," Violet finally said into the phone.

"I'm not sure yet. I had to um, well, leave the room." I winced.

54

"What? Why? Did the doctor not let you stay?"

I pulled on a stray strand of hair that had fallen on my face and tried tucking it back into my ponytail. "No. Not the Doctor."

"Then, who the hell told you…oh," Violet groaned, realizing who else it would have been who had told me to leave.

"Yeah, oh. He woke up, ripped into me and told me to get lost. I have to say any hope I had that Kurt would wake up a new man are out the window."

"Oh, Lee. I'm sorry, hon. I would say more, but I really don't know what you're dealing with since I only found out a day ago, that you were married," Violet lightly scolded. "Mitch still thinks Luke and I are playing a joke on him. He doesn't believe it at all that you two are married."

"Yeah, well, it is rather unbelievable."

"You going to tell me at least why you two got married?"

Ugh. Did I have to tell the truth? "I needed help." There, I answered the question, just not a detailed answer.

"Leelee, I'm going to get this damn story out of you if it's the last thing I do."

Judy peeked her head into the bathroom and motioned for me to follow her. "Uh, I gotta go, Vi. One of Kurt's nurses just came in. Tell Luke I'll call him as soon as I know anything about him going home."

"Okay. Sounds good. We love you, Leelee. Don't forget that," Violet reminded me.

Violet, Luke, Mitch, Scarlett, Frankie, and Levi had become like family to me, and it was crazy how much her saying that meant to me. "Love you guys, too," I mumbled back and hung up the phone.

"He's passed out again. He was complaining about pain and we had to give him some stronger meds to help."

"Oh, do you think he'll wake up again?" I asked, concerned he was going to be knocked out for another eight days.

"He should. As far as we can tell, he is firmly out of the woods now. Now, he just has to take it easy and let his body heal." Judy ducked out of the bathroom, and I was alone again.

I wished she would have come in and told me Kurt had changed his mind, and he was asking for me, but I knew it would be insane to expect it. Kurt wasn't going to ask for me. He didn't want me here, and I had no idea how to change that.

There had to be a way to prove to him I wanted to be here and there wasn't any other place I would rather be, but I was drawing a blank how.

I stared at myself in the mirror and realized it was time to be honest with myself.

I wanted Kurt Jensen, and I wasn't going to take no for an answer. I had made a mistake fourteen months ago, and now, I was going to do everything I could to make it right.

Kurt Jensen wasn't going to know what hit him.

****

CHAPTER 7

Kurt

"We're going to release you tomorrow, but you need to understand that you are going to have a lot of limitations, Mr. Jensen. You have multiple broken bones and won't be as mobile as you would like to be."

I rolled my eyes, and it took every ounce of control I had not to tell the doctor *no shit*. "Yeah, I kind of figured that." I held up my arm that was encased in a black cast that matched the black one on my ankle and foot.

"You are good to fly. I would just suggest to get up and try to walk when you can so you don't stiffen up."

"Fly?" I asked, confused as hell. I had no plans to fucking fly. All I planned on doing was blowing this joint, grabbing a taxi, and going to the hotel room I had been renting.

Three days after I had finally woken up and the doctor was now comfortable enough with me being discharged.

It had been three days of pure torture having to be around Leelee, also. She had insisted she was going to stay until I was released and there really wasn't anything I could have done about it. I guess I could have told the nurses and doctor I didn't want her there, but I didn't want to cause a scene, either.

"Yup, your wife said that she had tickets for you two headed back to the Chicago area." The doctor clipped his pen into the pocket of his coat and looked expectantly at me. "Are there any other questions you have for me? I would hook up with a physical therapist when you get settled. You'll need all the help you can get to get back to normal."

"No questions," I mumbled. Fucking normal was something I didn't think I would ever be again.

The doctor strode out of the room, and my eyes landed on Leelee who was looking at her nails in her lap. She rarely made eye contact with me and half the time, she seemed like this was the last place she wanted to be even though she insisted she wanted to be here.

"I'm not going back," I growled.

"That's what you think. You have no one to help you here, Kurt."

"I don't need help," I barked. I was fucking sick and tired of hearing her say that.

"Yes, you do. You can't drive, can't walk, and don't have a place to live here anymore. You're coming back." She stood and pulled her phone out of her pocket and pressed a couple of buttons. "I canceled your hotel. Our flight leaves in three hours. I'll leave you alone for a little bit to get used to the idea that you're going home."

"I don't have a fucking home. You can't make me stay with Luke and Mitch." I wasn't going back to being under Luke's thumb. I had left for many reasons, and one of them was I needed to do shit on my own without Luke and Mitch.

"I'm not," she smiled. "You're going to be staying at the place you've been paying rent on for months."

"What?" She couldn't mean that I was going to live with her.

"Jay is at football camp for the next three weeks or so. You can stay in his room until he gets back, and then we'll figure something else out."

"No. Hell no, Leelee." That wasn't going to happen.

"I'm calling Luke. You're being stupid and pigheaded." She swiped and pressed a couple buttons on her phone and put it to her ear.

"Put the fucking phone down, Lee," I growled.

"No. Only if you agree to come back with me."

"This is fucking shit."

She pointed her finger at me. "Promise you'll come home with me, or I'll sic Luke on you."

"As soon as I'm better, I get to leave. That is the only way I'll come."

She eyed me up and down. "Deal." She shoved her phone in her pocket and crossed her arms over her chest. "I thought you would be way tougher than that."

"What the hell! You started out the gate with calling Luke."

"No, I actually didn't. I just confirmed our flight. I didn't call Luke," she smirked. "I figured growing up the youngest of three brothers that you would know all the tricks in the book."

God dammit. "That's bullshit."

She shrugged. "Maybe, but you agreed to get on that plane."

I grunted and crossed my arms over my chest almost knocking myself out with my cast. I still wasn't used to the fucking thing. "As soon as the cast comes off, I'm gone."

"We'll see when that happens. You might need physical therapy."

"Leelee. I'm not fucking staying. There's nothing there for me."

She looked away but not before I saw her face drop. "You'd be surprised at the things that are waiting for you."

I shook my head. "Eight weeks. That's it, and then, I'm gone." I could go back home for two months. I could save up some money and figure out what my next move would be.

"Fine. I'll take what I can get at this point." She walked to the door, her back to me. "I'll find out how long till they discharge you." She slipped out of the room and quietly shut the door.

I laid my head back on the pillow and closed my eyes. Things were fucking weird.

For a second, it looked like Leelee didn't like the idea of me leaving when I was better. Why? I had no fucking clue.

Eight weeks. That was all she was going to get out of me. I had tried giving her everything she needed a year ago, and she had tossed it back in my face.

I wasn't going to play the fool again.

****

Leelee

We should be back tonight.

Let us know what time and we'll pick you up.

I was sitting outside of Kurt's room, my ass on the floor and my back to the wall, texting Violet. *My car is in long term parking. We won't need a ride.* Thankfully, I had thought ahead and parked in the long term. At least I knew my car wouldn't be towed.

We can still meet you there.

Ha, I think Luke and Mitch being at the airport was the last thing Kurt wanted. He was so mad at his brothers, I think just being in the same state as them was going to drive him crazy. *Nah, we'll be fine. You guys can come over tomorrow.* I knew once we landed, all I was going to want to do would be dive into my bed and sleep for a day.

OK. Just call if you need anything.

Thank God I had been able to ward off Luke and Mitch. I knew they wanted to be there for Kurt, but I think they were just as confused about everything that was going on and realized Kurt just needed distance.

I banged my head against the wall and ran my fingers through my hair. Ugh, this was exhausting. Not only was I trying to figure out how to get Kurt to forgive me, I knew I was going to be the mediator between Kurt and his brothers.

Kurt had never said anything to me before about wanting to get out of his brother's shadows, but I understood why he would feel that way. Everyone wanted to be known for what they were good at, except Kurt was known more for being a Jensen brother than he was for his skill on the track and his knowledge of what was under the hood. Luke had started the garage with the main idea being the brothers would work together, but it sounded like Kurt was over it. Add in me, who had fucked things up, and an idiot could see why Kurt didn't want to go back home.

"Hey, there you are, on the floor," Judy noted with a laugh. She stood over me, a huge smile on her face. "I've got some discharge papers here. I'm ready to spring you two out of here."

"Great," I murmured. I was ready to head home, but I knew once we got there, I was going to have an entirely different battle living with Kurt for the next eight weeks.

I shook my head, stood, and followed Judy back into Kurt's room.

I numbly listened to her as she went over all the paperwork with Kurt and realized if this was what I wanted, I was going to have to deal with the bad right along with the good.

I was getting Kurt back in the state of Illinois, but it was going to be an uphill battle trying to get him to stay.

The question was, how badly did I want Kurt?

****

61

CHAPTER 8

Kurt

I hurt. I'm talking, *I fucking hurt.*

I had been crammed into my seat on the plane for three hours on the nonstop flight back to Illinois, and I was in Hell. I had never been in so much pain in my life.

Leelee and I were sitting outside the baggage claim, waiting for our bags to show up. As we were waiting to get off the plane, Leelee had insisted on getting a wheelchair for me, and I didn't fight her on it. I was half an hour past the schedule for taking my pain meds, and I was more irritated with each second that went by.

Leelee looked like she was ready to fall over and I couldn't help but feel responsible for her being so worn down. "Here they come," she mumbled, as she grabbed a bag. Thankfully, the other two were close behind.

Leelee had parked in long term parking which was thankfully close to the baggage return, and we were headed to her apartment in no time. I pulled my pills out of my pocket and swallowed them dry. I was desperate to get some relief from the throbbing in my arm and leg.

"You're not supposed to take those on an empty stomach," Leelee scolded as she took an exit off the highway. She pulled into a fast food burger joint and ordered four burgers and fries.

"I don't need to eat. I just want to get out of this car and stretch my legs." I had only had a small reprieve from the plane to the car. Leelee drove an old Caprice, and while it looked like a tank, it wasn't as roomy as I needed. I needed a king size bed to sprawl out in right now.

"Eat it," she ordered, as she pulled off to the side in the parking lot and yanked a burger out of the bag. She partially opened it and shoved it in my face. "I don't need you throwing up all over my car."

I grabbed the burger out of her hand and took a huge bite. "It's not like you'd be able to tell," I mumbled around a mouthful.

"Hey, shut the hell up. I know my car isn't fancy, but it's mine, and it gets me where I need to go."

"You need a new car. Something that doesn't look like my grandma drives."

"Ha, ha," she growled as she rolled her eyes. "I guess I'm just glad my car doesn't look like a crushed tin can right now," she mocked as she batted her eyes at me.

I grunted and took another bite. I'd eat just to keep her off my back. Leelee unwrapped her burger and ate it in four bites. "Jesus, woman. Did you even taste that?"

She took a sip of her soda and rolled her eyes at me. "I'm ready to get home, but needed to feed you and my stomach was ready to start eating itself if I didn't eat, too." She started the car up and got back on the highway. "We still have forty-five minutes before we get home."

I polished off the rest of my burger and tossed the wrapper in the bag. I pulled out some fries and offered some to Leelee. She grabbed a fist full and shoved them in her face. "You do know you don't need to eat like I'm going to eat all the food on you."

"Habit. You've eaten with Jay and me before. Food doesn't last long. It was eating what was in front of you growing up because you never knew when and where the next meal was coming from." Leelee relaxed in her seat and grabbed the cardboard container of fries out of my hand. "I'll take my other burger," she mumbled around a mouthful of fries.

I handed the burger to her unwrapped, and she devoured it in four bites again. "Do you even taste the food?"

"Yeah," she mumbled. Her face was bright red, and she handed me back the wrapper. "I don't actually eat around people besides Jay," she said, embarrassed. She pulled her hood up and over her head and leaned back in the seat and put the cruise on.

I finished my food in silence. I hadn't meant to upset her, but damn. Luke, Mitch, and I had grown up rough too, but obviously, Leelee had it worse. I threw my garbage in the bag and kicked it on the floor. I stretched out as best as I could and leaned my head back. "You tell Luke we were coming back?" I asked, drowsiness hitting me.

"Yeah."

"I'm surprised he didn't insist on meeting us at the airport." Luke normally inserted himself into everything and tried to take charge.

"He tried. I told Violet to fend him off and let us get settled in before he comes in like a freight train."

"Freight train." I laughed. "That's a damn good description of Luke."

"He's just looking out for you, Kurt."

I scoffed and closed my eyes. "I'm twenty-eight years old, Lee. I don't need anyone looking out for me anymore."

"I don't know about that. I think we all need someone looking out for us, wanting the best."

"See, that is where you lose me because that is different from what Luke is trying to do. He wants to control my life and keep me under his thumb."

"So, that was why you flew halfway across the country because you can't stand up to your brother."

64

"Fuck this," I mumbled. I didn't need to justify myself to Leelee anymore than I did to Luke. It was my life to live, and I was going to live it the way I wanted. "Eight weeks can't get over fast enough."

Leelee scoffed but didn't say anything more.

Half an hour back in the state of Illinois, and I was all ready to get the fuck out of it.

I was fucking done.

****

Leelee

"I need to change the sheets."

"I need to go to fucking sleep."

I rolled my eyes and skirted past Kurt who was making his way down the hall. "It'll take five minutes. Trust me; you want me to change these sheets."

"Lee."

I waved my hand at him and quickly closed Jay's bedroom in door Kurt's face. "An almost seventeen-year-old boy lives here, Kurt. Two things happen in this bed, and only one of those is sleep."

Kurt swore under his breath, and I couldn't help but cringe. Jay beating his meat stick was one of the last things I wanted to think about, but there it was. "Just lean against the wall and try not to pass out on me," I yelled as I grabbed the sheets off the top of Jay's dresser. I had asked him to clean his room before he had left for football camp, but my request had been ignored.

As I peeled the old sheets off, I tried to ignore the stiff and sticky spots and tossed them on the floor. I would be glad as hell when Jay went off to college, and he would have to change his own damn nasty sheets.

"Lee, hurry the hell up," Kurt mumbled, as I spread the top sheet out and quickly tucked it under.

"This is for your own safety. Trust me." I kicked the old sheets in the hamper and tossed the comforter on top of the sheets. "I need to get you a clean blanket," I said as I opened the door. Kurt was leaning heavily against the wall while his left arm supported his right arm. "Come on." I grabbed onto his arm and helped him into the room. "Where did you leave your crutch?" Kurt wasn't a lightweight who was easy to haul around.

"It's by the door," he mumbled. His face was pale and his eyes were at half-mast.

"Are you okay?"

"I'm fucking tired," he slurred.

Apparently, Kurt wasn't up to traveling halfway across the country yet. I should have waited a couple more days before making him fly, and now I felt like an ass.

"I'm sorry, Kurt."

His legs gave out, and I half-carried, half-dragged him to the bed. He flopped down on his back and rested his broken arm on his stomach. "Did you flip my car over?" he asked as I worked on untying his shoelaces.

"Huh?" I grunted. Kurt was so tired that he wasn't even making sense anymore.

"I asked if you flipped over my car."

"No, of course not. I wasn't even there."

"Then, you have nothing to be sorry about," he muttered. "It was my own damn fault for taking that curve too sharp. I tried to drift it, but the tires caught and flipped me the fuck over."

I had wondered what had happened to make Kurt wreck, but I hadn't had a chance to ask him. "Do you remember it?"

"Every fucking second."

"Are you feeling better?" His color was returning to his face, and he wasn't slurring his words anymore.

"Still fucking tired, but I'm at least not standing up on one busted leg and a body that's fucked up." He grabbed the pillow that was under his head and laid it over his eyes.

"Um, did you want to take your clothes off?" I asked, hopeful he would say no. But also, that he would say yes. I was all messed up in the head right now.

"Yeah, but it's like trying to get an alligator in a dress. A broken leg and arm don't do easy work of getting dressed and undressed."

"Well, we're going to have to figure it out. I think Jay has a bunch of basketball shorts that we can fit you in, and I can always cut the arm holes on some of your shirts." I rummaged through Jay's dresser, avoiding the pile of Playboy's and found two pairs of shorts that would fit Kurt.

"How in the hell did they get your pants on?" I asked, looking down at his leg.

"Very fucking carefully. Why do you think it took me so long to get discharged? They were getting my pants on for fifteen minutes. Judy had to take a break for a couple of minutes to catch her breath," he chuckled.

"Damn. If it took you, and two nurses, to get into them, how in the hell am I going to get you out of them?"

"Grab scissors and cut them off."

"What? No. I can't wreck a perfectly good pair of pants."

"Yes, you can. Grab the scissors and do it. You have about five minutes before I pass out and I'm dead weight then."

I looked at his leg one last time, trying to figure out a better way to get his pants off, but the scissors looked like the easiest and fastest way. "Fine," I huffed. I quickly jogged to the kitchen, grabbed the scissors, Kurt's pills, and a glass of water.

"Okay. I think if we—" The pillow was still over Kurt's face, and he was lightly snoring. "Shit." I had only been gone two minutes. Three tops. How in the hell was I going to get him out of his pants now?

"Would you just cut the damn pants and stop staring at me?"

I jumped back, surprised he was awake. "I thought you were sleeping," I scolded as I grabbed his leg and started cutting up the seam of his pants.

"I was, but then I felt you staring at me."

"That's ridiculous. How did you feel me staring at you?" I was halfway up his leg, nearing his crotch. "I'm only cutting this far. I should be able to work them down your leg now," I mumbled, as I put the scissors down. My fingers fumbled with the button of his pants, and the warm skin of his stomach brushed against my fingertips. Holy hell. This was not how I envisioned getting Kurt out of his pants.

I managed to get the button undone and the zipper open with minimal blushing. "I finally get you to take my clothes off, and I can barely move. I think this is karma kicking me in the ass again."

"Uh…" Speechless. I felt the same damn way. I tugged the ripped jeans down and off his legs without hurting him any more than he was. "I'll go find you another blanket." I glanced up at Kurt, the pillow still covering his face, but this time, I didn't assume he was asleep.

Across the hall, I grabbed my extra blanket off my bed and spread it over Kurt. His feet were hanging off the end of the bed, but I didn't want to wake him up to move him a couple of inches up the bed. The pillow was still over his eyes, and he was lightly snoring again. "Kurt?" I whispered, testing to see if he actually was passed out. He didn't budge so I eyed up his arm wondering if I could get his shirt off him.

Jay had broken his arm when he was eight, and I had taken care of him, figuring out how to get him dressed and what not. But looking at Kurt, who was three times the size of Jay back then, I knew this was going to be a bit harder.

"Lee, stop staring at me."

"Son of a bitch!" I yelled. How in the hell did he do that?

"You were sleeping like ten seconds ago."

"Turn the light off and let me sleep. You can ogle me in the morning."

"Pfft, keep dreaming," I scoffed. "I'll wake you up in three hours to give you more medicine."

"Yeah," he sighed.

I backed out of the room, turning off the light. "Just yell if you need anything."

He grunted in reply, and I shut the door, leaving it open a crack.

"Well, that was a complete shit show, Lee," I mumbled to myself. Thankfully, getting him undressed went easier than I thought it would. Seeing Kurt in his underwear was more impressive than I assumed it would be, and the image of his firm and sculpted legs would be forever burned into my brain.

"Stop, Lee." Kurt wasn't here to stay. The least I could do was make the time he had here comfortable and not miserable. Kurt had been through hell, and he was here just to recover. I had to remind myself of that. Otherwise, I would make a fool of myself and be left with a broken heart again.

Kurt Jensen didn't want me anymore.

I wished I could say the same. Kurt Jensen seemed to be exactly what I wanted.

Shit.

****

69

CHAPTER 9

Kurt

"Luke is on the way over."

Fuck. I was sitting on Leelee's tiny couch, my foot resting on her coffee table and my arm resting on my stomach. I had finally found a comfortable position that didn't make my whole body ache, and now Luke was coming over to make me miserable. "Help me up," I demanded. Leelee had put my crutch next to the door after I had sat down and I was screwed unless she brought it over to me.

"What? Why?"

"I need that fucking crutch so I can get up and get the hell gone."

Leelee rolled her eyes and grabbed the remote I had in my lap. "You're not going anywhere. He's on the way over, Kurt. Talk to him and get it over with." She turned the channel to *Fast and Loud* and sat down on the couch next to me. "What's the worst that is going to happen? You said it yourself. You're twenty-eight years old. He can't run your life."

"Yeah, because Luke will listen when I tell him to get lost."

Leelee shrugged and turned to look at me. "He might if you tell him why you want him to get lost."

I had tried talking to Luke before, but he never heard what the hell I was trying to tell him. Knowing Luke, he wasn't going to listen to a word I had to say unless some of those words were I was coming home. That shit wasn't going to happen. "This is shit. I can barely fucking move. How in the hell is this fair?"

"It's not. At least, not for you." Leelee turned back to the TV and turned the volume up. "I don't know what to tell you, Kurt. Just listen to him."

"I have listened to him, Leelee. I don't like what comes out of his mouth."

"Fine. Um, tap me on the arm if you want me to get rid of him."

"You are going to get rid of Luke?" I laughed. "He's twice as big as you, Lee, and could probably bench press you."

"You want my help or not?"

I mulled it over, realizing it was better than nothing. If anything, she could distract him and then I could try to get the hell out of Dodge.

"I forgot to ask. Was my phone in the bag from the hospital?" I moved my leg to the right and leaned back further into the couch. I wasn't one of those people who was addicted to their phones, but I did use the damn thing.

"No. They couldn't find it after the accident. I asked."

"Then, how in the hell did they know to call you?"

"They said my number had been in your wallet."

Huh, I didn't even remember having Leelee's number in there. "Convenient."

"For you, not for me. I figured my first time out of the state of Illinois would be better than sitting in a hospital for nine days."

I was about to ask Leelee how she had never been out of the state when the door buzzed. We both looked at each other, neither one of us wanting to get the door. "You have to promise to listen to him. I know you don't believe it, but your brothers care about you. These past days have scared the living shit out of them. Remember that when he's talking."

I clenched my jaw, stopping myself from telling her to fuck off and nodded. The door buzzed again, and this time, Leelee got up to answer it.

Luke was standing on the other side with Violet to the side of him. They both looked worried and like they didn't want to be here almost as much as me.

Luke nodded at Leelee and ambled into the tiny apartment. When it had been Leelee, Jay, and me in the apartment, it hadn't seemed that small. Now, with Luke taking up residence in Leelee's living room, it felt like I was suffocating.

"Hey, Lee," Violet mumbled, as she wrapped her arms around Leelee.

Luke was standing in front of me; his arms crossed over his chest, and his eyes were on me, taking in all the cuts, bruises, and broken bones.

"I think the last time you were laid up for more than an hour was when you were seven and rolled over your go-cart."

He was right, but I wasn't going to tell him that. "I've had better days."

"Just the two broken bones?" he asked.

"Yeah. Ankle on the left and my right arm busted the hell up."

Luke nodded. "Won't be racing for a while."

I wished I could have told him I would be racing soon, but I knew he was right. Not having use of my right hand and my left leg meant racing wasn't anywhere in my near future. "We'll see."

"So, this was your big plan? You go halfway across the country to wreck your car that you've been building for a year? Fuck, you could have wrecked your damn car here," he growled. "You scared the living hell out of Mitch and me when Leelee called."

"Must not have been very concerned. I wrecked my car two weeks ago. This is the first I'm seeing or hearing from you."

"I didn't come to California because I knew I would want to fucking strangle you. I don't know what in the hell is going through your head, Kurt. You didn't act this reckless when you were a teenager. Now, you're almost thirty and acting like a punk."

I stretched my leg out and crossed my arms over my chest. My leg was fucking throbbing and Luke being here wasn't helping. "It's my life, Luke."

"So, that means I have to stand by and just watch you fuck up your life now? You don't have a job; you don't have a place to live. From where I'm standing, the only thing you have going for you is you were at one point smart enough to marry Leelee, although I'm sure you'll fuck that up if you haven't already."

"Funny, I'm not the one who fucked that up, but you might as well blame me. It's a well-known fact that Kurt Jensen is the fuck-up of the family," I sneered. I knew Luke had always thought that about me, but it was shitty hearing the words fall from his mouth. "You say everything you need to?" I grabbed the pillow out from under my arm and tossed it at the end of the couch. "I think I'll sleep the rest of the day instead of fucking it up like you think I do."

"Grow the fuck up, Kurt. Stop acting like the sullen kid who got his toys taken away."

"As soon as you stop acting like my fucking father. Dad died two years ago, Luke. He's gone; you don't need to try to fill his shoes."

"I'm not trying to be Dad. I'm just trying to keep you from killing yourself."

I laid down on the couch and propped my leg up on the small coffee table. "Well, you can breathe easy now. I have no plans of killing myself for the next eight weeks. After that, you won't have to worry about me. I'll be gone." I closed my eyes and tossed my arm over my eyes.

I could feel Luke staring down at me, but I was done with the conversation. "You're better than this, Kurt. Don't fuck up your life to the point where you can't fix your mistakes. I can't be there to pick you up anymore."

"I never asked you to be there."

"I know. I did it because I love you." He shuffled out the door, and it clicked shut behind him.

"Don't even start with me, Leelee. I'm not interested in what you have to say." I just had to listen to Luke bitch at me. I didn't need to listen to Leelee, too.

"I didn't plan on it. Plus, I don't have time to. I need to be back to work."

I peeked open an eye and saw Leelee's retreating back heading down the hall. Well, that was different from what I had expected. Luke had done exactly what I had thought he would do, but it was Leelee who was throwing me a curveball.

"I'll be home a little after five. Here are your pills, and a couple bottles of water." I watched as she walked back into the living room and set everything on the coffee table. "Here's the house phone also. If you need me, just call. I'll make sure to have my phone on me. After I get off work, if you feel like, we'll head to the phone store and see about getting your cell replaced."

Fuck. That was going to be a pretty penny. I had just gotten that damn phone a couple of months before I had left. "I'll be here," I mumbled.

"Take your pills, Kurt. Don't be an ass and think you can handle the pain." She grabbed her wallet off the counter and tucked it under her arm. "I'll be back around lunch to feed you. Try to get some sleep and just rest today." She slipped out the door without saying goodbye, snapping the door shut behind her.

That went a lot better than I thought it would have. Although, knowing Leelee, she was saving her speech for when she could hand me my ass without having to rush out the door to work. "Something to look forward to," I mumbled, as I reached forward and grabbed the remote off the table.

Today, I was going to make a plan. I had to figure out what my next move was and I already had a good idea what that was going to be. My eyes felt heavy with sleep, and I turned on the Discovery channel to watch the *Fast and Loud* and *Street Outlaws* marathon.

My eyes closed and I figured I could plan after I caught up on my sleep. After all, I had eight weeks to figure shit out.

****

CHAPTER 10

Leelee

"When you finish up the Supra, I'm going to need you to get the brakes done on the Mazda before you leave," Luke barked from the other side of the shop.

I glanced up at the clock, seeing it was half past noon and I still needed to run home and check on Kurt. I had already worked on three cars this morning, and Luke had just added two more to my list. "Sure thing. I'm just going to run home, make Kurt some lunch, and then I'll finish up the Supra." I wiped my hands on a shop towel and tossed it into my toolbox. "You want me to bring anything back?"

"No. Just get back here as soon as you can. We're backed up the next couple of days, and you need to be here more than you need to be there." Luke slammed the shop door shut, and I closed my eyes.

"Could this day get any shittier?" I muttered as I fished my keys out of my pocket. Luke had been acting like a pissed off bear all morning, and Mitch had called in because Levi was sick.

Violet had popped her head in when I had started work, but she was headed off to the library and couldn't stick around to keep Luke at bay. I thankfully only lived ten minutes away from the shop and planned only to make Kurt a quick sandwich and then head right back.

On the short drive to the house, I tried to diagnos the Supra, figuring out why it wouldn't start.

I could hear the TV blaring as I jogged up the front steps and unlocked the door. Kurt was flat on his back on the couch, passed out to the world. It looked like he hadn't moved since I left this morning except the bottle of pain pills was spilled on the coffee table.

His shaggy hair was mussed and pushed off to the side, and his bruised face was finally healing, the bruises that had been circling his eyes fading to yellow.

"You're staring at me again," he mumbled, making me jump back.

"What the hell? How the hell do you do that?"

He cracked open an eye and looked up at me. "Why do you keep staring at me?"

"I'm not staring, I'm just…just—"

"Making sure I'm not dead?" he suggested.

"Well, yeah." I dropped my keys on the coffee table and headed into the kitchen. "Sandwich okay for lunch?" I asked, as I pulled the bread out of the pantry and opened the fridge to grab the lunch meat. "Fuck," I whispered as I pulled out the bag of turkey that was now graying and had a patch of green on it. "Peanut butter and jelly okay?"

I grabbed the jelly and peanut butter, not waiting for his response and set them down next to the bread. I took two slices of bread out of the bag and realized any sandwich was out of the question. "New plan," I called as I opened the freezer. Thankfully, Jay always had a stash of Hot Pockets in the freezer, and I grabbed two. "Hot Pocket?"

"I'm not hungry," he grunted. I glanced back into the living room and saw he was sitting up, hunched over.

"Need help getting up?" I asked, as I unwrapped his lunch and popped it into the microwave.

"As much as I'd like to say no, I'm gonna have to go with yes. I don't think I moved an inch while you were gone." He rubbed his hand on the back of his neck and rotated his head, trying to work out the kinks.

"Bathroom?" I asked, as I grabbed his good arm and hoisted him off the couch.

"Yeah. Just give me my crutch," he grunted.

"No, I'm just going to help you. I need to get back to the shop as fast as I can. Luke is on the warpath, and I'm his target today."

"What? Why?" Kurt asked as we slowly made it down the hallway.

"Because I was gone for two weeks and Mitch didn't come in today because Levi was sick and Scarlett couldn't get off work. I'm five cars deep at the shop, and they all need to be done before five."

"Why the hell isn't Luke helping you?" We made it to the bathroom and Kurt leaned against the door frame. He looked down at me, irritated.

"Because someone has to take care of the front and I was gone for two weeks. I can pull my weight for a couple of days."

"You weren't gone on a fucking vacation, Lee. Luke can cut ya some slack."

I shrugged and reached in the bathroom and turned on the light. I didn't really want to discuss Luke with Kurt. I knew no matter what I told him about Luke, he was going to disagree. "You okay? Or do you need more help?"

"I'm good." He hobbled into the bathroom and shut the door in my face.

Ugh. Pissing Kurt off was the last thing I wanted to do when I had come home to make lunch, but it was evident I was meant to piss off every Jensen brother I encountered today.

I headed back to the kitchen when the microwave dinged, and I pulled out the plate of Hot Pockets. I had never gotten the hang of microwaving something without having the insides explode, and Kurt's lunch looked like it was my latest microwaving victim.

I grabbed a fork and set it on the plate, thinking they would still taste good, but just a bit messy.

"Lee," Kurt called.

"Coming," I yelled back as I quickly moved to the bathroom.

Kurt was leaning against the door frame again, but this time, his face was white, and there was a light sheen of sweat on his forehead. "When's the last time you took a pain pill?" I asked, as I wrapped his good arm around my shoulder and held him up.

"What time did you leave this morning?"

"Seven-thirty."

"I took a pill right after you left."

"Kurt, you bonehead. It's almost one o'clock. I'm surprised you're even standing right now. You need to take your medicine every three hours, even if you think you don't need it. You need to stay ahead of the pain," I scolded. I swear it was like I was dealing with a ten-year-old, not a man who was almost thirty.

"I was sleeping, Lee. Not like I was awake and decided fuck it." He groaned as I helped him down on the couch and he closed his eyes. "Just give me the pill."

I grabbed one off the counter and handed it to him. "If you didn't take a pill, then why are they spilled all over the table?"

"I don't fucking know. I think I woke up for two seconds and tried to get them open but passed out before I could take one."

"You think you didn't take one? Kurt, what the hell are you doing? I swear you're going to give me an ulcer."

"I know I didn't take a pill, Lee, because if I did, I wouldn't feel like death right now."

I twisted the cap off the bottle of water and handed it to him. "Don't mess with your pills, Kurt. It's not like you're taking Tylenol."

Kurt rolled his eyes and swallowed the pill. "I know, Lee. I'm not a fucking idiot."

Ha. I couldn't even count on my two hands the amount of times my dad had said the same thing. My dad always claimed he was in control of the pills and that only idiots let it take over their lives.

My mom and dad being idiots are what put me in the situation I was in now. I walked into the kitchen, grabbed a soda out of the fridge and the Hot Pockets. "Here," I said setting down the plate and drink. "I'll call you when you need to take another pill. I'll try to be off by five, but I don't know if that's going to be possible. When we go to do your phone tonight, we'll have to hit up the grocery store, too. Everything in my fridge is expired."

Kurt nodded and took a bite. "Holy hell. That shit is hot," he huffed as he popped open the soda.

"Microwaves aren't really my friend," I said as I shrugged. "Call if you need anything."

Kurt waved me off and took another bite. "I'll be fine, mother," he mumbled.

I flipped him the bird and headed out the door. I really didn't feel like putting up with his shit anymore.

My phone rang as I was getting back into my car and I saw it was Kurt calling. "What?" I barked as I started the car.

"You still here?"

"Yes, I'm still in the driveway. Did you need something?" I put my hand on the shifter but didn't shift the car.

"Yeah. Don't let Luke be an ass to you and thanks for lunch."

Huh, totally not what I expected him to say. "Um, you're welcome."

"I'm serious, Lee. Don't let him think he can treat you like crap. You haven't done anything wrong." I had never heard Kurt be so serious before.

"Okay, I hear you, Kurt." The phone clicked in my ear, and Kurt was gone as quickly as he was there. I tossed my phone in the passenger seat and wondered where in the hell that had come from. I didn't think his pain pill would have kicked in that quickly.

I backed out of the driveway and headed back to the shop. I don't know what had changed in Kurt to make him be nice to me, but I wish I did.

A nice Kurt Jensen was something I could get used to.

****

Kurt

I tossed the phone on the table and winced. Son of a bitch, this shit hurt.

I felt like an ass when Leelee had disappeared out the door. It wasn't her fault I had flipped my car and fucked up my life. Hell, she was flipping her life upside down now to help me, and all I was doing was acting like she was to blame. I ran my good hand through my hair and sighed.

Everything was so fucked up, and I had no idea how to fix any of it.

****

CHAPTER 11

Leelee

"Head home, Lee. I can finish everything up."

"'I'm not done with the Toyota yet," I said as I peeked out from under the hood.

"He's not picking it up until tomorrow. You can finish it up when you get here in the morning."
Luke slammed the hood shut on the car he was working on.

After I had gotten back from making Kurt lunch, Luke had come out from the office and started helping with all the cars that were backing up. He had grumbled something that had sounded like sorry and then took over half of my workload. It seemed all the Jensen boys were in an apologetic mood today.

"You want me here early to get this done before we open?" I asked, as I wiped off my hands.

"No. All you have left to do is change the oil, right?"

"Yeah. But it'll only take me twenty minutes to do. I can do it quick. It's only five-thirty." I had told Kurt we would get his phone done but if we had to wait until tomorrow or even the weekend, he would have to deal with it. Right now, I was the only one making money, and I needed to work as much as I could.

"I got it, Lee. I was a dick to you this morning and gave you way too much shit to do because I was pissed off at Kurt."

I nodded, not really knowing what to say. He had been a dick to me, but I understood his frustration with Kurt. Hell, I felt the same way about him. "He'll come around, Luke. You just need to give him time."

"Time for what, Lee? He's a fucking grown man who acts like a sullen teenager and doesn't think about anyone but himself."

He was right, but only to a point. I knew Kurt didn't only think of himself. Jay and I were a prime example of how selfless Kurt could be. "He may not make the best decisions, Luke, but in his defense, he's had you making all of his choices for him so long, you have to realize he's going to make a couple of mistakes starting out."

"I don't make his decisions for him."

I crossed my arms over my chest. "You don't try to tell Kurt what to do all of the time?"

"I'm just looking out for him. He should be thankful that I care enough about him to help make his life better."

"You know you sound like an ass, right?"

"I'm not trying to be. I just want what's best for Kurt."

"And you don't think he wants the same thing? You need to give him more credit than you do. He's smart, and I don't think he's going to run his life into the ground. He may not make the same choices as you, but that doesn't make all of his choices wrong."

Luke looked me over and nodded. "You mean like the choice to marry you and not tell anyone?"

I swallowed hard. "Yeah. That would be one of those choices."

"You gonna say anything more about why you two are married or are we just gonna walk around the elephant in the room?"

I shrugged and pulled my keys out of my pocket. "Let's just say Kurt and I being married proves everything you just said wrong. He didn't marry me for his own benefit; he did it to help me. He hasn't gotten anything out of it."

Luke nodded. "Just don't let him bring you down, Lee."

I sighed. Luke was a lost cause at this point. He wasn't going to see anything past the mistakes Kurt had made. Hell, had he really made any mistakes that were that bad? Yeah, he had moved to California without a word to anyone, but I understood why he did. Luke had the best of intentions when it came to Kurt, but those intentions were quite misguided.

"Kurt's going to surprise you, Luke."

"I hope he does, Lee, because I'm sick of rescuing him."

I ducked through the front office just as Violet was coming in. "Hey, what are you still doing here?" she asked.

"Long day. I'd love to talk, but I need to run." I didn't want to talk. Talking with Luke had pissed me off, and all I wanted to do was go home.

"Oh, okay. Give me a call, yeah?"

I nodded and headed out. I didn't need to be so short with Vi, but I had a feeling she wanted to have the same conversation I had just had with Luke, and I wasn't up for that twice in one day.

My car purred to life, and I rested my hands on the steering wheel.

How in the hell had my life turned around from a year ago, where I wouldn't say one word to defend Kurt, and now, all I wanted to do was tell Luke how wrong he was about Kurt?

Luke was wrong about Kurt and I couldn't wait for the day when Luke would realize it.

****

CHAPTER 12

Kurt

Well, this was a fucking disaster. Who would have thought trying to make dinner would be so hard? Granted, all I was trying to do was warm up some Hot Pockets, but that was seeming to be more than I was capable of.

I took the plate out of the microwave and looked down at the spattered and exploded pockets of pizza. They looked like the ones Leelee had made for lunch, but when I touched them, they were rock hard and likely to break every tooth in my mouth if I were to try to take a bite.

After Leelee had left to go back to work, I hadn't been able to fall back asleep and with every passing hour, I felt like a caged animal with no way out. I still felt like hell, but I knew if all I did was lay around and not move, there would be no way I would loosen up and not be so stiff.

I had paced the living room fifty times, trying to get used to walking with the crutch. The problem I had that most people didn't when they had crutches was, I also had a broken arm. It just went to show when I did something, I did it one hundred percent.

At five o'clock, I became even antsier, waiting for Leelee to get home. By the time five forty-five rolled around, I was pissed off at Luke for making her stay late, and I was upset at myself for caring so much.

Making dinner was supposed to distract me, but all it had done was piss me the hell off.

"Wow, you're up." I spun around as fast as I could and saw Leelee walk through the door in her Skid Row uniform and bend over to untie her boots. "What is that smell?"

I held up the plate of rock hard Hot Pockets. "That is supposed to be dinner, but I think the microwave won this round."

Leelee laughed and toed off her boots. "Now you know my struggle. I never seem to be able to cook anything in that damn thing without it having explode on me."

"Yeah, I had the same problem except I went one step further and petrified it." I took one of the pockets off the plate and hit it on the counter. It sounded like I was banging it with a rock.

"Wow. That's a talent I have yet to conquer." She laughed. "How about I get changed, and we'll grab something to eat on the way to the phone store, then when we hit the grocery store, we won't buy everything we see because we're starving."

"Sounds like a damn plan to me." I dumped my ruined attempt at dinner into the garbage can and dropped the plate into the sink.

"Give me five minutes," she muttered and headed down the hall to her room.

I looked down at my feet and realized I had no idea how I was going to get my shoes on. But then I realized I had an even bigger problem. I didn't even have pants on. "Jesus Christ."

I hobbled down the hallway, bracing myself on the wall. I was so fucking out of it, I hadn't even realized I was just wearing boxers. I pushed open the bedroom door and was greeted with the sight of my jeans from last night, complete with a cut up the seam of the leg, and now, useless to me. "Fuck."

"What's wrong?"

"The only pair of pants I had are cut to the fucking crotch." I bent over and picked them up. "I know it's nice out, but I don't think airing out my crotch to the phone store is ideal."

Leelee laughed and grabbed some shorts off the floor. "I grabbed these last night, but you passed out before I was able to get them on you. I think Jay has some Adidas sandals in the closet too that'll be better than the work boots you were wearing." Leelee tossed the shorts at me then rummaged through the closet looking for the shoes.

"Sandals?" I wore tennis shoes and work boots; that was it.

"Yeah. I know they're not exactly manly, but with a broken leg and arm, you need something that is easy to slip on and has no laces. If you want, we can try to find you some other slide-on shoes. Jay has a pair of DC slide-on shoes he wears all of the time that are pretty cool."

"I'll figure out how to get my shoes on. I'm not wearing sandals." No fucking way.

"Yes, you are," she insisted. She grabbed the shorts out of my hands and held them out to me like I was a toddler. "Step in them." I tried to balance on my good leg and almost fell on my ass. "Put your arm on my shoulder to steady yourself, Kurt."

I lightly grabbed her shoulder and managed to wrestle one of my legs into the shorts. "Now, how the hell do I get my other leg in?"

She pushed on my stomach, throwing me off balance and I fell back onto the bed. She worked the shorts up my other leg and pulled me back up before I could catch my breath. She grabbed the sandals off the floor and set them next to my feet. "Put those on and then I'll find you a new shirt to wear. You're starting to smell a little ripe, but we don't have time for you to take a shower."

Fucking great. Not only was I a fucking cripple, but I also smelled like shit. "I'm going to have to call the hotel I was staying at and ask them to pack up all of my shit and send it to me."

"No need to. When you were passed out, I figured out where you were staying and checked you out. They weren't going to let me in at first, but once I told them I was your wife, they let me in."

"Funny how we went to no one knowing we were married, and now everyone knows, even the hotel clerk." I slid my feet into the sandals, thankful they weren't the ones that went between my toes.

"Yeah. There seems to be more benefit to it than we thought." Leelee laughed. "I left your bag in the car. Here's one of Jay's shirts. You two seem to be the same size." She held up a plain white shirt, and I knew it was going to be too small.

"Lee, that isn't going to fit."

She looked down at the shirt and shrugged. "So, it'll be a little tight." She tossed it on the bed and made her way over to me. She grabbed the hem of my shirt and worked my arm that wasn't broken out of the shirt and then pulled it over my head and slid it down my broken arm.

"Well, that was a hell of a lot easier than when the nurses had tried to get me dressed."

She grabbed the white shirt and worked it up my broken arm. "Jay broke his arm when he was younger. Mom and Dad were out on a bender and weren't around to help." She stretched my shirt out to my good arm, stuck it through the hole, then pulled it over my head. "It really was amazing that CPS didn't come sooner than they did."

"Did you ever wonder if maybe they would have come that your parents might have snapped out of it?"

"I wish. I think if that had happened, they would have just hidden it better. I think the reason they took off now was because Jay is older. He just turned seventeen, and they think he can take care of himself now."

"That's bullshit."

"Yeah, well, I can't argue with you on that one. Jay and I definitely didn't win the parent lottery." She pulled the shirt down my body, and it felt tight as hell.

I looked down. "Lee, you can see my God damn nipples through this thing."

She shrugged. "Eh, you'll survive. If anything, you'll have to beat the ladies off."

"I'm not looking to talk to anyone and especially not looking to attract any attention."

She propped her hands on her hips and smirked. "Well, I hate to break it to you, Kurt, but even with a broken leg and arm, you're still going to have to beat the ladies off."

"Well, then we better bring the crutch along. I'm not interested." I hobbled down the hallway, the damn sandals on my feet trying to trip me. "You do know that I was already struggling with the crutch, right? Now that you threw in these fucking sandals, you'll be lucky not to have to scrape me off the sidewalk. Men are not meant to wear fucking sandals."

"Just get in the car, Kurt." Leelee grabbed her keys off the coffee table, bending over in front of me and it finally registered what she was wearing.

Leelee was fucking hot. There was no other way to put it. Even in her Skid Row uniform, you could tell she had a hell of a body, but seeing Leelee in cutoff jean shorts and a tight green tank top had me stopping to take notice. She had miles of long, tanned legs, and I could go on for days about her lush ass that just begged for me to grab. She slipped a pair of sunglasses onto her face, shielding away her dark brown eyes that always saw too much when she looked at me. "You ready?"

I blinked twice, trying to process the question. "Uh, sure."

Leelee quirked her eyebrow at me. "Are you feeling okay? Do you need another pill? When was the last time you took one?"

"An hour ago, I should be good for another two."

Leelee reached over and grabbed the bottle off the coffee table. "I'll bring them along in case this takes longer than we think."

"Lee, we're only going for a phone and then the grocery store."

"Always be prepared, Kurt." Leelee headed to the door, swung it open and motioned for me to move. "Your chariot awaits, oh crippled one."

I hobbled out the door, tripping on the rug and almost landed on my ass.

I had a feeling this quick trip was going to be much more than I had bargained for.

****

CHAPTER 13

Leelee

"Red or green?"

"Huh?"

"Red or green?"

"Lee, I don't know what the hell you are talking about."

"Grapes, Kurt. Grapes." I held up two packages, one red and the other green.

"Is there really a difference?"

I rolled my eyes and put the red grapes in the cart. "Yes. The red taste better."

"Then, why in the hell did you ask me red or green, when you knew that you wanted the red?"

"Just being nice," I mumbled. We had only been at the grocery store for five minutes, and Kurt had already said seven times that he was ready to go. "Did you want to wait in the car?" I could be in and out of the store much faster if I didn't have Kurt with me.

"No. I'm here to hurry your ass up."

I looked Kurt up and down. "You gimping behind isn't exactly hurrying up."

Kurt turned his head and looked at the registers. "I'll be right back." He circled around and headed back the way we had just come.

"Kurt, where in the hell are you going?" I called. He waved his broken arm at me and headed out the front entrance. "Whatever," I mumbled to myself.

I had made it to the end of the produce aisle when I heard a loud buzzing. I set down the bunch of carrots I had in my hand and turned around to see Kurt cruising past the display of apples, barely missing clipping them with the back tire.

"Out of the way, woman, we're grocery shopping the fast way now." He grabbed a bunch of bananas as he flew past me and dropped them into the basket in front of his cart. "Move it or lose it, Lee." Kurt sped around the corner, and I could hear him dropping stuff into his basket.

"Lee, can we get Pop Tarts?" Kurt called from down the aisle.

I hung my head and couldn't help the smile that spread across my lips. "I only eat cherry," I yelled back.

"Sweet, me too." I heard him buzz further down the aisle and knew I needed to catch up to him if I wanted any chance of having more than Pop Tarts and bananas.

"Where do they keep the pizza rolls?"

Holy hell. I grabbed the carrots and ran down the aisle. "Are you actually grabbing things we need, or just filling the cart so we can leave?"

"Both." Kurt grabbed a box of taco shells and sailed it over his shoulder at me.

"Jesus Christ." I snatched the box out of the air and tossed it into my cart. "Do you think you could not throw shit at me?"

"No rules to speed shopping, Lee. Pick up the pace, or you'll be left behind." Kurt cruised to the end of the aisle, grabbing three more boxes of Lord knows what, then disappeared around the end and into the next aisle.

"That seems to be your motto."

"Hasn't failed me yet. That and bang shifting are the keys to my success."

I turned the corner down the next aisle and saw Kurt pulled over to the side, studying a box. "Bang shifting, really?"

Kurt shrugged and tossed the package back at me. "Gotta hammer through those gears as fast as possible. Bangshift, baby."

"Jesus, how many times have you used that line?" I snatched the pack of Rice-a-Roni he threw at me and put it back on the shelf.

"Enough. It's not really as effective as you would think."

"Hmph, I'm pretty sure you saying bang shift is enough." I passed Kurt and glanced in his basket. "Do you think we can get more than junk food and shit that is going to make my ass even bigger?"

"I wouldn't worry about that," Kurt mumbled.

I rolled my eyes and turned my cart to the right, cutting off Kurt, and looked down at him. "More healthy food, less shit."

"I'm paying, we buy what I want." Kurt twisted the throttle and rammed into my cart. "Out of my way."

"You're not paying."

"Yes, I am."

"Kurt, knock it off." He rammed into my cart again. "I'm paying for my own groceries."

"No." He rammed into my cart again, knocking me out of the way enough to sneak past me before I could recover. "And yes, I'm paying for the groceries. I'm eating the shit, too."

I wheeled my cart around and chased him down the aisle. "You're not working, Kurt. You don't have the money for groceries."

"You're right, Lee, I don't have a job, but you are wrong about not having money. Winning nine races this past year has cushioned my bank account. Not to mention the past eight years I've been racing. I can buy groceries for the next two months, and a new car for you," Kurt scoffed. "Put what you want in the cart, so we can get the hell out of here." He zoomed to the end of the aisle and cut over to the meat department. I knew the Jensen boys made their money racing and fixing cars, but I had no idea it was that lucrative. "Lee," Kurt called. "Move your ass."

I rolled my eyes but couldn't help but laugh. At least with Kurt on the motorized scooter, he was moving a lot faster. He had yet to master walking with his crutch. "I'm coming. I'm trying to grab food that isn't going to kill us."

By the time I made it over to Kurt, he was in the frozen food aisle, eyeing up the pizza rolls and Hot Pockets. "I'm determined to learn how to work the microwave. We need a shit ton more Hot Pockets for me to figure it out."

"Well, I guess that will give you something to do during the day." I opened the freezer door in front of Kurt and grabbed four boxes of Hot Pockets.

"Grab four more. They're actually not half bad if you don't turn them into rocks."

"You've never had a Hot Pocket before today?" Jay and I grew up on Hot Pockets. They were fast and easy to make when Mom and Dad weren't home. Which often happened, so Hot Pockets had become their own food group for us.

"Once or twice. Not often. I figure Jay liked them since you had so many in the freezer. Might as well restock him before he gets home." Kurt motored down a bit farther in front of the ice cream and crossed his arms over his chest. "Now, who in the hell decided to call an ice bar Magnum?"

"Hey," I protested. "Don't knock them until you try them. Those are my number one guilty pleasure. You have to savor them because they're so good."

"All right. I guess you better grab one of each kind. I have to see if you are right." Kurt opened the door and reached in, grabbing whatever his hand touched.

"Are you insane? These suckers are expensive." I grabbed the boxes out of Kurt's hand and put them back on the shelf. "There are like eight different kinds. You can't buy all of them."

"I can't? Is there a sign stating you can only buy one box?" Kurt looked around like a smart ass searching for a sign.

"No, there's not a sign, but it's a Leelee rule."

"A Leelee rule?" I nodded and crossed my arms over my chest. "I can't wait to hear this bullshit," Kurt muttered.

"You can't spend that much money on ice cream, Kurt. I won't let you. These things are like five bucks a pop. You're going to spend forty dollars on ice cream alone. No. Leelee Rule Number One: You cannot spend more than five dollars on ice cream."

"Fine. Move out of the way so I can follow the Rules of Leelee." I stepped back, and Kurt opened the door and quickly grabbed all eight different kinds and tossed them in the cart. "I've found a loophole."

My jaw dropped. "What do you mean you found a loophole?"

"Well, my loophole is that I don't give a shit about the Rules of Leelee. I want ice cream, and you said this was the shit. Now, it's in my cart, and we're leaving before it melts. Move, Lee," he ordered.

"I still have to get butter, milk, and cheese. When I say there is no food in the house, I mean there is *no* food in the house."

Kurt swung a U-turn, and three frozen pizzas and a box of ice cream bars fell out of his basket. "Pick that up, and I'll meet you by the milk," he replied, as he zoomed past me.

"Seriously," I mumbled. "How in the hell did I get stuck with this man?" I grabbed the pizzas and ice cream and tossed them into my cart.

"You signed up for this when you married me, and stop talking to yourself, Lee. You sound crazy."

"How in the hell did you hear me?" I asked, as I turned the corner and saw Kurt grabbing three gallons of milk and setting them by his feet.

"I hear you talk to yourself all of the time. Especially at work." He moved down further, grabbed a huge tub of butter and handed it to me.

"What? I do not talk to myself at work!" That was a bald-faced lie.

"You do, Lee. Let's not even get into your horrible taste in music when I walk past and hear the shit spewing from your headphones."

I slammed the butter down in my cart, squishing all the food beneath it. "My music is not crap."

Kurt smirked, twisted the throttle on the scooter and moved away. "It's shit, Lee. It's hard to believe a girl like you listens to boy band garbage." He grabbed two packs of processed cheese and three bags of shredded cheddar cheese and precariously balanced it on the mountain of food in his basket.

"I don't listen to boy bands." I didn't. At least, now I didn't.

"Ya do. All that pop shit is just that, shit. You need anything else?"

I looked at my overflowing cart and Kurt's teetering tower of junk food. "I have no idea. I was just as bad as you toward the end of those two aisles. I was just tossing in whatever. I can always run to the store tomorrow if we forgot anything."

Kurt nodded and made his way to the checkout. "For the record, I will stay home if you need to come back to the store. One night of grocery shopping a month is enough for me." Kurt rammed into the checkout and started throwing all the food onto the belt.

"You really can't tell you race cars by the way you drive that scooter." I laughed as I grabbed the milk from his feet.

"This damn thing has the worse steering ever. You can't compare this to a car. I'm surprised there aren't more accidents with these damn things with Grandma taking out the watermelon display on the way to the Depends."

The cashier scoffed. "You just described every Thursday. Senior discount day. It's a miracle they make it out without running into something."

"See, told ya," Kurt said, laughing. "I'm a stellar driver."

I rolled my eyes and grabbed my cart. "If you say so. I think your accident says otherwise."

Kurt growled but didn't say anything.

By the time we had everything up on the belt, the cashier already had ten bags full and was filling up Kurt's scooter. "I'm gonna run this out to the car. I'll be back for another load." He handed me his wallet. "Pay if I'm not back by the time she's done."

He zoomed out of the store, barely making it through the sliding doors before they closed on him and I watched him weave in and out of the cars.

"Boyfriend?" the cashier asked.

I opened Kurt's wallet and saw a wad of money. "Holy fuck."

"What was that?" she asked.

I snapped his wallet shut and looked up at the cashier. "Um, boyfriend? No."

"Roommates?"

Why in the hell did this woman care? "I guess so."

"Does he have a girlfriend?"

Then, it clicked. This chick was trying to figure out if Kurt was single. I really shouldn't be surprised, but I was. Kurt and I weren't really a couple, but it still stung that this woman was interested in Kurt. "No."

A smile spread across her lips, and she kept glancing at the door as she swiped all the items, waiting for Kurt to come back in.

"Three hundred eighty-nine dollars and seventy-seven cents."

I'm sure my eyes bugged out, shocked how all of this added up. I opened Kurt's wallet, hoping he had enough money because I knew, for a fact, I couldn't even afford half of these groceries. I handed her four one-hundred-dollar bills and tried not to cuss when Kurt came wheeling back through the door. I had been hoping I could beat him out and I wouldn't have to watch the cashier drool over him.

"Everything paid for?" he asked as he grabbed a bunch of bags and started loading them into the cart.

"Um, yeah. It was almost four hundred dollars, Kurt." I handed him back his wallet and waited for the cashier to give me the change.

"I kind of figured it would be, Lee. I think we bought half of the store."

I grabbed the change the cashier held out to me and noticed she wasn't even looking at me. Oh Lord, here we go.

"So, uh, what happened to you?" she asked.

Kurt didn't say anything, and I rolled my eyes. How the hell Kurt was clueless to this woman drooling all over him was beyond me. "Kurt, she's not talking to me." I grabbed the bags out of his hand and nodded at the cashier.

"Oh," he said, glancing over at her. "Car accident. I was going too fast for the turn."

"That's too bad. I could always come over and cook some of this for you." She batted her eyes at him, and I couldn't help but roll my eyes again.

"Thanks, but I think I'm good. Lee has that covered." Kurt gave her a panty-melting smile with his polite refusal.

It was like the girl hadn't even heard a word he said as she leaned over the register and gave Kurt a coy smile. "I could always come over and just keep you company."

Oh, sweet Jesus, the shit was getting thick in here. I grabbed the last of the bags and waited for Kurt to get her phone number so we could get the hell out of here. Hopefully, Kurt would have her come over when I was working. I didn't think I could handle him having girls coming over to the apartment.

"Thanks, but I'm going to have to pass."

"But she said you don't have a girlfriend," the girl pouted.

Kurt looked at her name tag and leaned in. "She's right, Kelly. I don't have a girlfriend. I have a wife. Thanks for the offer, though." Kurt hit the reverse on his scooter and backed away.

I had to pick my jaw off the floor and gave the cashier a sheepish grin. She glared at me, and I swear I heard her hiss at me.

"What the hell was that?" I asked Kurt as we made our way over to the car.

"What?"

"Why the hell did you tell that chick you're married?"

Kurt stopped his scooter by the car and gingerly stood. "Because I am married, Lee."

"Since when did that stop you from dating and getting girls' phone numbers?"

"Since the day we got married, Lee." He opened the back door of the car and laid the bags in the backseat. "I know it may not mean much to you, but that day meant something to me."

I was speechless. I stood there watching him load the car up, and I couldn't move. Kurt Jensen hadn't dated since we got married? "You haven't done, well, anything?"

Kurt shook his head and sat back down on the scooter. "Nah. I'm gonna take this back and grab a soda from the vending machine. I need another pain pill." He took off to the front door, not realizing he had just rocked my whole world off its axis.

Kurt Jensen hadn't been with anyone since he married.

Eighteen months and counting and Kurt Jensen had stuck by his vows.

Holy hell.

****

CHAPTER 14

Kurt

"This where you've been hanging out?"

I opened the door wide and stepped to the side. "Yeah. At least, for the last two weeks."

Nos stepped through the door and clapped me on the back. "You don't look too bad for almost dying."

I had to agree. My face had healed completely in the past two weeks, and the only remaining evidence of my crazy ride was my arm and leg. "Yeah. If only I could fucking drive, I'd be golden."

"Eh, give it time, brother." Nos sprawled out on the couch and spread his arms across the back.

"Of course, you would say that. With me out of the scene, you've got a better chance of winning."

Nos shrugged. "It definitely isn't hurting me having you out, although I still need to contend with Mitch."

"How's he been doing?" I sat down in the recliner and rested my arm on my stomach.

"I beat him last week, but the two races before that he wiped the floor with me."

"AZ still around?"

Nos laughed and shook his head. "AZ. Where do I even begin with that asshole?" Nos kicked his feet up on the coffee table. "Last I heard, he was trying to piece together a car on the south side. He's low on cash, though, so he's taking any and all work he can get."

"Oh yeah?" I could only imagine the shit AZ was doing.

"Last night, I saw him at the club, slinging fucking drinks. He served me the weakest rum and coke I've ever had."

"AZ, a fucking bartender?" I couldn't picture AZ behind the bar.

"Yeah. At least, for now. He keeps serving shitty drinks; I doubt it'll be for long." Nos looked around. "So, whose house is this?"

"Lee's."

"Leelee? Leelee Perez?"

"Yeah, one and the same."

Nos whistled low and shook his head. "Word on the circuit is you two can't stand each other, and now you two are shacked up together?"

"Ha, Lee and I are far from shacked up. She's just helping me until I get back on my feet."

"Hell. She's pretty fucking helpful. Letting you shack up with her goes beyond helpful."

"Whatever, Nos. You think we can talk about why I asked you to come over?" Nos shrugged. "I need your help."

"Sure. Whatever you need."

I knew I could count on Nos. We had been racing each other for years, competitors on the track, but off the track, we were good friends. "I need a car and a place to work on the car."

"Why can't you work on it at Skid Row?"

Apparently, word of my falling out with Luke and Mitch hadn't hit the streets yet. "I don't work there anymore."

"I kind of figured that when you ran off to California, but I thought you'd fall right back in there."

"Naw, there's nothing there for me. It's time I made something that's just mine."

Nos nodded. "I get that. Make a name for yourself."

At least Nos understood what the hell I meant. "I don't plan on hanging around for too long. At least until I'm cleared by the doc, and then I don't know where I'm going, but I know no matter what, I'm going to need a car."

"What are you in the market for?"

"Something they aren't gonna see coming. A good base that I can build off."

"I know a guy who's looking to unload his GTO."

"Year?"

"'06. Base model. V8, 6.0L. That car in the right-hand lane could definitely win some races. There is one thing, though."

Great. He was probably going to tell me it was in pieces or some bullshit. "What is it?"

"It's purple."

"Purple?"

"Yeah, brother. Fucking Barney purple."

"Jesus Christ. It sounds like I'll be changing that."

Nos laughed. "Could be a cool thing. Spin it to work in your favor."

I would cross the purple bridge when I got there. Right now, I was trying to figure out what motor I could drop in it and everything I needed to make this car a winner. "You know of a place I can work at?"

"My uncle just closed down his shop. He couldn't keep up with the new cars."

"You didn't want to take over the business?" If I were Nos, I would have jumped at the shot to own my own shop.

"Nah, that shit ain't for me. I'm good with working for Neal. He deals with all the business bullshit, and I just work on the cars."

"I'll pay rent."

"I'll pass it on to Nick. I'm sure he'll appreciate anything you throw at him. The building is just sitting empty right now."

"Tools?" I had no idea where the hell my tools were. I was going to have to rebuild my stockpile I used to have.

"All there. You're basically walking into a fully stocked garage. Three lifts, and all of the tools you could need."

"When do you think we can head over to the GTO? I need to find out as soon as possible if the car works for me."

"I'll give the guy a call tonight. See if we can meet up tomorrow." Nos stood and pulled his phone out of his pocket. "What are you up—"

"Thank Christ that day is over. I swear to God, I was ready to kill—" Leelee barged through the door and stopped in her tracks when she saw Nos.

"Sup," Nos grunted.

"Uh, hi," Leelee murmured. "I can go." She backed out the door, and I shot up out of my chair.

"No. You're good, Lee. Nos and I were just talking, but he's headed out right now."

"Oh, well, I'll let you two talk." She headed down the hall to her room and slammed the door.

"What the hell was that about?" Nos asked.

"Not a clue, brother. We've actually been getting along pretty well."

"I always thought you two would be good in the sack. It's only a matter of time with you two shacking up that you'll see it, too."

"What in the fuck are you talking about?" I laughed. "You sound like a damn woman right now."

"Fuck off, man. I see shit, and I know something is going on with you two."

Fucking Nos couldn't be more right. "There's nothing. Now, why don't you find out about my car and the shop and stop worrying about Lee and me."

Nos flipped me off and headed out the door. "I'll call you tomorrow, asshole."

I closed the door behind Nos and shook my head. I have to do something, and I knew Nos was going to come through with exactly what I needed. I had been trapped in Lee's house for the past two weeks, and I was already going stir-crazy." Getting a new car and souping it up was the thing that was going to help me. I had plenty of time to sit around and figure out what I wanted to do, and this was the first step in my plan.

I glanced down the hallway, wondering why Lee had fled to her room so quickly when she had seen Nos. She had to know him from the races, so I didn't get why she didn't want to stick around.

I hobbled down the hallway, finally able to get around a little better, and knocked on her door. "Yo, Lee. You know what you want for dinner?"

"Whatever you want," she yelled. "Just let me know when Nos leaves."

"He's gone." Why the hell was she hiding in her room because Nos was here? "Are you coming out?"

"Um, yeah," she muffled.

"Lee, what in the hell is going on?"

"Nothing. Just give me a second, Kurt."

"I want to know wha—" Leelee flung the door open and was standing there in just a tank top and lime green underwear.

My gaze dropped to her legs, and I couldn't rip my eyes off her. I swear to Christ, she had legs for days. I couldn't tell you how many times I had pictured those legs wrapped around me while I plunged into her body. Leelee snapped her fingers and my eyes regretfully moved to her face. Her arms were folded across her chest, and she was glaring at me. "I've had a shit day, Kurt. You think you can give me five minutes to myself before I have to start waiting on you?" She stepped back and slammed the door in my face.

"What the fuck?" I whispered. I raised my hand to pound on her door and demand she tell me what in the hell was going on but stopped before my fist hit the door. She thought she waited on me? Where in the hell was that coming from?

I headed back to the kitchen and leaned against the counter. I didn't want to be here as a burden to Leelee. I had been trying to pull my weight as much as possible, but I still wasn't up to one hundred percent.

Making dinner was something I should be able to handle myself. She was working eight to ten hours at the garage every day and making dinner wasn't that hard.

I checked over the fridge, trying to figure out what I could make that wouldn't taste like shit. "Think, Kurt. What the hell can you make that won't kill Lee?"

I grabbed the eggs, milk, and a pound of bacon from the freezer. You couldn't go wrong with breakfast for dinner. My culinary skills only extended to the microwave and grill, but I could also make a mean breakfast.

"I'm sorry."

I glanced over my shoulder and saw Leelee leaning against the wall; her arms crossed over her chest. I could still see her amazing legs, but she at least had shorts on now. I turned back to the cabinet and reached up to grab a bowl. "No need to be sorry."

"Yeah, there is. I shouldn't have taken my shitty day out on you."

I shrugged and started cracking eggs into the bowl. "You wanna tell me why your day was shitty?"

Leelee walked to the fridge and pulled out a Corona. "Men are assholes. That about sums up my crappy day pretty well."

I chuckled and shook my head. "Luke in a shitty mood today?"

"Nah. He wasn't even there for half of the day. Every other guy I came into contact with today though was an ass. When is the time going to come when a fucking guy is okay with a chick changing his oil?" Leelee took a long drink of her beer and wiped her mouth with the back of her hand. "They act like I should be in the kitchen making a pie or some shit."

"You know you're one of the best mechanics in the city, Lee. Why the hell are you letting these asshats get to you?"

"Because those asshats are threatening to take their business away from Luke if I work on their car."

"What? How in the hell do you know that?"

Leelee set down her beer and glided over to see what I was making. "Because they told me on the phone today. They wanted to request that only Luke, Mitch, and Kurt work on their cars. I told them they obviously didn't get the memo that you were out and they were stuck with me."

"You tell Luke? You know he isn't going to put up with that shit."

"Yeah, but I'm pretty sure he's not going to put up with losing half of his customers because of me. It looks like I'm going to have to find a new job before Luke cans me."

I set the pan on the stove and shook my head. "He's not going to can you, Lee."

"Yeah, he is."

"Luke isn't going to get rid of the best mechanic he has because a couple of guys don't like chicks. Brush it off and prove 'em wrong."

"That's so easy to say when you have everyone in your corner. This isn't the first time I've had to deal with assholes, and I'm sure it won't be the last."

I sprayed the pan and then dumped the eggs in.

"Aren't you going to cook the bacon first?" she asked.

"Fuck. Yeah, I probably should." I turned off the stove and moved the pan off the heat.

"Here, I got it. You work on the eggs, and I've got the bacon." Leelee pulled another pan from the cabinet and set it on the stove. "You want toast with it, too?"

"Yeah, but I can get it. You don't need to make the bacon, either." Leelee was taking over making dinner when my plan was to make dinner for her.

"Um, I can help. You don't need to make me dinner."

"Lee, I don't need you waiting on me. I can get around and take care of myself more now. You don't need to worry."

"Kurt, I didn't mean what I said before. I was just taking out my frustration on you. You're a man and an easy target." She laughed, pulled open the package of bacon, and laid four pieces in the pan. "You're doing more than I thought you would be able to do."

"I'm trying. Nos was over helping me figure out what my next move is. I need to get moving more." I pulled the eggs back onto the burner. "He's helping me line things up."

"Oh, like a job?"

"I guess you could call it that."

She nodded but didn't ask anymore.

"When does Jay get back?" I asked, as I grabbed the bread and popped a couple of slices into the toaster.

"Wednesday."

"He knows I'm here?"

Leelee grabbed a couple of paper towels, spread them on a plate then laid the cooked bacon on it. "Yeah. I told him I was helping you out."

"He okay with me being here?"

"He doesn't really have a choice. Besides, school starts soon. He'll barely be home between classes and football." Leelee laid out four more pieces of bacon in the pan then wrapped up the rest of the bacon and put it back in the fridge.

"I'll take the couch when he comes back. I don't want to put him out in his own home."

"You won't have to do that if you don't want to. Jay is young. He can handle sleeping on the couch."

"We'll see." I stirred the eggs, thankful I hadn't burned the hell out of them.

"I'm gonna grab another beer; you want one?" Leelee opened the fridge and pulled out two beers.

"I probably shouldn't with all of the pain pills I've been taking."

"More for me to drink." Leelee set the one beer down and popped the top on the other. I grabbed two plates down from the cabinet and loaded them full of eggs and bacon. Leelee grabbed the toast out of the toaster and slathered them with butter.

"You tell Luke about what happened?" I grabbed two forks out of the drawer and handed one to Leelee.

"No. He doesn't need to know."

"I think you should tell him."

"Well, it's a good thing you don't work there anymore because I don't have to listen to you when it comes to work shit."

I shook my head and picked up my plate. Leelee handed me a piece of toast, and we headed into the living room. Leelee sat on one end of the couch, and I sat on the other. This had been our routine for the past two weeks. Leelee came home from work, she made dinner, we sat in the living room watching TV until about ten and then we would both go to bed. It was boring, but I didn't mind it. I liked hanging out with Leelee. Before the whole CPS situation and getting married, Leelee and I used to hang out quite a bit. Normally, it was after a race or when we would run into each other at the bar, but we at least hung out.

I had missed her the past year when we were both at each other's necks, neither of us knowing what the other was thinking.

"What do you want to watch? I don't know if there is a new *Fast and Loud* on tonight."

"There isn't. I checked the TV guide earlier. It looks like it's a movie night." I shoveled a mound of eggs into my mouth and chased it down with a bite of bacon.

"I have like ten movies, and I've seen them all five times."

"You can do what Luke, Mitch, and I always do. Pop in one of the *Fast and the Furious* movies. Those never get old."

"I heard Frankie complain about you guys always watching those movies. I guess she wasn't over-exaggerating."

"Nah," I mumbled. "They're classics, and every time we watched them, Frankie was sitting right next to me on that couch." I finished off my eggs and bacon and set my plate on the coffee table. "You want one of our ice creams?" I asked, as I stood and headed into the kitchen.

"Um, maybe in a little bit." Leelee followed me into the kitchen and dropped her plate into the sink. "Leave the dishes. I can do them before I go to work in the morning."

"You know I'm not going to argue with you on that one, Lee." I set my plate on top of hers and headed back to the living room. Our dinner only managed to last five minutes tops because we both ate so fast. "I'm picking a movie," I hollered. "You have all of them, right?"

"Yeah. They are under the TV. I think Jay might have worn out the first two, though."

"Oh yeah? He still into cars?" I blindly grabbed one of the DVDs and pulled out the third movie in the series.

"Yeah. He's always bugging me to teach him, as he likes to say, everything."

"Smart kid."

"Not really." Leelee walked back into the living room and flopped down on the couch. "I'm not someone to look up to. I barely finished high school and everything I know, I learned watching other guys work on cars."

"I've always said I'd rather be street-smart than book-smart." I popped the disc into the player, turned off the lights, and sat down next to Lee, who now had her legs propped up on the couch. Her leg was bent at the knee, trying not to touch my leg. I grabbed her foot, stretching her leg out and rested it on my lap.

"What are you doing?" she protested as she tried to move her foot out of my hand.

"You had a shit day, Lee. Just watch the movies and don't worry about what I'm doing." I lightly kneaded her foot and watched the opening scene.

"This is crazy. I don't know why you are doing this." Her whole body was tense, and I could feel it all the way down to the tips of her toes.

"Lee. For once in your life, could you just keep your mouth shut and let me do what I want to do?"

Leelee scoffed and tried snatching her foot out of my grasp again. Thankfully, her feet were dainty, and they were easy to hold on to. "Rude," she mumbled under her breath as she turned her head back to the screen. "I feel like you're sucking up for something you did."

"There isn't much these days that I do, that you don't know about. If I needed to suck up for something, you would know about it. Although, I do need to make it up to you for letting me stay here for so long."

"Well, your name is technically on the lease. I'm just the tenant that lives here."

I shook my head. "That's shit, Lee. You know that this is your place. My name being on the lease means nothing."

Leelee relaxed further into the couch and kicked up her other foot and put it in my lap. "Keep telling yourself that. One day, I'll have something that is just mine. I could always open my own shop, but then I wouldn't have any customers because no one would come seeing that I'm a woman."

I nodded and filed away what she said so flippantly. "Maybe someday, Lee."

She rested her head on the armrest of the couch, and I pulled the blanket she had draped over the back of the couch and laid it over her legs and half over my lap. "That is a dream that I don't see becoming a reality anytime soon."

"You never know, Lee. When you least expect shit, it fucking happens."

She closed her eyes and a small smile spread across her lips. "You mean how you didn't expect me to fall asleep, but here I am, ready to start sawing logs and we're not even ten minutes into all the Vin Diesel goodness."

"You mean his badassery, right?"

"Badassery?" she asked, laughing.

"Yeah, Lee. You can't sit there and say that Vin is not the most badass guy ever. The way he drove that Challenger at the end of the first movie should be considered a highlight in all of cinematography."

"Crazy, Kurt. You're out of your mind." She burrowed under the blanket and hummed as my hand continued to rub her foot. I wished my arm wasn't busted so I could rub both of her feet at the same time, but that wasn't an option to me right now. "I'm going to fall asleep," she said around a yawn.

"Go for it, Lee. I can watch this by myself."

She hummed low and turned her head to look at the screen. "Oh darn. This is the one that doesn't have Vin in it except for the very end when he shows up in Japan to race that other guy."

"It's still fucking good, Lee. Go to sleep, so I can watch the movie in peace and not have you interrupting the movie every ten seconds."

Her eyes fluttered shut, but a smirk played on her lips. "Be thankful my day was so hectic."

I switched feet and started rubbing the other one. Her body relaxed, and I knew she had finally fallen asleep. I laid her feet in my lap, and my eyes watched the TV, but I didn't really see what was going on.

I didn't know how I had ended up here—Leelee and I watching a movie and her sweet body touching mine—but here I was. Finally, able to get the girl who hadn't left my mind the last year next to me, and she wasn't running away.

I just hoped it would stay that way.

****

CHAPTER 15

Leelee

"Are you coming to the race tonight?"

I was leaned into the engine bay of a suped-up Camaro when Violet asked the question I had been trying to avoid. "Um, I'm not sure."

"What is there not to be sure about? You need to come. Scar and I are clueless when it comes to cars. You being there helps to make us look better."

"You don't need me to look good," I mumbled, as I tighten the oil cap.

"Yes, we do. Everyone knows that I'm clueless about cars and it's ridiculous that Luke is dating me." Violet leaned against the fender and sighed. "I feel like an idiot at the races."

"Number one," I said as I slammed the hood shut. "Luke could care less about the fact that you know nothing about cars. He knew from day one that you didn't know a dipstick from a banana and he was okay with it."

"This is true," she muttered.

"Number two," I held up two fingers in her face, "don't give a fuck about what anyone thinks at that race."

"Easier said than done. Ginny has been at the last two races, and I've wanted to scratch her eyes out anytime I saw her."

"Then, do it. Bitch needs to be put in her place." I wiped my hands on the rag in my back pocket and tossed it on the workbench.

"Luke isn't fond of the idea of me getting into a fist fight with Ginny."

"It'd be more of a cat fight with you two. Lots of scratching and hair pulling. I bet you could get people to pay to see that." I laughed knowing what kind of assholes hung out at the races.

Violet rolled her eyes. "Still, not something Luke would like me to do. But that is beside the point. You need to come to the race. If not to make me look better, than just to be there so I have someone to talk to."

"I really don't think Kurt wants to go to the race, Vi. Luke and him still aren't talking."

"Then, don't bring him. Or, kidnap him and bring him along. I don't care what you do as long as you're there." Violet pointed her finger at me. "Make it happen, Lee, otherwise I'm calling in reinforcements."

"Luke?"

"No, Levi. No one can say no to that kid." Violet headed out of the shop and closed the door behind her.

I rested a hip against the Camaro and closed my eyes. Dammit, I really did want to go to the race, but I also wanted to stay home and spend some more time with Kurt before Jay came home. I only had four more nights alone with Kurt.

I had no idea what was going on with Kurt and me, but we had called a truce of some sorts, and I had no interest in breaking the ceasefire. Kurt being nice, cooking dinner, and just hanging out with me was better than the Kurt who hated to see me and scowled every time he did.

Even if I decided to go to the race, there was no guarantee Kurt would come along. It wasn't that I couldn't leave him alone, it was I didn't *want* to leave him alone. I repeat, Kurt was nice to me, and I didn't want to mess it up.

I glanced at the clock over the door and pulled my phone out of my pocket. It was going on five o'clock, and I figured I would give Kurt a heads up about the race. If he didn't want to go, then I wasn't going to go, either. I would just have to lock my door and not let anyone in if we stayed home. Violet's threat of sending Levi after me was a good one and I knew I wouldn't be able to say no to him.

What are you doing? I was too chicken to call him and ask. Text messaging was the easy way to go.

Just got back to the house. I was with Nos all day.

I still had no idea what Kurt was doing with Nos. *Wanna go out tonight?* Yes, I was crossing my fingers hoping Kurt wouldn't ask what I wanted to do and just get in the car with me. A girl could dream, right?

What did you want to do?

Damn. *I thought we could grab a bite to eat and then head over to the race. Violet wants us to come tonight.* I mentioned Violet, hoping that would guilt him into going. I was not above laying a guilt trip on the man.

Really?

Uh oh. That wasn't the answer I was hoping for. *You don't need to talk to Luke or Mitch at all.*

And what the hell do I get out of this?

Um, anything you want. I looked down at what I had just sent and felt a heart attack coming on. Anything could be, well, *anything.* "Oh hell." *Within reason.* I sent off quickly.

Deal.

Fuck. Shit. Fuck. One minute ago, I was worried he wouldn't want to go, and now that he was going, I was terrified not knowing what he was going to want in return.

"Everything okay, Lee?" Mitch walked into the shop and tossed a clipboard on his workbench.

"Uh. Sure. I was just making plans with Kurt."

Mitch nodded and crossed his arms over his chest. "What are y'all up to?"

"I think we're going to the race tonight."

"No shit? How in the hell did you manage that one? Luke has been calling him all week trying to set something up to get together, and Kurt keeps blowing him off."

Really? I had no clue about any of that. Kurt told me he hadn't heard from Luke in weeks. "I just asked him if he wanted to go and he said yes." There was no way I was going to tell Mitch I told Kurt he could have anything he wanted if he came with. That was a detail I would keep to myself. "Is Scarlett going to be there tonight?"

"Yeah. Frankie volunteered to watch Levi for us overnight, so we plan on going to the race and then out to the movies after. You and Kurt should come with us."

"I'll have to ask Kurt. I'm surprised that he said yes to the race tonight."

"How are you two doing?"

"Um, what do you mean?" Why was it no matter who I talked to, they had to know something about Kurt, me, or Kurt and me? Thankfully, Violet hadn't pressed me for too many details so far, but I knew she was chomping at the bit to find out what was up with us.

"I mean, I'm sick of walking around the elephant in the room. You're married to my brother, and not one of us knew about it. I say you start with how in the hell that happened, and then from there, I can figure out what my next question will be."

"Kurt helped me when I needed it."

"Lee, I helped Scar when she needed help, but I didn't fucking marry her."

"Well, marrying me was the only solution to my problem. At least, it was the only solution Kurt, and I could come up with."

Mitch ran his hand over his head. "You think you might tell me what that problem was that Kurt solved?"

I hung my head and knew there was no way out of telling Mitch everything. "Both of my parents took off and left Jay and me behind. Their leaving didn't really affect me since I didn't live at home anymore, but it really fucked over Jay."

"Where in the hell did your parents go, and how the fuck do they leave their fifteen-year-old to fend for themselves?"

I shrugged and shoved my hands into my pockets. "Drugs will make ya do some fucked up shit, Mitch. It wasn't the first time they left, but it was the fact that they didn't come back after a weeklong bender. Jay moved into my house and things were going fine until word got out that Mom and Dad left and then the school came knocking wondering who was taking care of Jay."

"That's fucking bullshit. You were probably giving that kid more than your shit parents ever did."

I laughed and shook my head. "I have never heard a truer statement."

"So, you and Kurt got married to get CPS off of your back?"

Ding, ding, ding. I guess it was pretty obvious why Kurt and I got hitched after I told the story of how shitty my parents were. "Yeah. It was supposed to be just for show, but then Kurt and I started to spend time together even more, but I ended it before it became anything."

"That's why he hates you. He wanted more, and all you wanted was to get CPS off your back."

Well, when put that way, it sounded like I was a heartless bitch. "No."

"Then, why in the hell did y'all breakup?"

"We're not broken up. At least, not to the state of Illinois, we're still married. Kurt never got a divorce, and I couldn't afford one."

"You could have asked Luke and me for help. You know we would have helped you no matter what."

"I know that now. Back then, I didn't even know you or Mitch. Kurt, I met at the races, and we would hang out every now and then. He surprised the hell out of me when he suggested that we get married, and I went along with it because I didn't know what else to do, and I would have done anything to keep Jay with me."

"Obviously."

"Look, Mitch. This is all fucked up, and I have no idea how to fix any of it. Now, not only does Kurt hate me, he hates you and Luke, too."

"You're wrong, Lee. He doesn't hate any of us; he's just trying to figure out who he is. I know from experience, being behind Luke can be daunting. He built this garage from the ground up, giving us all a better life. It's hard to compete with something like that."

"But you guys don't need to compete. You're brothers. Luke may have started this garage, but you're all keeping it going."

Mitch pointed the finger at me and a smirk spread across his lips. "Right on, Lee. Now, all you need to do is convince Kurt of that."

"Wait." I held up my hand and shook my head. "Why in the hell do I need to be the one to convince him of that?"

"Because you're the only one he's going to listen to."

None of this made sense. Why in the hell did Mitch think Kurt was only going to listen to me? We were getting along, but I knew it was only a reprieve until Kurt was back to one hundred percent. "Did you hit your head today?"

Mitch laughed and crossed his arms over his chest. "No, Lee. I just know what Kurt is thinking and what he is going through. I felt the same way at one point."

"Yeah, but you didn't completely disown your family, run off to California, and then almost kill yourself in a car accident."

"No, I didn't. But that's what makes Kurt. He flies off the handle and doesn't think before he acts. But, once he cools down and takes a chance to think, he knows what he needs to do."

"Hell, I don't even know what he should do. How am I supposed to help him figure it out?"

Mitch laughed and headed to the overhead door and pressed the button to close it. "Honestly, Lee? I don't know what the hell you are going to do, but whatever it is, you need to do it before Kurt gets a hair up his ass and decides to leave again."

I grabbed my car keys off my toolbox and headed out the back door to where I had parked my car. After I unlocked the doors and slid in behind the wheel, I stuck the key in the ignition and cranked it on. "What in the hell are you going to do, Lee?" I asked out loud.

If I wasn't careful, Kurt was going to slip through my fingers again, and I would be back where I started.

Kurt wasn't going to leave again. I was going to make sure of that.

Hopefully.

****

CHAPTER 16

Kurt

"I changed my mind. We don't need to go to the race tonight."

I slipped my feet into the sandals Lee had given me two weeks ago and grabbed her keys off the coffee table. "We're going."

"You do know that Mitch and Luke are going to be there, right?"

"Yeah. I kind of figured that out."

"Are you sure you want to see them?"

I hobbled over to the door and tossed it open. "I'm a big boy, Lee. I can handle seeing my brothers."

"Can you handle seeing your brothers and not punching them? I'm not in the mood for a bloodbath tonight, Kurt." Leelee grabbed the sweatshirt she had tossed over the back of the couch and pulled it on over her head.

"I don't plan on talking to them, Lee. So, I don't think you have anything to worry about. Now, let's go. We can grab something to eat after the race if that's okay with you. I'm meeting Nos at the race so we can go over some things." Progress on the GTO had been slow, but things were hopefully going to start picking up in the week to come. The thing I needed to talk to Nos about was the garage I was working in.

Nos hadn't told me how state of the art the damn thing was when he offered to let me work there. The garage was amazing. I had an idea, and I wanted to run it past Nos to see if he was down with what I was thinking.

"You and Nos have been hanging out a lot lately."

I shrugged and headed down the sidewalk to the car. "We've always been friends. He's just helping me with some things."

"Oh, well that's cool." Leelee slid into the driver's seat and cranked up the car.

I fell into my seat, still not as graceful as I should be. I knew it was killing Leelee not knowing what was going on with Nos and me, but I didn't want to say anything until I knew what the hell I was doing. Right now, everything was an idea in my head. I didn't want to open my mouth until everything was concrete. "The race is over on 5th tonight."

"I heard." Leelee backed out of the driveway and headed over to the race. "That's the first time they've raced over there, right?"

"Yeah. I've been wanting to race over there for years and wouldn't you know when they finally decide to race there, I can barely fucking walk, let alone drive a damn car. Fuckers." 5th street was one of the curviest and hardest roads to drive in the city, and everyone was afraid of it. Everyone but me. 5th street was where I had learned how to drift. If you could drift on 5th, you could drift anywhere.

"You drift over there all the time."

"Yeah, but I've never raced there. I'd love to beat all those fuckers over there. Most of them would spin their tires and crash on the fourth curve."

"You think so? I hope Mitch doesn't crash tonight." Leelee turned onto the main road and headed west out of town.

"He won't. He's cautious. Now, if AZ were racing, I would bet good money that fucker will crash."

"I haven't heard much about AZ lately. Did he finally get sick of getting his ass whipped by the Jensen boys?"

"That, and I don't think he had the money to keep racing and wrecking. It's one thing to do a little damage to your car; it's another to completely annihilate the damn thing."

"I guess you would know how that goes." Leelee glanced at me, a smirk on her face.

"Yeah. California was me not knowing the course and driving like an ass."

"I'm surprised you'd admit that. Most guys would blame the track or something asinine like the weather."

I shrugged and glanced out the window. I wish I could blame the road, but I crashed because I was driving pissed off, trying to prove myself to everyone. "I was driving for the wrong reasons in California."

"Money?"

"No. I was driving for everyone but myself."

"Oh."

Yeah, oh was right. I had fucked up that night, and now I was paying for it. Crashing my car and almost dying was not the way to prove to Luke and Mitch that I could make it on my own. "You think we'll be able to get a close parking spot? I'm getting better at walking, but I'm not really up to walking my ass off."

"I called Pedro. He said we could park behind his truck."

"Huh?" I asked, wondering who in the hell Pedro was. Not that I had a right to know who he was, but I was jealous of the guy all the same.

"The taco truck."

"You got an in with the taco guy?"

Leelee turned the corner onto 5th, and we instantly hit a crowd of people. She slowly crept down the street, urging the crowd to part with the bumper of her car. "We went to school together, and he hooks me up with tacos."

I nodded, but I still was jealous. What in the hell was going on?

We finally made it to the area where all the food trucks were parked, and Leelee pulled her tank behind the taco trailer.

"Yo, Lee. I haven't seen you in a while," a guy called from the back of the truck as I opened my door and swung my legs out of the car.

"I was out of town for a bit and just been working my ass off," Leelee said as she walked over to the guy and gave him a hug. He wrapped his arms tight around her and lifted her off the ground.

My stomach tightened as I watched him run his hands over her back and she wrapped her arms around his neck. "You want your usual, babe?" he asked as he set her back on the ground.

"Yeah. Throw in a couple extra. I'm extra hungry tonight."

The guy threw his head back laughing and disappeared into the trailer.

"You need help?" Leelee asked as she turned back to me.

I was still sitting in the car like an idiot, paralyzed by what I had just seen. "Uh, no. I'm good." I braced my hands on the door and hoisted my ass out of the car and prayed my arms wouldn't give out.

"No need to stop for dinner on the way home. Pedro is hooking us up with dinner."

"I heard. How much is it?" I pulled my wallet out of my pocket and grabbed a fifty out.

"Nothing. Pedro owes me."

I was holding the fifty up to Lee, ready to ask her what the hell she meant by Pedro owing her when he jogged down the steps of the trailer with a box overflowing with food.

"Here you go, babe. If you need anything more, just let me know." He winked at Lee and headed back into the trailer.

I was beginning to see what kind of arrangement Leelee and Pedro had, and I didn't fucking like it.

"Hungry?" Leelee asked as she held up the box to me.

"No." I was fucking starving, but I didn't want a damn taco from Pedro. "I need to find Nos. You coming with me, or you want me to drop you off with Vi and Scar?"

"Um, you don't want to watch the race with me?"

"I do, but I'm going to watch it with Nos."

Leelee looked around, and I knew she was torn on who she wanted to watch the race with, but I wasn't going to hang out with Luke tonight. "Can we stop by and say hi to Violet and Scarlett before we find Nos?"

I nodded over her shoulder. "Yeah. I saw them back that way." When we had driven through the crowd, I had spotted Luke and Mitch leaning against Mitch's Vette. "Nos is over there, too."

"Okay. Lead the way. I figure if anyone gets in our way, you can whack them upside the head with your cast."

"Really, Lee? If that was your plan, then I should have brought my crutch. That's a much better weapon."

"Duly noted for our next excursion."

I slowly made my way through the crowd with Leelee following close behind, bumping into me every time I had to stop for someone crossing our path. "You need to get your brake lights checked." Leelee laughed when she smashed into me. "You're going to be wearing our dinner on your back soon."

"Well, if these fuckers would just get out of my way, we wouldn't have a problem." A guy in a blue shirt who had cut me off glared at me over his shoulder. "Yeah, I'm talking to you, fucker," I growled under my breath.

"Kurt," Leelee gasped. "You agreed on no bloodbaths tonight."

"That was before I saw how rude these fucking people are." Another guy skirted around me and bumped into my shoulder. "Watch where the hell you're going," I grunted as I accidently elbowed him in the stomach.

Leelee half-laughed and scoffed as the guy turned to yell at me but then saw I was a fucking cripple. "Uh, sorry, man," he mumbled.

I grunted at him, and Leelee hit me on the back. "He said he was sorry, Kurt."

"He wouldn't have to be sorry if he would have just watched where the hell he was walking. I can't believe you and the girls walk through this every Friday and don't deck someone."

"The guys tend to get out of our way a bit more than they do for you."

I growled low as another fucker bumped into me and I was ready to take a swing at him when Leelee wrapped her arm around my waist and pressed her lips to my ear. "Down, boy," she whispered. She pressed her body against my back, and I couldn't help but notice the way her breath floated across my neck and the feel of her soft lips against my ear. "You okay?"

Was I okay? Hell no. I had Leelee pressed up against me, and I was standing in a sea of people unable to do anything about it. "I'm good."

She hesitated, her body still pushed against mine and then she pulled away. "Um, I see Vi and Scarlett over here," she mumbled.

They were across the road and were both looking at us, along with Luke and Mitch. Of course, they had just seen Leelee pressed up against me. Fucking great. I didn't know what the hell was going on with Leelee and me, but now they were all wondering the same thing.

I reached behind me, grabbing Leelee's hand that wasn't holding the box of tacos and pulled her across the road behind me.

"Hey," Violet said, smiling. "I was wondering when you were going to get here. I was beginning to think that I was going to have to deploy Levi" she threatened with a laugh.

Leelee held out the box of tacos to everyone and shook her head. "No need to deploy the secret weapon. We were fighting the crowd to get over here. I swear it's busier than it normally is."

"That's 'cause we're on 5th tonight. They're all waiting for the accidents," Luke replied, as he grabbed four tacos out of the box and handed one to Violet. "Thank fuck I'm not driving tonight. Give me a Christmas tree and a straight shot any day. Y'all are fucking crazy." Luke chomped into his taco and finally looked at me. "Well, if it isn't Mr. Crazy himself."

"Hey, Kurt," Scarlett chirped. "You're looking really good."

"Thanks, Scar." I couldn't be mad at Scarlett and Violet. It wasn't their faults they were dating my brothers, who were asses to me.

"When are we going to see you back behind the wheel?" Violet asked.

"At least another four weeks. I go to the doctor next week. I'm hoping they'll let me out of this early." I held up my arm and shrugged. I hoped it would happen, but I doubted it would.

"Come on, sit down." Violet scooted over on the tailgate of Mitch's truck and patted the spot next to her for Leelee.

Leelee looked over her shoulder at me, and I shook my head. If she wanted to stay, she could. But there wasn't a way in hell I was going to.

"We were actually going to find a couple of Kurt's friends. But I can leave the tacos with you guys." Leelee set the box of food next to Violet and grabbed a couple of tacos. "We'll try to make it back before the race starts."

"Okay, we'll be right here," Violet replied.

Leelee waved to everyone and grabbed my hand as we headed further down the road.

"You could have stayed, Lee."

She glanced over at me and shook her head. "I know I could have. I didn't want to."

I didn't know what to say. I had never had someone pick me over someone else before. I knew that Lee, Vi, and Scar were tight, so it was a big deal for her to choose to watch the race with me. "Thanks."

She squeezed my hand, and a small smile played on her lips. "Don't make me regret it."

****

CHAPTER 17

Leelee

"So, how long have you and Kurt been dating? The last I knew, he was single."

I was in Hell. Absolute Hell. I don't know how the fuck I ended up in a group of track bunnies while Kurt wandered off and talked to Nos.

"We're not dating." It was the truth. We were married, not dating.

"Oh, really? Then, why is he staying with you?"

Because we're married, but I knew I couldn't say that. "He needs a place to stay, and I'm helping him out until he gets back on his feet."

"Jesus, Nila, you're giving her the third degree. Just let the girl breathe." The one girl who seemed like I could have a conversation with without her saying *like* fifty times rolled her eyes and leaned against the white car behind us. "I'm Del," she said as she held her hand out to me. "I'm with Nos."

I shook her hand and felt a little bit better. While this girl was dressed like all the other track bunnies, I could tell she was different. Although I couldn't figure out why in the hell she was hanging out with a bunch of track bunnies.

"I better go, it looks like the race is about to start." The girl who had been grilling me about Kurt pulled down her tank top, revealing the tops of her breasts and pulled up her skirt. "Gotta give 'em a show." She winked at me and flounced over to the cars that were lining up. "She's actually harmless, I swear," Del said as we watched the girl walk away.

"I'm going to have to take your word for that."

Del laughed and shook her head "My word is a good promise." She winked at me, and I again felt like this chick and I could be friends.

"You know what Nos and Kurt are talking about?" I looked over my shoulder and saw Kurt and Nos huddled next to Nos' car with a bunch of papers spread out on the hood.

"I really don't know. I've been working my ass off at the nursing home the past two weeks. It's a miracle that I even remember what Nos looks like."

Well, that didn't really help me. I was afraid Kurt was falling into things he shouldn't be doing to get out from under Luke. "They've been hanging out a lot lately. From the way Kurt talks, he spends all day with Nos."

"Yeah, I think they're working on a car or something. Nos knows that I can only take so much car talk stuff until my eyes glaze over and I fall asleep."

I nodded, acting like I knew what she was talking about, but in reality, I had no idea what she meant. I loved anything to do with cars. Whether it was a TV show, a drag race, or ripping an engine out of a car. I loved it.

"Not wanting to sound like Nila, but what is going on with Kurt and you?"

"Honestly, Del? I don't have a fucking clue. There was something there between us a year ago, but now? Now, I am lost."

"Well, I'm sure you'll find your way. Just try to act interested when he starts talking about cars. That is the best piece of advice I can give to any of these girls that are looking to land a gearhead."

I threw my head back laughing, unable to act like a track bunny anymore. "I don't think that will be a problem for me at all. I'm a mechanic at Skid Row Kings. Cars are my thing."

"No shit?" Del laughed and ran her fingers through her hair. "Well, now don't I look like an ass. Telling a mechanic to act like they care about cars."

"Hey, I assumed you were a track bunny until you told me you were dating Nos. I think we are even." We both burst out laughing and the awkwardness that had been surrounding us faded.

"What the hell are you two laughing about?" Nos asked as he walked up and wrapped his arms around Del. "You causing problems again, woman?"

"No, just fixing some misunderstandings Leelee and I were having about each other." Del pressed a kiss to Nos' cheek and wrapped her arms around him.

"She thought you were a track bunny, didn't she?" Nos asked me.

"Um, yeah. But in her defense, I thought she was one, too."

Kurt and Nos both busted out laughing. "Leelee is the furthest thing from a track bunny, babe. She could fine tune and work on each and every car here tonight and not even break a sweat."

"No shit?" Del asked, sounding amazed.

"Um, yeah. I tend to know a thing or two."

"Stop being modest, Lee. You're one of the best mechanics in town. Hell, probably the whole state." I turned to look at Kurt because I couldn't believe he actually said that. He had said it to me in private before, but I never thought he would actually admit it in public.

"Good, you can help figure out what the hell is wrong with my car. Nos said he doesn't have time to look at it."

"What? Woman, I can look at your car," Nos said as he pulled away from Del. "You're making me look like I don't take care of my woman."

"Oh, you take care of your woman, it's your woman's car that you tend to neglect." Del turned on her heel to storm off, but Nos pulled her back into his arms and buried his face in her neck. She tried fighting him off for about ten seconds before she surrendered and relaxed into him.

Kurt leaned against the front of the Charger that was next to us and pulled me next to him. "Everything okay?" I asked.

"Yeah. Just going over some stuff with Nos."

"Am I ever going to hear the stuff you and Nos keep going over?"

"Maybe someday, Lee."

"I hope whatever it is; it's not trouble."

Kurt shook his head and crossed his arms over his chest. Well, he tried to cross his arms as best as he could with a broken arm. "You had me for a second there, Lee. I thought you got me, but then you go ahead and think that I'm fucking stupid."

Huh? Where in the hell did he get that from? I was just worried he was so desperate to get out from Luke that he would do anything.

"Yo, race is starting," Nos called.

Kurt pushed off the car and hobbled over to the side of the road where everyone was waiting for the start.

"Kurt," I called as I followed him. "I didn't mean it the way it came out. I jus—"

"Lee, just stop. I hear you loud and fucking clear." Kurt turned away from me and focused on the cars that were lining up next to us. "You just helped me to remember why the hell I was done with this place."

I didn't know what to say to make things better. I didn't want Kurt to be done, but I also didn't want him to do something stupid and get in trouble. There were lots of ways to make quick money on the streets, and I just hoped Kurt didn't get caught up in them.

I focused on the cars while I tried to figure out what to say. Mitch had the far lane with three other cars slowly pulling up to their spots. I only recognized one other car that Mitch was racing against. "Who is in the Supra?"

"Fucking AZ. Fucker somehow managed to scrape up enough money to get back in the running," Kurt growled.

AZ was racing? Oh hell. I was surprised AZ hadn't tucked his tail between his legs and disappeared after the last race when Kurt and Mitch both beat him.

I glanced over to where we had left Scar and Violet and saw Luke glaring at AZ. Ever since AZ had smashed into the back of Luke, wrecking both of their cars, AZ had been on all the Jensen brothers' shit list. It seemed that wherever AZ was, trouble followed.

"It looks like Luke is about to bust that big ole' vein in his neck."

"Can't really fucking blame him," Kurt mumbled.

"Is AZ still with Ginny?"

Kurt shrugged and nodded further down the road. Ginny was standing in the middle of a group of track bunnies, but her eyes were focused on Luke and Violet. "Ginny is with whoever she can use. She's still got her sights set on Luke, but she's a dumb bitch if she thinks she's any competition for Vi."

"Damn straight," I murmured. I never understood people who felt the need to wreck a perfectly good relationship because they thought they were better.

One of the girls who were surrounding Ginny broke away from the group and sauntered in front of the cars. She pulled a handkerchief out of her bra, and I couldn't help but roll my eyes. "Ho," I mumbled under my breath. It was a miracle I didn't titty punch some of these chicks.

"There's only one lap," Nos said as he stood next to Kurt. Del was tucked under his arm, and I couldn't help but feel a twinge of jealousy at how well they seemed to get along.

"It's only going to take one lap. I'll be surprised if any of these guys make it to the finish line with no damage on their cars." Kurt shifted his weight, and I saw him grimace.

"You okay?" I asked. Kurt had a walking cast on his leg, but the doctor had recommended he use the crutch as often as possible just to help to take the stress off his ankle.

"I'm fine," he grunted. "You gonna eat those tacos in your hand?" he asked as he looked at me out of the side of his eye.

I held them out to him and shrugged. "I grabbed them for you." He took them and ate one in two bites. "Did you even taste that?"

"Yeah, mostly," he mumbled around a mouthful.

I couldn't help but roll my eyes and grab the empty wrapper from him.

"Alright, brother. Time to place your bets. Who do you think is going to win?" Nos asked.

"Mitch. He's cautious enough that he won't crash like these other fuckers. When 5th crosses over Johnson, I bet at least two cars spin out and crash. None of these guys know what they are getting into." Kurt sounded confident in Mitch even though he was pissed off at him.

I had driven 5th plenty of times before going the speed limit, and even I could realize it was one of the most dangerous courses that had been raced.

"You don't think AZ has it in him?" Nos laughed.

"He's too desperate." Kurt again shifted his feet, and I could tell that he was in pain.

I leaned over, my shoulder brushing against him. "Did you take a pill before we left?"

"No. I fucking hate how they make me feel. It's like I'm walking around in a God damn fog. I'll deal with the pain."

"Did you at least take some Tylenol?" I understood what he was saying, but I didn't think his leg was healed enough to be walking on it the way he was.

"Lee, I got this. Don't worry about me."

I stepped back and rolled my eyes. "If you can handle, then stop looking like you're about to pass out."

"Here we go," Nos called.

I shifted my attention back to the cars on the line and crossed my arms over my chest. If Kurt wanted to be a moron with a stick up his ass, that was fine. I would be here ready to pick him off the pavement when he passed out.

The track bunny who was standing in front of the cars raised her arms over her head, dropped the handkerchief, and each car took off from the line with Mitch in the lead.

Nos pulled a walkie-talkie out of his pocket and held it up to him mouth. "They just took off, Mouse. They're headed your way."

"Who is he talking to?" I asked.

"He's got guys all on the track that report back to him letting him know who's in the lead and if there have been any crashes."

"Oh, well that's pretty handy. Does he do that for every race?"

"Only the really dangerous ones."

"You don't think Mitch is going to crash, do you?"

"You never know what's going to happen out there, Lee. You could drive clean and safe, but then you have the guy next to you who doesn't give a fuck and drives like an asshole."

"AZ," I whispered. When AZ was out there, no one was safe. "Why do they let him race if they know how he drives?"

"It's not like we have a panel of judges and shit, Lee. If he's got the cash to race, then he's in. Every race you have to put in five hundred. The winner of that race gets half of the cash and then the other half goes into the pot for the final race of the season."

"So, the winner tonight gets one thousand? Holy hell. Now, I know I'll never be able to race. I don't think I could put in five hundred and not know if I'll get that money back."

"It's all part of racing, Lee. You have to put in big if you want to win big. Just like life. You get back what you put in."

"Damn brother, that shit is deep. That your new motto for the shop?"

"Shop?" I asked.

"It's nothing, Lee. I've just been helping Nos out at his Uncle's shop."

Nos shook his head and started to talk, but Kurt shut him down right away. Kurt was working at a different body shop? Why the hell would he be doing that? Working for Luke's competition would not be a good way to mend fences with his brothers. "Kurt, do you rea—"

"No." Kurt shook his head. "I'm not talking about it, Lee. I need out; you know that. I'm making moves to do that. When it all comes together, then I'll talk about it. But now? No." Kurt shut me down and turned to talk to Nos.

Del looked over at me, and I shrugged. I had no idea what to say or do. I stood next to Kurt, feeling like I was completely left out of everything and that I didn't matter. But I didn't have a right to feel that way because I had chosen over a year ago to step away from Kurt. A lot of good that had done me. Now, I just felt hurt and left out.

"They've all cleared the fourth section. AZ has a lot of damage to his car, but he's in the lead." Nos' radio went off with crackling and static. "Mitch is in second with Blade and Tiny right behind."

"I don't know, homie. Your brother might not pull this one out." Nos shook his head. "AZ drives dirty, but that might be the edge he needs to win this race."

And that right there was the problem with street racing. There were no rules. "How many sections are there?" I asked, hoping Mitch would still be able to pass AZ.

"Seven. Five and six are the toughest. This race is still anyone's." Kurt turned to look at me, his eyes traveling over me. "AZ still has time to fuck it up."

"Doesn't he always?"

"So far, he hasn't proved me wrong. He doesn't drive smart."

"They're headed into the 6th section."

Knowing what was going on during the race was great, but it was also driving me crazy. Typically, we would see the cars take off and then five or ten minutes later, we'd watch them cross the finish line.

"Hey, you know how Mitch is doing?" Luke had made his way over to us and was standing next to Nos.

"Second place, right behind AZ," Nos rattled off. "AZ is driving fierce, but Mouse said the race is anybody's still."

"He's gonna fucking kill someone," Luke growled.

"Holy fuck!" Mouse crackled over the walkie-talkie. "They just entered the 6th section. AZ just slammed into Blade, forcing him into the old flower shop. Fucking glass everywhere."

"Oh my God," I gasped. What in the hell was going on? AZ was completely out of control.

"Blade is getting out of the car. He's okay, but he is out of the race."

Really? Who in the hell cared if he was out of the race. Thank God he was all right. "Something has to be done about that asshole." I turned to face Kurt and crossed my arms over my chest.

He held his hands up and shook his head. "Don't look at me, babe. There isn't a damn thing I can do sitting on the sidelines."

"If you were racing, you could stomp his ass into the ground. Lord knows you can drive this course better than he can."

Kurt shrugged but didn't argue. Kurt was damn good, and he knew it.

"They're headed into the final section. Mitch is in the lead with AZ right behind him banging into his bumper."

"Keep me posted, Mick," Nos said.

"How long is the last section?" I asked.

"They are just down the road. There are three curves, the last one being a one hundred and eighty-degree turn that slingshots them over the finish line," Luke explained.

We all turned to look down the road and waited. We could hear screeching tires and engines revving but no sign of any of the cars yet.

"Final turn. Mitch is ahead by two car lengths, with AZ gaining on him. He's headed into the turn way too fucking fast if he's not caref—" The walkie talkie cutoff, and then there was pure static pouring out of the device.

"What happened? What was he trying to say?" I asked frantically.

Screeching tires cut through the air, and the crowd gasped as we watched Mitch safely make it around the last corner. His ass end swung out dangerously, but he managed to keep the car under control and cross the finish line first but not before AZ's car went airborne, launching inches away from Mitch's before it flipped over at least a dozen times.

The car crumpled like a tin can as it smashed into the concrete.

"Holy fuck!" Luke yelled as the car finally came to a stop on the sidewalk where a crowd of people had just been standing.

Smoke rolled out from underneath the hood, and you couldn't even tell what kind of car it was anymore. "We need to get him out," Kurt called as he started hobbling to the wreck.

"Stay here," Luke ordered as he ran past Kurt to the car. Mitch's car slid to a screeching stop, and he killed the engine and jumped out of the car to follow Luke.

"Kurt, just stay here," I pleaded. I grabbed his arm, trying to stop him from going to the accident but he shrugged me off and quickly limped over to the car.

"Oh my God!" Violet called as she and Scarlett ran over to me. "He didn't land on anyone in the crowd, did he?" she asked nervously.

"No. Not that I saw. Everyone moved out of the way." Time had stood still when AZ's car had started to roll, and I had watched everyone scatter like ants.

"What the hell is Kurt doing? He's not well enough to be helping. He's going to hurt himself again," Scarlett said, her voice laced with concern.

Kurt had made it to the car where Mitch and Luke were trying to pry the door open. It didn't look like AZ was moving inside and there was a crowd gathering around the wreck.

"They need to get him out of there before the car blows." I pulled my phone out of my pocket and dialed nine-one-one. I figured other people had already called the police, but it wouldn't hurt for me to call too. Maybe it would make them get here faster.

I rattled off where we were and what had happened to the dispatcher, and she told me the police and ambulance were in route. She asked me if I wanted to stay on the line until they got here but I told her I was fine.

Smoke billowed out of the engine and Mitch ran back to his car and yelled to Scarlett, Violet, and me to get back because the car was about to catch on fire.

We stepped back on the curb and huddled together, watching everyone run around. Mitch grabbed his fire extinguisher out of his car and ran back to AZ's car. Luke managed to pry open the passenger side door, and Kurt disappeared into the car. "What the hell is he doing?" I demanded. I stepped off the curb to go yank Kurt out of the car, but both Violet and Scarlett grabbed my arms and wouldn't let me move. "Let me go. He's in the car."

"Lee, stop. There isn't anything you can do. Luke and Mitch are right there with him." Violet wrapped her arms around me, anchoring me.

"He's hurt, Vi. He shouldn't be over there." The man was insane. He had just been in a car accident just like this a few weeks ago, and now he was playing hero trying to save AZ.

Flames started shooting out of the hood, and I knew it was only a matter of time before the car exploded. I closed my eyes and tried to quiet the scream that was begging to rip from my mouth.

"They've got him. Kurt got him out." Scarlett grabbed my arm and shook me. "He's okay, Lee."

I opened my eyes to see Luke and Mitch carrying AZ to the other side of the street where they laid him down on the sidewalk. Kurt limped behind them; his head hung low. "Is he okay?" I asked. It seemed like he was limping worse than he normally did and he was holding his broken arm to his chest.

"I'm sure he's fine, Lee. Don't worry."

"Let's go ov—" The car exploded, cutting off Scarlett's words and deafening my ears. Shrapnel flew, landing all over and the car was engulfed in flames. Luke and Mitch fell to the ground with AZ in their arms while Kurt kneeled and covered his head with his arms.

I heard sirens in the distance and knew the ambulance was only blocks away. "I need to go over there." Scarlett and Violet tried to hold onto me, but there was no way they were going to keep me away from Kurt.

"Are you insane?" I ranted at him as I stood in front of him.

"What are you talking about?" he asked. His voice was raspy, and he coughed hard, almost hacking up a lung.

"Why the hell did you come over here? Luke and Mitch could have helped him."

Kurt shook his head and tried to stand up. "I wasn't going to stand by and watch someone burn up in their car."

"There are hundreds of people here who would have helped him, Kurt. Why in the hell did you think that you need to be the one to rush in and save him? You scared me half to death. That car could have blown up at any time."

"You think you could save your lecture for later, Lee?" Luke asked as he leaned over AZ. He pressed his ear to AZ's mouth, trying to hear if he was breathing.

Kurt smirked at me but grimaced as he tried to stand up. I put an arm around him and helped him off the ground. "You've given me a heart attack twice in the last month, Kurt. You think you're done for a while?"

"I'll try," he mumbled.

The ambulance showed up, pushing us all out of the way and the paramedics started working on AZ.

"You think he'll be okay?" I asked, as they loaded him up the stretcher. AZ's face was covered in blood; his arms were cut all over, and he had yet to regain consciousness.

"I don't know, his car looks about the same as mine and I made it."

I looked at AZ's car that was now just a rolling ball of flames and a shudder rocked my body. I had never thought about what Kurt's car had looked like and thankfully, I didn't have to see it. "That's what your car looked like?"

"Yeah."

The fire department rolled up and started to put water on the car, trying to put the blaze out.

"Everyone seems to have scattered, but from what I gather, you three helped to get him out of the car?" Kurt and I looked to our right and saw a police officer standing next to Luke and Mitch.

"Yeah. We managed to get him out of the car before it exploded," Luke said.

"You wanna tell me how it is his car became a ball of fire?"

Kurt, Mitch, and Luke looked from one to another, and they all shrugged. "Not sure," Mitch replied. "We were just driving by, saw the taco truck and decided to stop. The next thing you know, this car came flying around the corner."

"You really mean to tell me that you all are here for tacos?"

Luke shrugged. "You ever have one of Pedro's tacos? Things are legendary."

"That so?" the cop asked.

"Yeah. Thankfully, we were around or that guy, whoever he is, probably would have died," Kurt added.

The cop closed the small notebook he was holding and shook his head. "Should have known," he mumbled, as he walked away.

"You think he bought it?" I asked.

"No," Mitch said as he brushed off his jeans. "But there isn't much he can do. Everyone he ends up talking to is going to say the same thing. They have no idea what happened and they were just passing through."

"We all better get out of here. There isn't anything else we can do." Luke looked around and saw Violet and Scarlett still standing on the sidewalk. "You okay to get to your car?" Luke asked Kurt.

Kurt brushed him off and nodded. "I'm good," he said as he limped off in the direction of the car.

"Is this really how it's going to be, Kurt?" Luke called after him.

Kurt raised his hand in the air but didn't turn around. "It is what it is," he yelled back.

"Jesus. You think he's ever going to pull that stick out of his ass and start acting like our brother again?" Mitch asked as he ran his hand over his head.

"You just need to give him time," I said as I watched Kurt disappear into the crowd.

"I don't need to fucking do anything, Lee. We haven't done anything but try to help him, and now he's treating us like the fucking plague," Luke bit off.

He was right, but then I also understood what Kurt was feeling. "You need to cut him some slack, Luke."

Luke shook his head and stormed off. Storming off was one of the Jensen boys' signature moves.

"Things getting any better?" Mitch asked.

"I thought they were. I was surprised he came tonight, but then I found out he just came so he could talk to Nos about whatever the hell he's been doing during the day." I ran my hand through my hair and realized how wrong I was about things getting better with Kurt. I swear to God; the man was bipolar.

"What's he been doing with Nos?"

"Not a clue. He said he'd tell me what it is when he's got everything in place. What that means, I have no clue."

"You don't think he's getting into something he shouldn't be, do you?" Mitch asked, his voice laced with concern.

"Honestly, Mitch. I know Kurt is smarter than that. I just wish he would let me in on what he's doing. Nos picks him up before I even leave for work, and then he's home right before I get home."

"See what you can find out, Lee. I know it seems like Luke is a huge dick, which he is, but the reason he is acting that way is because he's worried as hell about Kurt."

I ran my fingers through my hair. "I know. Just try to keep him off Kurt's back like I asked. Hopefully, he lets me know what he's been working on." I pulled my keys out of my pocket and turned to look at Mitch. "Kurt's smart, and you guys don't give him enough credit."

"I think there are things we all need to change, even Luke and I." Mitch walked over to Scarlett and tossed his arm over her shoulder.

Well, this was a different twist to how I had seen the night ending. Kurt was pissed off again, and AZ was carted off in an ambulance.

"Never a dull moment," I mumbled to myself.

I picked my way through the crowd, dodging what was left of the group who were standing around gawking at AZ's car.

"You should really lock your car," Kurt said as I slid into the driver's seat.

"Eh, if they need it that bad, they can take it. A nineteen eighty-seven Caprice isn't exactly on the list of most stolen cars." I shoved my key in the ignition and shifted the car into reverse. I slowly inched my way back, careful not to peg any of the people still milling around and pulled out onto the road.

"You know that is something I have never understood about you. You know your way around a car like no one I have ever seen before, but you drive the biggest piece of shit I have ever seen."

"Hey, I wouldn't talk so bad about this piece of shit while you're in it. It might decide to break down and then we'll both be shit out of luck."

"Hell, you could pick up an older Supra for a couple grand and fix it up better than this thing."

"That would be nice if I had an extra couple grand just lying around, Kurt. Some of us don't have pockets lined with fifties and hundreds."

Kurt scoffed and shook his head. "Then I guess it's a good thing you married someone who has pockets like that."

"If you're offering to buy me a new car, Kurt, the answer is no. This car is fine. I don't race, and I don't need some flashy car. I build other people flashy cars." I turned onto the road to my apartment and stopped at the red light. "I'm still hungry. I didn't get to eat any of the tacos."

"Head home, and we can order a pizza. I need to take a fucking pill." Kurt rubbed his shoulder and winced.

"Told ya that you shouldn't have climbed into that car after AZ."

Kurt leaned his head back against the headrest, and I glanced over at him. "So, how old were you when you realized you knew everything?"

I scoffed, ready to yell at him when a smile spread across his face, and I knew he was joking. "I think I was six. You know. Once you have the potty training and being able to feed yourself, you basically have life figured out."

"If only that were the truth," he said with a laugh. "I'm almost thirty and don't have my life figured out."

"I think you have it more figured out than you think."

"I'm getting there. Each day I get a little bit closer to where I want to be."

"And where is it you want to be?" I asked, as I pulled into the driveway.

"I want to be where everything I have is mine and no one else's. I'm not afraid of hard work and getting dirty, Lee. I just feel like everything I've had has been handed to me, and I'm done with that shit. Luke built that garage from the ground up, and it's his no matter how many times he says it's all of ours. I want it all to myself."

"That seems kind of crazy to go from the top of the pile all the way to the bottom."

Kurt turned his head to look at me as I turned the car off and pulled the keys out of the ignition.

"It's not crazy. It's what I want."

"And what happens when you get everything you want?"

Kurt reached over and cupped my face in his hand. "There's one thing I don't think I'll ever get."

The warmth of his hand spread across my cheek and left me speechless. Kurt slipped out of the car before I could form a coherent sentence and slammed the door behind him.

I brushed my hand against my cheek where he had touched me. "What in the hell just happened?"

****

CHAPTER 18

Kurt

"Can you hand me that wrench?"

"Which one?" Nos asked.

I shook my head and walked over to the tool box. "You know for being such a good driver; you don't know shit about cars."

Nos shrugged and leaned against the workbench. "The way I figure, you open this shop again, and I'll be your number one customer."

"You know, I had an idea." I headed back over to the GTO and dropped the radiator in. "You know my plan of what I want to do when I have the ink dried on the paperwork, but I know we are going to need someone to run the office and all of the paperwork."

"Yeah, you will definitely need that. You don't seem to be the type of guy to sit behind a desk."

"What about you coming to work for us and taking care of the front end."

"You just said I don't know dick about cars. Why in the hell would you want me to work for you?" Nos folded his arms over his chest and shook his head. "You're fucking crazy, brah."

I shrugged and mulled over the idea in my head. The more I thought about it, the better it sounded. "I'm not crazy. I believe that this is a fucking brilliant idea. I don't want to have to interview people and end up hiring some douche I can't stand."

"I really shouldn't be surprised about this. I mean, you are building up the shop and then giving it away."

"I'm not fucking giving it away."

"Could have fooled me. I'm pretty sure if your name isn't on the building, then it doesn't belong to you."

I tightened up the bolts on the radiator and slammed the hood shut. "That's just a fucking detail. So, are you in or what?" I asked.

"When are you planning on opening up?"

"I figure I'll need to wait at least until I'm able to drive. I go to the doctor in two weeks and should hopefully have everything taken off. I'd say the beginning of September."

Nos shook his head. "I'm giving you a tentative yes. You know I've got to talk to Del about this."

"Ah, another one who bows to the power of the pussy." I threw my dirty rag at him and slammed the hood shut on the GTO. "That's all I plan on doing today. Ready to drive my ass home?"

"You mean to the pussy that you bow down to?"

"That's fucking different." I flipped off the lights in the shop, and we headed into the front office.

"You wanna tell me how the hell it's different? I see you bending over backward for this chick and from what I can tell, you ain't getting nothing out of it. At least with Del, she warms my bed every night."

"How about you don't worry about Lee and I, alright?" I fell into Nos' car and slammed the door shut. Damn asshole had been giving me grief for the past two weeks since the race about Leelee and I was about done with it.

Something had changed that night. Leelee was running scared again and was barely talking to me. She would come home from work every night, make dinner, hang out with Jay, and then she would spend the rest of her night in her room.

Jay had come home a few days after the race and I was surprised at how well he took me being there. Leelee had warned me

Jay might have a problem with me staying in the house but so far, he hadn't said or done anything to say he was pissed off.

"You coming to the race this week?"

"Nah. AZ's crash two weeks ago was enough for me. I think Lee might be going tonight with Vi and Scar, though."

"Yeah, that was some crazy shit. Heard he just got out of the hospital and is going to be laid up even longer than you were."

"Hell, I'm still fucking laid up." I held up my broken arm and wished like hell I could get the fucking cast off. "Two more weeks of this bullshit and then I'll be behind the wheel again."

"You gonna get back to racing right away?" Nos turned down the street to Leelee's house, and I leaned my head against the headrest.

"I don't know, brah. I kind of feel like racing may just be something I do when the mood hits. I've been working on the GTO for weeks, and I've really come to realize that I love working on cars. Even more than racing."

"No shit?" Nos glanced over at me, and I could tell he was shocked as hell. I had been too when I sat down and thought about it.

"Yeah. I think I finally figured out what my next move is."

"The garage?"

"Yeah, definitely the garage. Although, the garage all hinges on one person."

"Lee?"

"Yeah." It had finally come down to this.

I wanted Leelee, and I wasn't going to let her go again. I had a plan for my future, and Leelee was the center of it.

I wanted Leelee.

****

Leelee

"School starts Monday. You have everything you need?" I pulled the meatloaf out of the oven and set it on the stove.

"I think so. Junior year, you basically need pens and paper." Jay plopped down at the kitchen table and kicked his feet out. "I'll check everything before bed."

"Don't you think that is something you should do sooner?"

"I've only been back for a little over a week, Lily."

I turned around and leaned against the counter. "You do know you are the only one who calls me Lily, right?"

"That's because I'm the only one who knows that's your name."

"And you are the reason you are the only one who knows. I swear, you couldn't say Lily until you were ten and by that time, everyone thought my name was Leelee." I rolled my eyes and grabbed the loaf of Italian bread off the counter. "So, keep that Lily business to yourself."

"Hey, I did you a favor. You are more of a Leelee than a Lily any day." Jay grabbed a soda out of the fridge and popped the top. "You going to the race tonight? I had heard about the accident before I got back. You know the guy?"

I sliced into the loaf of bread and set it on the sheet pan. "Knew of him. He was kind of an ass. Grab the butter out of the fridge." I finished cutting the bread and grabbed a butter knife. "And no, I don't plan on going to the race. Violet was begging me to go at work today, but I really don't feel up to it."

"You haven't felt like doing anything since I've been home."

"I've just been tired. The shop has been crazy busy since Kurt quit." Busy was an understatement. I had been running around trying to fix every car that came into the shop, and at the same time,

152

I was dodging all the questions Luke and Mitch kept asking me about Kurt.

"I was going to go to Mike's tonight if that's okay with you."

I shrugged and grabbed the garlic salt down from the cabinet. "I guess that's fine. You planning on staying the night there?"

"I don't know. We were going to GTA or maybe hit up the mall. I'm not sure."

"I'm fine with either, just let me know what you're doing."

"Yes, mother," he mockingly joked. "What time is Kurt going to be home?"

"I'm assuming the usual time." I heard the front door open and shook my head. "Which would be right about now." Kurt had been getting home later from whatever the hell he was doing, and the only good thing was he would come home looking like he had been actually working—grease on his hands, pants, and sometimes on his face. I swore the man never looked in the mirror.

I finished buttering the bread, sprinkled some garlic salt on them and shoved them in the oven. "Go wash up, Jay."

"I played video games all day, not played in the mud," Jay complained.

I pointed down the hallway, and he stood, shook his head, and grumbled all the way to the bathroom.

"Smells good," Kurt said as he walked into the kitchen.

"Meatloaf, carrots, and garlic bread. I was going to make mashed potatoes, but I didn't have time to boil them. Jay thankfully stuck the meatloaf in the oven, or we would just be having carrots and bread." This was also new. I rambled. A lot.

"Whatever you make is good, Lee." This was Kurt's new thing. He was nice. Like, I'm talking super nice. Not that he had been mean to me since his accident, but it was like he was walking on eggshells around me and I had no idea why. "I'm gonna wash up quick."

I turned back to the stove and bowed my head while I listened to Kurt's footsteps down the hallway. I was losing it. I didn't know what to do anymore. Ever since the race, I had barely been talking to Kurt and staying in my room most nights. I was trying to give him the space he wanted, but it felt like I was running away again. Running was the last thing I wanted to do, but I didn't know how to give him his space but still be in his space.

"What's burning?" Jay asked as he came back into the kitchen.

"Son of a bitch," I cursed as I opened the oven and pulled out the bread. "I only had it on broil for two minutes. How in the hell did they burn?"

"Because you can't make toast, Lee. You burn it every time," Jay noted, laughing.

"They're not that bad. Just the edges are a bit crispy." I set the pan on the stove and turned off the oven. "Put a piece of meatloaf on it, and you won't even be able to tell."

"Burn the bread again?" Kurt asked as he glided into the kitchen and grabbed a beer from the fridge. "You want one?" he asked as he turned his head to look at me.

"Yeah, please." He used the hem of his shirt to twist off the top and handed a Corona to me. "Dinners ready. Burnt bread and all."

Kurt shook his head and laughed. "I'm acquiring a taste for burnt bread, Lee." He winked at me and sat down at the table next to Jay.

I tossed the bread on a plate and tried not to let the butterflies take over my stomach from the wink Kurt had given me.

"Trust me, Kurt. No one gets used to burnt toast. Especially Lily's." Jay slapped his hand over his mouth. "Shit," he mumbled.

"What?" Kurt asked looking at me as I sat down.

"Carrots?" I asked, as I held up the bowl.

Kurt grabbed it from me and set it down next to his plate. "Please, Lily," he said, smirking.

Jay laughed, and I tossed a piece of burnt toast at his head. "Ass," I hissed as he snatched it out of the air and bit a huge bite out of it.

"It's your damn name. You can't be mad at me."

"It's not my name," I fussed. I cut off a huge chunk of meatloaf and forked it onto my plate. "My name has been Leelee for the past sixteen years." I grabbed my fork and knife. "Use it," I said pointing my knife at Jay.

Kurt had his elbows on the table and one arm holding his head up as he looked at me "Lee, we got married. I saw your name on the marriage certificate."

Jay laughed and slid half of the meatloaf onto his plate. "He's known this whole time, and you didn't even know?"

"Lee is hard to picture as Lily, but I'm getting used to it," he said. "But now I need to know the middle name to make this complete. Lee only put a C in that line."

"It's C—"

"Don't you even dare," I said, pointing my fork at Jay. "You'd be amazed at the things I can do with a fork."

Jay held his hands up and tried not to laugh.

"It's hard to believe," Kurt said. "But I am oddly turned on right now."

Jay busted out laughing and picked up his fork. "This is some strange foreplay going on right now."

I felt a blush rise on my cheeks but tried to keep my focus on Jay. I didn't need to think about Kurt being turned on. "You shouldn't even know what that word means."

"What word?" he asked, baffled.

"Foreplay."

Jay scoffed and popped a carrot into his mouth. "Lee, come on. I knew what that was years ago. Redtube and Pornhub have been great teachers to me."

"I'm gonna need something stronger than beer," I mumbled, as I grabbed my bottle and downed half of it.

"And that is the difference between when I grew up and now. I had to sneak nudie magazines into the house and hide them from Luke and Mitch, so they didn't steal them."

"Really? That would suck. I can watch all of that shit on my phone."

"That's it. I'm cutting off the phones tomorrow." I didn't want to think about Jay watching porn, let alone knowing he was doing it on the phone I paid for.

Jay scoffed and stuffed his mouth full of meatloaf. "I think you might be overreacting a bit, Lee." Kurt laughed as he grabbed the carrots and piled some onto his plate. I handed him what was left of the meatloaf, and he scrapped it onto his plate.

"I may be, but I don't need to hear about my brother watching porn."

"Hey, you're the one who wanted to know where I learned about foreplay." Jay shrugged. "I know a lot more than foreplay." Jay winked at Kurt, a smirk on his lips.

"I think that's enough about this. Why don't you talk about something else, Jay," Kurt said, trying not to laugh.

I rolled my eyes but thanked God Kurt had told him to change the subject. "You think I can use the car the first day of school?" Jay asked me.

"If you give me a ride to work and then you have to pick me up." I knew Jay was getting to the age where he didn't want to walk to school anymore. I couldn't blame him. When I had turned sixteen, I saved every penny I could to get my first car. It was an even bigger pile of crap than the Caprice I was driving now.

"Monday the first day of school?" Kurt asked.

"Yeah."

"Leelee can drive my car, you take the Caprice and then you don't have to worry about dropping and picking her up."

"What?" Jay and I said at the same time.

"Since when do you have a car?" I asked.

"I've had one for a month. I've been fixing it up." Kurt finished his meatloaf and piled more carrots onto his plate.

"What kind of car is it?" Jay asked.

"GTO. Newer body style. She was wrecked but fixable." He grabbed two more pieces of bread and used them to shovel carrots into his mouth.

"Sweet. You planning on racing it?" Jay was sitting on the edge of his chair, clearly excited about Kurt's new car.

"Probably, but who knows." Kurt shrugged.

"When can I see it?"

"I can't drive yet, so you and Lee are going to have to help me get it here."

"Where is it?" Jay was playing twenty questions with Kurt, and I was just sitting there, speechless.

Kurt had a car? Kurt had been building the car the past month? Why in the hell didn't he want to tell me? What this the secret he had been keeping the whole time?

"Shop over on Meadow."

"You been doing the work?"

"Yeah." Kurt finished off his plate and pushed it away.

"Cool. Well," Jay said as he pushed his chair back, "I'm going to head over to Mike's. Okay if I take the car?" He held his hand out to me for the keys.

"He lives two blocks over, Jay. I think you can walk."

"Come on, Lee," he pleaded. "You said you weren't going anywhere tonight."

"I had planned on going to the race, but I really don't feel like it. You can take the car, but if you spend the night at Mike's, you need to be home by nine so I can do the grocery shopping tomorrow." I fished the keys out of my pocket and placed them in his hand.

"Sweet. Thanks, Lee." He brushed a kiss to the side of my head, waved to Kurt and he was out the door.

"I'll clean up the dishes. I thought we could watch a movie tonight." Kurt grabbed the empty plates and took them to the sink.

"Um," I muttered. "I'm kind of tired."

"That's fine. You can lay out on the couch, and I'll take the chair."

I helped grab the rest of the dishes and dumped them into the sink. "You don't have to do the dishes tonight, Kurt."

"I know. I plan on doing them tomorrow." Kurt put his hands on my shoulders and pushed me into the living room. "Pick out a movie to watch. Don't worry about the dishes."

What in the hell was Kurt up to? I turned around and watched him walk back into the kitchen and finish clearing all the dishes off the table. "Did you hurt your head or something?"

"Huh?"

"Did you fall and hit your head? Is this like side effects from your accident?" I strode up to Kurt and put my hand on his forehead. "Do you have a fever?"

"Lee, knock it off." Kurt brushed my hand away and shook his head. "I don't have a fever, and I didn't hit my head."

"Then why are you so nice to me again?" I propped my hands on my hips and tilted my head to the side.

"I'm always nice to you."

My jaw dropped, and I rolled my eyes. "Sure, and I'm the queen of England."

"I just figured some things out, Lee. That's all."

"And what is it that you figured out?"

"Just things."

"You're crazy if you think I'm going to be okay with that answer. I need to know what things changed so I can make sure those things don't change back to the way they were when you were a royal douche to me. Tell me."

"Lee, no. Just go with it."

I shook my head no and crossed my arms over my chest. "Hell no. I am not going with it. I've done that with you before. Not falling for it again."

"You were the reason I changed the last time, Lee. You told me to get lost."

"I didn't tell you to get lost. I just didn't want you to feel that you *had* to stick around for Jay and I. I was a burden to you."

"I think you should have let me decide if you were a burden."

"But you didn't know I was a burden then. You would have gotten sick of me, and then you would have started resenting me and then we never would have talked again."

"Do you know how crazy you just sounded, Lee? You thought that you were going to be a burden so you decided to end us before we could even start. That's fucked up." Kurt shook his head and reached for the light switch. "Go find a movie to watch."

"Why?"

"Jesus Christ, Lee." Kurt ran his fingers through his hair and shook his head. "I'm going to need to spell it out for you, aren't I?"

I shrugged and shifted back and forth. "I don't know what to do, Kurt."

"I wanna spend time with you, Lee. Not because I have to, but because I want to." Kurt limped down the hallway and disappeared into Jay's bedroom.

"I thought you said you wanted to spend time with me," I called.

Kurt steps out of Jay's room and into the bathroom across the hall. "I'm gonna shower, Lee. Like I said before, find a movie to watch." He shut the door behind him, and I heard the water in the shower turn on.

I stared down the hallway, my eyes on the spot I had last seen Kurt and my mind was racing. "Where am I?" I asked, dumbfounded. Kurt Jensen had just admitted he wanted to spend time with me and I couldn't wrap my head around it. I was half-tempted to walk into the bathroom and make sure it was Kurt in there.

Although, if I did that, I'd probably make an ass of myself by just staring at him as the water cascaded over his body. "Hmm, that idea isn't half bad," I contemplated.

I shook my head and made my way back into the living room. As much as I'd love to see Kurt naked, I first needed to figure out this while being nice to Leelee business.

Was it a fluke, or was the new Kurt here to stay? I picked up the remote and flipped on the Hallmark channel. A sappy romance I never watched was playing, and I flopped down on the couch.

It was time to find out what I was dealing with.

****

CHAPTER 19

Kurt

I wanted to gouge my eyes out with a dull knife and wish for a slow death.

Leelee was passed out on the couch, and some sappy romance bullshit was playing on the TV. Leelee had the remote, and I was too lazy to get up and change the channel.

This is what I got for being nice.

When I had walked out of the bathroom after taking the world's quickest shower, Leelee was sprawled out on the couch, a smug smile on her face and she told me to take a seat. As soon as I glanced at the TV, I knew she wasn't playing fair.

Ten minutes into the movie, she had passed out, and I was left to watch the shitty movie by myself.

The credits were now rolling on the screen, and I stood, knowing I couldn't sit through another movie like that. Leelee had the remote in her hand, a firm death grip on it, and I knew I wouldn't be able to pick it up without waking her.

I glanced at the clock, saw it was barely nine o'clock and knew I wasn't ready for bed, although even if I was, I couldn't go to sleep since Lee was asleep on my bed. The couch may look uncomfortable, but it was actually perfect to sleep on.

So, now I had to decide my next step. Grab the remote from her hand and wake her up, or wake her up and tell her she needed to go to her room. Each option ended the same, Leelee awake and possibly pissed at me.

"Now who's staring at who?" she mumbled sleepily. Her eyes were still shut, but there was a small smirk on her lips.

"I'm trying to figure out what to do, and I wasn't staring at you."

"Mmhmm," she hummed as she grabbed the blanket off the couch and pulled it over her body. "You don't get the remote." She tucked it under her body and rolled away from me.

"That's fine, Lee, but you're on my bed."

"I'm not moving. You can sleep in my bed."

"Nope. I want the couch. Get up or move over."

She snuggled into the couch and lifted the blanket. "This invitation lasts for five seconds. One…two…"

She barely made it to three before I tossed the blanket back, slid in next to Lee and wrapped my arms around her. Her body went stiff against mine, and she gasped as my hand lifted the hem of her shirt and touched the soft, warm skin of her stomach. "I'll never say no to that invitation, Lee," I whispered into her ear.

"What are we doing, Kurt?"

I brushed the hair back from her neck. "What I wanted to do a year ago, but you wouldn't let me."

"And what makes you think I'll let you now?"

"Because we both want the same thing, Lee. Each other."

She rolled over in my arms and looked me in the eye. "You really think this is a good idea?"

I shrugged. "We're married. I don't think holding my wife is something I shouldn't do."

"Don't you think it's crazy you have a wife, but you've never kissed her?"

"Crazy, yes. But I think that's something we can fix right now." I cupped her cheek and stroked my thumb across her soft skin.

"Please don't kiss me if this is all a dream and I'm going to wake up tomorrow, and you're going to act like nothing happened."

"Something happened between us over a year ago, Lee, and I haven't been able to forget since."

"You're gonna do this, aren't you?" Her voice shook, but she didn't move away from me.

"You want it just as much as I do, Lee. I'm done acting like I don't care about you."

"This is going to chan—"

"Lee, just shut up and let me kiss you." I brushed my lips against her sweet mouth, and she gasped. "Don't tell me to stop, Lee. I won't be able to," I said against her lips.

"I don't want you to stop," she whispered.

That was what I needed to hear. Leelee was what I wanted, and now, I finally had her.

My hand gripped her hips, pressing her lush body against mine. She tangled her feet with mine, getting as close to me as she could. "We're going to mess this up, Kurt, because I'm a bit of a bitch, and you're a sometimes ass."

I chuckled under my breath and pressed a kiss to her neck. "I think as long as we both know that, we'll figure our way through."

She wrapped her arms around my neck and delved her fingers into my hair. "You have this all figured out, don't you? We've been running from each other for so long that it seems surreal to be here with you."

"I don't have a damn thing figured out, Lee, but I know that this is the only place I want to be right now." I pressed my lips against the pulse in her neck and felt her skin warm under my touch. "Softer than I ever imagined," I whispered. Goosebumps rose on her skin, and she sighed under my touch. "Are we done talking?"

"For now."

My hands traveled up the back of her shirt as her lips moved against mine. I moaned when her tongue traced the seam of my lips, and I ground my hips against her and opened my mouth. Our tongues glided against each other, teasing and tasting with each caress.

I let my fingers roam over her body trying to touch her all at once. "Fuck me, Lee. I've never wanted someone so much in my life." My dick was rock hard and begging to be let out of my jeans.

Her hand traveled down my body in between us and grazed my dick. "The feeling is mutual," she purred into my ear.

My mouth devoured her, needing to have her all at once.

I reached up, my cast banging against her shoulder. "Ow." She laughed against my lips. "You should really register that thing as a weapon."

"Two more weeks and I can get the damn thing off."

Leelee grabbed my fingers on my broken arm and lifted them to her lips. "You seem to be doing pretty well the way they are." She pressed a light kiss to each finger and my already rock hard dick almost exploded.

"How long have you wanted me, Lee?" I asked, as I leaned in and whispered in her ear.

"Um...when you offered to marry me. But, I thought you were hot as hell before that. I always wondered why you took the time to talk to me."

"Because you're different, Lee. I love that I could talk to you for twenty minutes on how to tear down an engine, but you were also easy on the eyes and knew how to stroke my ego."

"Stroke your ego?" she asked, apparently shocked.

"I guess it wasn't really stroking my ego, but you just made me feel like you were actually listening to what I was saying." Jesus, I sounded like a sap.

Leelee reached up and cupped my face with her hand. "Kurt Jensen, if I didn't know any better, I would think you have a soft side to you," she purred.

"Don't tell anyone, gorgeous. I might have to punch them in the face just to prove them wrong."

"You promised no bloodshed," she reminded me with a laugh.

"That was only that one time." I pressed my lips to her soft mouth, unable to stay away from her any longer. "I don't think I'll ever get enough of your kisses, Lee."

"Why did you stay away from me for so long, Kurt? Even when I asked you to stop, why did you if you wanted me so bad?" She laid back into the couch and partially pulled out of my arms.

"Don't pull out of my arms, Lee. I've waited for a long time to have you here. Don't leave yet." She sighed deep but came back willingly into my arms. She nestled into my chest, and I rested my chin on top of my head that she had cuddled into my neck.

"Spill, Kurt."

"Fuck. It actually stopped having much to do with you, Lee, but it did." She scoffed, and I'm sure that sounded as clear as mud. "For all my life, I've been behind Luke and Mitch. I always got their hand-me-downs, or I couldn't do something because Luke or Mitch had done it and they were moved on from it so then I couldn't do it."

"That's pretty shitty, but that has nothing to do with me."

I chuckled and squeezed my arms tight around her. "Patience, Lee. I'm not sure how much sense this is going to make." I took a deep breath and tried to figure out what the hell to say. "When I asked you to marry me, you were mine. No one else knew, and I didn't have to share you with anyone. You broke it off with me, and even then, I still felt like you were mine even though no one knew about us. When you started hanging out with Violet and then got a job at Skid Row, I felt like I had lost you to Luke and Mitch.

You were just another thing that I had to share with them. You weren't mine anymore, and it pissed me the fuck off."

Lee pushed back and looked up at me. "I wasn't Luke and Mitch's. I only got the job at the shop because I didn't want you to think that you had to support Jay and I. I've told you before, I didn't want you to be with me because you were trapped. I wanted you to be with me because you wanted to be there."

"Lee, you really don't know me very well if you think I'm going to stay somewhere I don't want to be."

She shrugged and laid her head on my shoulder. "I guess that was me going back to believing the worst in people."

"I guess we both fucked up and didn't know how to fix it."

"That would be a good guess," she agreed with a laugh "Although, I think that next time we fight, we need to find a better way to figure things out than you crashing your car and almost killing yourself."

"I'll keep that in mind." My hand traveled over the swell of her hip and cupped her lush ass. "Although, from where I'm laying right now, it's been well worth all of the pain and broken bones."

"Mr. Jensen, I do believe you're just trying to get in my pants." She batted her eyes at me and wound her arms around my neck.

"Is that something you'd be against, gorgeous?"

"I like when you call me that," she murmured.

"I just call 'em like I see 'em, Lee, and you are the most gorgeous woman I have ever laid eyes on."

"That definitely gets you a peek into my pants."

I threw my head back laughed and held her body against me. "Are we keeping track of points now?" I asked. "How many points until I get to see you naked, spread out on your bed."

"Oh, Mr. Jensen, that is going to cost you a lot." She rolled on top of me and straddled my waist.

"Are you going to keep calling me, Mr. Jensen, because it's hot as fuck when you say it?" Every time those two words came out of her mouth, I swore my dick was going to take off like a rocket.

Her hands went to the hem of my shirt and worked it up my stomach. "If the mood strikes me." She leaned down and flicked her tongue against my nipple. "Mr. Jensen," she whispered as she looked up at me, lust filling her face.

I clamped my eyes shut. "You're gonna fucking kill me, Lee, because all I want to do right now is pick you up, carry you to your room and have my way with you all night."

"What's stopping you?"

"A fucking broken leg and a bum arm, Lee. I'm fucking dying here." I tried to wrap my arms around her and almost clocked her on the head.

"I think we can manage to work around that," she purred in my ear. She slid off, her feet touching the floor and she held out her hand to me. "You might not get to carry me, but I promise to follow you to the bedroom."

This was it. This was what I had fucking wanted for the past year, and now I finally had it. She pulled me off the couch, and I wrapped my arm around her and looked down into her eyes. "I don't—"

"Why the hell are all of the lights off?" The lights flew on around Lee and me. "Oh shit." Jay was standing in the open door; his jaw dropped to the floor.

Leelee buried her face in my neck and squeaked. "Shit!"

"Is this what I think it is?" Jay asked.

"Well, it's definitely not a tea party," Leelee said, muffled.

"No, I would say not. Well," Jay turned off the lights and shut the door. "I'll just leave you two to whatever you were doing and be headed to my room." He winked at me and pumped his fist in the air as he strode down the hallway.

"Is he gone?" Leelee asked when she heard his bedroom door shut.

"Yeah," I sighed.

"Thank God." She relaxed into my arms and pressed a kiss to my neck. "I guess we won't have to awkwardly tell him we're dating, will we?"

"No, I don't think we'll need to, Lee. I'm pretty sure he got the picture."

"Oh, shit on a stick. I wanted to keep this between us for a bit."

I put my hand under her chin and tilted her head back. "Why?" The first thing that came to mind was she didn't want anyone to know we were together.

"Jay...I don't care if he knows. He would have found out sooner than later anyway. I know he's going to tell Frankie and then it's only a matter of time before it gets back to Vi and Scar who are going to go apeshit with hundreds of questions wanting to know everything."

"So, it's not you wanting to hide me?" I smirked.

"Hardly. I'd like to fast forward to where we aren't some strange new thing where people ask so many questions that my head spins."

"How about if they ask you any questions, you just send them my way."

"And what exactly are you going to tell them?"

"Whatever that will get them to shut the hell up."

"I think us hiding out for the next couple of months might be better."

"In bed?"

"That could be arranged," she coyly said. "Although, with Jay in the house, I don't see that happening too often."

"What? He lives here, Lee. How are we going to get around that?"

"I don't know. It just seems weird doing, you know, with him here."

"Oh, Lord. You can't even say sex when he's in the house."

She slapped her hand over my mouth and shook her head. "Too fucking weird, Kurt. I can't do that shit with my brother in the house. Not happening. All I need is for him to hear us one time getting it on and I'll never live it down."

"Does that mean you're a moaner?"

Leelee slugged me in the stomach. "Oomph, what the hell was that, woman?"

"Sounds like you're the moaner, Kurt," she said with a laugh as she danced out of my grasp and into the kitchen. She grabbed a bottle of water from the fridge and twisted off the cap. "But it looks like you won't be finding out about me being a moaner anytime soon." She took a small sip of water and turned to walk down the hallway.

"Hold on," I hollered before she took two steps. "You're still going to make me sleep on the couch tonight?"

"We just started dating, Kurt."

"Leelee, we've been married for over a year." What in the hell was she thinking? We were God damn married, and I didn't want to spend another night without her.

"I think I need some woo in my life, Kurt."

"Woo? What in the fuck is that?"

170

Leelee shrugged. "I guess you're going to have to figure it out." She sauntered to her bedroom door and looked over her shoulder at me. "I'd start with Google. Goodnight, Kurt." She slipped into her bedroom and closed the door behind her.

Woo?

What in the ever-living hell was that?

I pulled my phone out and laid down on the couch.

If Lee wanted woo, woo is what she was going to get.

As soon as I figured out what in the hell it was.

****

CHAPTER 20

Leelee

"Wow! Whose car is that parked in front of the house? Did you see it, Lee?"

I grabbed my cup of coffee out from under the coffee pot and leaned against the counter. I had seen the car outside and had a pretty good idea whose it was. "I saw." I glanced in the living room, seeing the crumpled blanket Kurt had used last night, but didn't see Kurt.

"You think it's Kurt's?" Jay grabbed the orange juice from the fridge and drank straight from the carton.

"You do know that we have cups, right?"

Jay shrugged and put the carton back in the fridge. "Whatever."

I shook my head and took a sip of my hot coffee. "It's Kurt's. Has to be, although I have no idea where he is."

"You check your bed?"

"Shut the hell up." I grabbed the dish towel off the counter and chucked it at him. "He is not in my bed."

"That's surprising. I put my headphones on last night, so you know, I wouldn't hear anything." Jay wiggled his eyebrows, and I died a little bit inside.

"Jay, I swear to God, you are going to have a short life if you keep giving me shit about Kurt."

"Come on; I gotta give ya hell a little bit. That's what little brothers are for." Jay grabbed a Pop-Tart out of the pantry and ripped it open with his teeth. "I'm gonna head over to Kyle's for the day. We're going to run over some football plays then meet up with some other guys at the movies tonight."

I nodded and thought that this was exactly what Kurt and I needed. Time alone without Jay around. "Sounds good. Call me when you're on the way home." I did not need a repeat performance of last night.

"Trust me; I'll give you guys plenty of warning to get your clothes back on."

I looked for something to chuck at him, but he ducked out the front door before I could find something. I heard my car start up and hoped that really was Kurt's car outside. Otherwise, I was going to have to walk to the grocery store today.

I finished off my coffee, turned on the radio and turned to the sink to start the pile of dishes still there from last night.

I heard the front door open and figured it was Jay back, grabbing something he forgot. "What did you forget this time?" I asked, as I filled the sink full of water.

"My good morning kiss." Kurt wrapped his arms around me, and I jumped in his arms.

"Holy hell, I thought you were Jay."

"Does Jay generally kiss you good morning?" Kurt asked as he nuzzled my neck.

"No, you ass. I meant I thought it was Jay coming back in the house because he forgot something." I relaxed into Kurt's body and enjoyed the feel of his lips against my skin.

"Nah, I passed him at the stop sign. Where was he headed?"

"Over to a friend's house." I knew Jay had told me which friend but I couldn't remember anything when Kurt was kissing me.

"Does that mean I can start my wooing?" he whispered in my ear.

"So, you figured out what woo is?" I laughed.

"Yeah, I finally figured it out. There was some weird shit that popped up, but I managed to figure it out."

I turned around and wrapped my arms around his neck. "I think we have a little time for woo, but I do have to go to the grocery store."

"Well, in that case, let the wooing commenc." Kurt pulled out a set of keys from his pocket and held them in front of my face.

"What is this?" I asked, grabbing them.

"Those are the keys to my GTO that you get to drive."

"Really?" To a normal person, this wouldn't be that big of a deal, but to me, getting behind the wheel of a new, suped up car I'd never driven before was like Heaven.

"I fucking love that about you. Cars excite you as much as they do me."

"What can I say? I'm easy like that." I tossed the keys in the air, caught them and pressed a kiss to Kurt's cheek. "Wait, am I getting to drive your car before even you get to?"

Kurt shrugged. "Yeah, but not for lack of trying. I tried to drive it this morning, but Nos talked me out of it. There's no way with this damn boot on my leg that I can drive yet."

"Well, that makes this even better."

"So, my wooing is doing pretty good?" he asked, winking at me.

"Your woo is strong so far."

"Only because I know you, Lee. If it's got an engine, your eyes light up, and I swear I can see your mind going a mile a minute thinking about it."

"Eh, what can I say? I'm a simple girl." I pressed a kiss to Kurt's cheek and bounced to the door where I slipped my shoes on. "I'll meet you at the car," I called, not waiting for Kurt.

I was standing in front of the car when Kurt came out, a smirk on his lips. "You do know you left the water running, right?"

"Oh shit. I totally forgot. Your woo threw me off."

"No worries, Lee. I got you covered." He laughed. "You ready to take her for a ride?"

"Yeah, except you do know the car is purple, right?" I couldn't help the giggle that escaped.

"I know. I haven't had the time to get it into paint yet, although I have to say that the purple is starting to grow on me."

"At least it's a dark purple. If it was a lilac, I don't even think I would drive it."

Kurt shook his head and ran his hand through his hair. "I knew you were going to give me shit about the color. I'm painting the damn thing black and blacking out the wheels. We'll see how much shit you can give me then."

I shook my head and moved around to the driver's side. "Even if you paint it black, I'll always know that it was once purple."

"Then it stays purple, but I'm still blacking out the wheels."

I nodded. "I think that might help downplay the purple a little bit."

"Just get in the car, Leelee, and you'll forget what color the damn car is when you shift into first and press down on the gas."

We both got in the car, and I ran my hand over the dash and the steering wheel. "I could definitely get used to driving this every day."

"How bad is it that I'm jealous of my damn car? You're touching it more than you've touched me."

"I think we did enough touching last night," I reminded him, laughing.

"There's always more where that came from, Lee." His hand slid across the center console and caressed my leg.

175

"I don't think you really needed to look up woo, Mr. Jensen. You seem to be doing pretty well."

"You know, I never got that good morning kiss, Lee." He reached over with his hand that was in the cast and a giggle bubbled out of me.

"I think your woo will be even better when you get that cast off." I leaned over, brushing my lips against his mouth and couldn't resist the pull I felt to him. Kurt deepened the kiss, giving me everything we both wanted and I didn't want it to end.

"Do you really need to go to the store?" Kurt mumbled against my lips.

"Unfortunately, yes. I promise to be quick."

Kurt gave me one last kiss and settled into his seat. I sat there staring at him, wishing he hadn't moved away from me.

"Lee, drive before I take you right here and we break-in the back seat." I glanced in the back, contemplating if that was something I wanted. "Lee, drive," he growled.

I shakily stuck the key in the ignition and shifted the car into reverse. I eased the clutch off while I gently pressed down on the accelerator. "Driving is something I can do, Kurt."

"I know you can drive me crazy, Lee. Now, let's see if you can drive my car."

I looked over at Kurt and gave him a wink. "Buckle up, Mr. Jensen, I'm gonna take you for a ride."

****

Kurt

Leelee could drive. Holy hell could she drive.

"I think that was the longest but quickest drive to the grocery store."

176

Leelee laughed and turned off the car. "Come on; you knew I had to see how she drove."

"The whole way through town and back before you headed to the store?"

"I could keep driving if you want me to."

I shook my head and opened my door. "It's a good thing I think you're sexy as hell driving my car, Lee."

Leelee hopped out of the car, rounded the hood and was standing at my door before I even hoisted myself out of the car. "I move like I'm ninety."

"Aw, you kind of do," Leelee agreed with a laugh, "but you at least don't look ninety." She smirked.

"That smart mouth of yours is going to wind you up bent over my knee, Lee."

"Promises, promises," she tsked.

I slammed the car door shut, leaned against the car and crossed my arms over my chest. "Remind me again why we were too stupid to get together before?"

"Because I suffer from 'Everyone Leaves Syndrome,' and you're the last born and think you have to share and get everyone's seconds."

"I think we were both wrong, Lee."

She stepped into my space, and I spread my legs so she could cuddle up to me. She wrapped her arms around my neck and looked me in the eye. "I think I came around before you did, though."

"How do you figure that?"

"I don't remember you flying halfway across the country to be with me while I was in a coma for a week."

I shrugged and brushed her hair off her neck. "I guess I just needed some sense knocked into me."

"Hmm, next time you need that, just tell me, and I'll smack ya upside the head. Flipping your car and almost killing yourself seems a bit over the top."

I caressed her cheek, and she leaned into my touch. "I'll remember that, gorgeous." I pressed a kiss against the warm, soft skin of her neck and she gasped under my touch. "I think we should have stayed home and gone to the store later. This might be the only time we have alone."

"Oh, but Mr. Jensen," she purred, "this is all part of the woo, and I have to admit, I'm loving it."

"I bet you are." I nipped the lobe of her ear and wrapped my arm around her waist. My broken arm awkwardly rested on her hip, and I again couldn't fucking wait to hold Lee like she deserved to be held. "You think we can speed shop and get back home before Jay does?"

"I think that sounds like a perfect idea," she murmured. "Although, no scooter."

I leaned back and looked down at her. "No scooter? Come on! There's no way I'm going to be able to walk fast with this damn cast on. That scooter saves us so much time. I'll even let you ride in my basket." I wiggled my eyebrows at her and squeezed her waist.

"As tempting as that sounds, I'm going to have to take away your scooter and take a raincheck on that basket ride." She pressed a quick kiss to my lips and pulled out of my arms. "Come on, Mr. Jensen. The sooner we get done, the faster we can get back to the house, and you can try a different kind of woo on me."

I laced my fingers through hers and limped to the front of the store. "And what kind of woo is that?" I asked.

"The kind where we don't have any clothes on." She winked at me and skipped to the cart rack.

Now that was the kind of woo I could get behind.

****

CHAPTER 21

Leelee

"Four packs of Oreos, Kurt? Really?" How in the hell did Kurt keep the rock-hard body I had glimpsed before and still eat like a hormonal teenager?

"Yes. I would normally only get two packs, but Jay ate over half of them last time. Damn kid. I'm going to have to start labeling my shit."

"Is that what this has come down to? Labeling and hoarding your food?" I laughed as I grabbed a pack of crackers and tossed them in the cart.

Kurt was pushing the cart, complaining the whole time that having the scooter would be better but I was standing my ground we didn't need the damn thing. "Two things you need to know about me, Lee."

I stopped walking and turned to look at Kurt. "And those would be?"

He popped a grape into his mouth that he had been munching on and pointed his finger at me. "Number one. Don't come between my Oreos and me. We've had a close relationship for the past twenty-five years, and I am not above hoarding and labeling."

"That has been duly noted," I said, motioning to the cart. "Now, what is number two?"

"Number two is...see rule number one."

I couldn't help but laugh. "You really are a simple man, aren't you, Kurt?"

He shrugged and pushed the cart forward. "I'm sure there's more, but it's all clouded by Oreos now."

"I'll be waiting for number two." My phone rang, and I pulled it out of my pocket. "Hell, it's Violet."

"Answer it," Kurt said as he tossed a pack of Nutter Butters into the cart.

"You don't mind?"

"Why the hell would I mind? She's your friend, Lee. Answer it."

I swiped left and put the phone to my ear. "Hey, Vi."

"Leelee! You answered," she said, sounding surprised.

"Yeah, you called."

"I called last night, and you didn't answer. I thought maybe you were mad at me or something."

I shook my head at Kurt who was about to throw another pack of Oreos in the cart. "Four is enough," Kurt growled but put them back on the shelf.

"Four of what?" Violet asked.

"Oh, not you. I was talking to Kurt. We're shopping, and I'm discovering his love affair with Oreos."

Violet laughed. "We still have one pack in the pantry that is his. You can pick them up when you come over for dinner tonight."

I laughed. "Smooth, Vi, real smooth."

"Eh, I'm not very subtle. So, be here at six, bring a pie and Kurt." She hung the phone up before I could tell her she was crazy and I looked at the phone dumbfounded.

"What did she want?" Kurt asked.

"She invited me to dinner and told me to bring a pie and you."

Kurt shook his head and cursed under his breath. "You going?"

"Only if you go."

Kurt shook his head. "Is that how you're going to guilt me into going there?"

"I haven't actually seen Violet in a while," I said meekly.

"That's a lie, Lee. I know you see her every day at work."

"Yeah, but that's different. I'm normally all greasy and under the hood of a car. I do like to see my friend when I'm not working, and we can have a drink or two."

"Or ten," Kurt snickered.

I bumped into him with my hip and rolled my eyes. "You're coming, Kurt."

"You can't make me, Lee."

"No, I can't, but I can withhold naked woo."

Kurt stumbled over his feet and abruptly stopped. "But we haven't even naked woo'd yet? How the hell are you going to keep that from me, woman?"

"Well, man," I said, moving his arms out of the way and standing between him and the cart, "come with me tonight, and I promise you will be rewarded accordingly. But, you have to agree, no arguing and no punching Luke or Mitch."

"I don't know what you have against bloodshed. Sometimes, a well-placed punch is all you need to break the ice."

"No. Don't even think about it, Kurt. I get why you're pissed off at your brothers, but you also need to see where they are coming from."

"Siding with my brothers would not bode well for us, Lee."

I shook my head and wound my arms around his neck. "I'm not, Kurt. I'm just saying, I think you need to knock that chip off your shoulder and just listen. I think you might be surprised at what you hear if you just give them the time of day. Your accident made you wake up and see things differently. It did the same thing to them."

"Why can't we just stay at home tonight and go to Luke's next year?"

"Because you need to talk to your brothers. We're going, Kurt. And I'm bringing a pie."

"You can bake?"

I slipped out of Kurt's arms and headed back down the aisle we had just been down. "No, but how hard can it be?" It couldn't be that hard. Not that I had actually seen someone make a pie, but they didn't look hard. Jay and I typically bought a pumpkin pie from the grocery store for Thanksgiving, and it looked simple. Dump stuff in a bowl, stir it up, dump it into a crust and let it bake. Easy as, well, pie.

"Lee, I don't think you know what you're getting yourself into," Kurt called.

"Kurt, I can tear apart an engine and put it back together in no time. I really think I can figure out a pie."

I glanced over my shoulder and saw Kurt had turned the cart around and was following me. "I don't doubt your ability as a mechanic, Lee. I'm just saying, I think you at least need a recipe to make a pie."

I pulled out my phone and held it up over my head. "Google, Mr. Jensen. It never fails." I opened the app on my phone, but my finger hovered over the search bar. "What kind of pie do you like?"

"Your's."

"But what kind."

Kurt shook his head and laughed. "I can tell you're serious about this pie because you completely missed my high school joke."

I thought back on what he said and rolled my eyes. "You haven't even tried that pie yet, so you might want to withhold judgment."

Kurt put his arm around my shoulder and guided me over to the baking aisle. "I like banana cream pie, and I really doubt I'm going to change my mind about your pie, Lee. Although, if you want to do a taste test when we get home, I'm more than willing."

I slugged him in the shoulder. "There's the crude Kurt Jensen I know."

"You know you like it, Lee."

I did, but he didn't need to know that. I didn't want a relationship where I had to be all prim and proper and being with Kurt was the furthest thing from that. "Now, shh. I need to find a recipe for banana cream pie." I typed in the words and was bombarded with hundreds of recipes. "Holy hell. Who knew there were so many ways to make a pie?"

"I know how my mom used to make it," Kurt volunteered

"You mean to tell me you know how to make a pie?" I asked, amazed.

"Yeah. Follow me, Lee. I'll show you the ways of the easy banana cream pie." Kurt wandered down the aisle, and I followed him because, let's face it, I was so lost that I didn't even know where to start. Was Kurt Jensen the best person to help me make a pie? Probably not. But as of right now, he was my only option.

And besides, who was I kidding? I'd follow Kurt Jensen anywhere. Even down the baking aisle.

****

Kurt

"Just slather the whipped cream on top, put some more bananas and we're good to go." I handed Lee the cream and leaned against the counter.

184

"You do know you just made this whole pie, right?" Leelee looked at me like I was a god and I couldn't help but think I could get used to her looking at me like that.

I shrugged and swiped my finger through the cream when she opened it. "It's not so much making it as just putting it together. We could have done an even quicker step and bought the already made pudding instead of the instant."

"Now that really would have been cheating. I want Vi to think I actually put some thought and time into the pie." She laughed as she gobbed the whole container on top. The cream was mounded up an inch higher than the crust, and all it looked like was a pie shell filled with whipped cream. "I wonder how much this thing weighs." She laughed as she tossed the empty container into the garbage and started cutting up the last two bananas.

"Probably close to five pounds," I guessed.

"Holy hell, is that the time? We only have twenty minutes to get to Luke's." Leelee tossed the bananas on top, threw the dirty knife in the sink and sprinted down the hallway into her room.

I grabbed a banana off the top, popped it into my mouth then put the pie in the fridge. We didn't need the damn thing melting before we got to dinner.

"Lee," I called as I hobbled down the hallway. "It takes five minutes to get there. Why in the hell are you freaking out?" I opened her bedroom door and leaned on the frame as I watched her toss clothes out of her closet onto the bed.

"Because I need to change, but I have nothing to wear." She dropped to the floor and started pulling out shoes, looking for what, I had no idea.

"What is wrong with what you have on?" She was wearing tight cutoff jean shorts and a dark green tee shirt with an old dragster on it. She looked hot as fuck with her pitch-black hair piled on top of her head, and her miles of long legs on display.

"I look like I went to the store."

"Uh, isn't that what you did? I didn't know you were trying to look fancy at the store."

"I don't want to look fancy, Kurt. I just want to look like I care and I know what I'm doing." She stood and started tossing clothes again.

"Lee, you have completely lost me. You're trying to impress Vi and Scar who you have met and hung out with before."

"I'm not trying to impress them, Kurt, I'm trying to show that I know what the hell I'm doing."

"Yeah, that made everything clear as mud. You're speaking in tongues, woman."

Lee huffed and tossed her hands in the air. "It's hopeless. Everything I have looks like I'm a twenty something that doesn't have a clue and married a guy I didn't know."

I pushed off the door and sat down on her bed. "Come here, Lee."

She shook her head at me and crossed her arms over her chest. "No. You can't fix this, Kurt."

"Lee, come here now," I growled as I pointed to where my legs were spread.

She scuffled toward me and looked down. "Naked woo is not happening right now, Kurt."

"Woman, I'm not looking for naked woo, although, for the record, if you were offering it, I would not decline it."

Leelee rolled her eyes and took a step away from me. I wrapped my arms around her legs and pulled her back to me. "Work with me here, Lee. You know my right arm works worth a shit. Stay."

"I'm going to ignore the fact you just told me to stay," she snarled. She rested her hands on my shoulders and sighed.

"And I'm going to ignore the fact that you're tossing clothes around like a mad woman."

"Kurt, what in the hell are we doing?" She looked exhausted and ready to cry.

I tugged her into my lap, and she curled her arms around me. "We're together, Lee."

"But what *are* we?"

"Together." I didn't know what else she wanted me to say. She was it. That was it for me. I wasn't going anywhere but where she went.

"I don't know why that doesn't feel like enough."

I tilted her head back and looked into her eyes. "I'm done, Lee."

Her eyes got huge, and she sat up straight. "What? What do you mean you're done? You can't be that mad—"

"No, stop. That's not what I meant." I turned her in my lap, putting one leg on each side of me and had her straddle me. "I mean, I'm done doing whatever the hell we were doing before. Being married but not fucking being together. I'm done." I brushed her hair out of her face. "It's you, Lee. It's always been you since the first time I saw you bent over the fender of a car at the track, grease all over your hands and face and acting like it was the most natural thing in the world to tear apart a tranny."

"I don't even remember that," she whispered.

"That's because you didn't see me that night. Or the next five nights at the track. I watched you, Lee. I wanted to know you, but I was afraid the girl you were wouldn't live up to the girl I thought you were."

187

"I'm afraid to ask what you thought of me when you met me."

"Smart as hell, loves cars more than I do, can turn a wrench better than anyone I know, and I'll be damned, but also the most gorgeous woman I've ever laid eyes on. You're everything I wanted and more. You pushed me away before, and I let you. But that's not going to happen this time. You can sit here and say this isn't right or you don't like, and I'm not going to listen to a word of it. We're fucking married, Lee, and it's about time we start acting like it."

"But...you married me because you were doing the right thing."

"No, stop that bullshit right there. I married you because I knew it was the way to make you mine forever. I knew the second you signed those papers and took my name, that you were mine. Endgame. The whole enchilada. Hook, line, and sinker. Mine."

"But—"

I delved my hands into her hair and looked into her eyes. "Do you like where you are right now, Lee?"

"In your lap?"

"Yes. Right here. In my arms, our bodies touching and no one but you and I. Do you like it?"

"I love it," she blurted out.

"Then, what is the problem?"

"What if Violet and Scarlett think we're crazy for staying together? We may have been married for months, Kurt, but we've only been together for two months tops between our wedding day and now."

"Are you happy?" I didn't know how else to get this through her head.

"Yes, we've already gone over that."

"Tell them that, Lee. You're fucking happy, and you don't plan on changing it. Why are you letting your happiness depend on Violet and Scarlett? Who, by the way, aren't going to judge you the way that you think they will. They're friends, Lee."

Leelee leaned forward and rested her forehead against mine. "I'm so scared that this isn't going to work and then I'm going to look like an idiot."

"If this doesn't work out, the only one who is going to look like an idiot is me for letting you go. There is no one else on the Earth for me, Lee. There's only one other way to say it, but I'm pretty sure that'll send you running for the hills right now."

Leelee shook her head and whimpered. "Please don't say that, at least not yet."

I rubbed her back and pressed a kiss to the side of her head. "I know, Lee. Just know I feel it."

She wound her arms tight around me and clung to me like I was about to disappear.

I held onto her even though I wanted to scream that I was in love with her, but I knew she needed to just figure things out on her own and I could tell her out loud when the time was right.

I just hoped I gave her enough time until she figured it out.

I was here to stay, and she needed to wrap her head around it quickly.

****

CHAPTER 22

Leelee

"Mama said I can sit by you while she and Violet do the dishes." Levi set his plate of banana cream pie on the coffee table and climbed on the couch next to me. "Can you hand me my plate, please?"

"You think you got a big enough piece?" I joked as I handed it to him. Half of his plate was full of pie, and he also had three Oreo cookies. "Where did you manage to snag the cookies from?"

"Kurt. He was in the pantry when I walked by. His mouth was full, and he had cookie crumbs on his shirt."

That definitely sounded like Kurt. "Did you happen to see where Kurt went?" After the huge meal Violet had made, I managed to make it over to the couch where I was sprawled out and wondered when I was going to give birth to my food baby.

"He went downstairs with Luke and Mitch. I was going to go with them, but mama told me to come keep you company."

"Well, that was very nice of you, Levi. I know it's more fun to hang with the boys."

Levi shrugged and picked up an Oreo. He twisted off the top and licked all the cream off from the inside. "I like you, though. You're like a guy but totally a girl."

I laughed. "Thanks, I think."

"It's a compliment. You're, like, the best of both worlds." Levi dropped the two cookie halves into the pie and stirred it around. "Like pie and cookies together."

"I'm gonna have to take your word on that one, little man." I watched as Levi stirred and the cookies were starting to make black skid marks all through the pie. Not my idea of the best of both worlds.

"Mama said you and Kurt are married."

Oh, Jesus. Even Levi knew now. I didn't want to keep hiding it, but I just wish it was a non-topic when people found out. "Yup, we sure are."

"How come I didn't get to be your ring guy?"

"Huh?"

"You know, the guy who keeps the rings and then gives them to you after you tell Kurt that you love him."

My throat tightened at the thought of telling Kurt I loved him. That was a whole other mountain I needed to climb. "You mean a ring bearer?"

"Yeah, that too. How come you didn't have me carry your rings?" He spooned a huge bite in his mouth and waited.

"Uh, that would be because Kurt and I didn't get married like that."

"That's dumb. Everyone knows you need a ring guy and a flower chick."

"Chick?" I giggled. Hearing a five-year-old say *chick* was comical.

"Yeah, I take care of the rings, and she takes care of the flowers. You can't have a wedding without either of them."

"You can. When Kurt and I got married, it was just us two and then a judge."

Levi shook his head and handed me his plate. "When Mitch marries mama, I'm gonna be the ring guy and then I find a girl to be the flower chick." He hopped off the couch and headed back into the kitchen. "Mama, Leelee didn't have a ring guy at her wedding *or* a flower chick," I heard him tell Violet and Scarlett. They both busted out laughing, and I couldn't help but laugh too.

"That's too bad. Maybe they can have another wedding, and you can be the ring guy," Scarlett suggested.

"Leelee," Levi called as he ran back into the living room. "You're getting married again, and this time, I'll plan everything since you messed up the last time." Violet and Scarlett cackled in the kitchen, and I ruffled Levi's hair.

"If Kurt and I ever renew our vows, you'll be my first call."

"Sweet," Levi beamed.

"Alright Mr. Wedding Planner, how about you grab your plate and head into Mitch's room. You can watch some TV before bed," Scarlett pointed down the hallway and Levi pumped his fist in the air.

"Heck yeah. I am so watching Transformers."

Scarlett shook her head and followed him down the hallway. "Why am I not surprised," she mumbled.

Violet laid down on one end of the couch, propped a throw pillow under her head and looked at me. "We'll wait for Scarlett to get back out here."

I rolled my eyes and tucked my legs underneath me. "Is this really going to happen?"

"Damn straight it is. We've got questions, and you are going to give us the answers."

I had been hoping I had bypassed the twenty questions. Dinner had gone surprisingly well with Kurt not punching Luke or trying to trip Mitch. I really did need to give the man more credit. Although it had been a bit tense the first couple minutes, Levi had broken the ice when he informed Kurt that he made his mama buy special metilalicy markers just to sign Kurt's cast and then demanded one from Luke. After we had figured out metilalicy was metallic, Levi then made all of us sign it.

Violet had asked me to help her in the kitchen, and she didn't take no for an answer when I tried to fend her off. Mitch had been watching drag racing on TV, and the boys had all sprawled out on the couch and watched TV until dinner had been made. Violet and Scarlett had kept their questions to a minimum, but the second Kurt walked into the kitchen to get a soda and pressed a kiss to my temple, both of their eyes bugged out of their heads. I should have known I wasn't going to be that lucky to miss their interrogation.

"Alright, sister, spill," Scarlett demanded as she sat on the other end of the couch and crossed her arms over her chest. Looking back, I should have sat in the chair because now I was surrounded.

"Spill what?" I asked. I wasn't going to give them any information unless they asked for it.

"The kiss," Violet chirped.

"And the way his hand lingered on your waist after dinner," Scarlett put in.

Jesus, they were watching me like a hawk. No one had been around when Kurt had put his arm around me and asked if I was okay. I think I had scared him during my rant on not having anything to wear and the breakdown of not knowing what the hell I wanted. "It was a kiss, and he put his arm around my waist. Next question."

Violet grabbed the pillow out from under her head and chucked it at me. "Duh. We mean, what in the hell changed for him to kiss, touch, and look at you like you're the only person in the room?"

I clasped my hands in my lap and tried to figure out when everything changed.

"Hold on," Scarlett interrupted. "I think we need to start from the beginning. Like the beginning where you and Kurt got married and decided not to tell anyone."

Ugh, the beginning. They were going to have to get the condensed version because I really didn't want to talk about the part where I pushed Kurt away because I was an idiot. "CPS was going to take Jay away because my parents skipped town and we had no idea where they were. Kurt was there the day I found out, and I had no idea what to do. It came down to Kurt suggesting we get married, and we did because there was nothing else to do. Jay had already lost the parent lotto; he didn't need to lose me too."

"Jesus, Leelee. You know if we would have been friends, I would have helped you. Scar and I both would have helped you." Violet looked like she was ready to cry for me and that was the last thing I wanted.

"So, we got married, Kurt started hanging around, I got scared, told him to leave, and then Kurt got pissed. That about covers the last year or so." I looked at Scarlett who was shaking her head.

"Girl, why the hell did you push him away?"

"Because I didn't know what the hell was going on and I felt like he was there because he felt he had to be, not because he wanted to be. The last thing I want to be is an obligation to someone."

Scarlett smirked. "Well, from the way that boy is looking at you, I'm going to have to say that you guys got over whatever the hell was keeping you two apart."

I still didn't see what they did when Kurt looked at me, but it was nice to know Kurt wasn't trying to hide us being together, although I wouldn't be against a little more discretion. "It's a bit awkward, especially with you two noticing everything."

Violet rolled her eyes and waved her hand at me. "We're happy for you, Leelee. I'll try to keep my gasping and aweing to myself."

"Does this mean Kurt is going to come back to the shop?" Scarlett asked.

"Um, I don't think so."

"What? What is he going to do, then?"

"He's not going back to California, is he?" Violet piped in.

"No, as far as I know, he's not going back to California. He plans on staying here, and he has a plan, but he hasn't shared with me what that plan is yet." Which was another thing that was annoying the hell out of me. Kurt still disappeared all day, and I didn't know what he was doing. I figured he had been working on his car before, but I had a feeling he was doing more than that.

"So, are you two together?" Violet and Scarlett asked at the same time.

Violet laughed. "Great minds think alike."

"Yeah. I'm pretty sure we are. Kurt told me he's done doing whatever the hell we were doing before."

"Thank God," Scarlett whispered.

Violet giggled. "I do have to tell you, you and Kurt sure do know how to keep a secret. I swear, Luke's head was going to explode when he found out you two were married."

"Mitch just kept saying he knew something more was going on with you two. Vi and I had the same feeling, although it sure wasn't that we thought you two were married." Scarlett laid her head back on the armrest and crossed her arms over her chest. "Here I had thought that Violet and Luke would be the first to get married. Hell, you beat them before they even knew each other."

"You missed so much by getting married at the courthouse." Violet sat up and a huge grin spread across her face. "You two need to get remarried, and this time, you need to do it right."

"Hell yes!" Scarlett agreed. "A bachelorette party and everything."

I stood and shook my head. "No. I really doubt Kurt would want that. I think we need to get to know each other before we renew

195

our vows. Hell, Kurt could really get to know me, you know, the real me that no one had ever seen before, and decide that he's out."

"Nonsense," Violet hushed me as she strode out of the kitchen and sat back down on the couch with a notepad in her hand. "Do you plan on staying with Kurt?" she asked as she opened the notebook and grabbed a pen off the coffee table.

"Well, yeah," I stuttered. I had no plans of breaking up with Kurt, but I couldn't tell the future.

"Then, you need a wedding to match the happily ever after you plan on having." Scarlett clapped her hands together and sat in front of Violet. "Sit down, Lee, and start acting like the blushing bride you never got to be."

I sat down, not knowing what else to do and listened as Scarlett and Violet tossed around ideas of what kind of dress I should wear and where we should have the party.

I was apparently having a wedding re-do. I just hoped my groom showed up.

****

CHAPTER 23

Kurt

"So, when are you coming back to work?" Luke asked.

We were standing outside of the shop looking at the GTO, and for a second there, I thought things were going to be different between Luke and me. Except he still figured I was going to come back to work and fall into the life he had planned for me. That wasn't going to happen. "Not planning on coming back, Luke."

He crossed his arms over his chest. "So, what are you going to do then?"

"I got something going. It's looking to be a good thing." I shoved my hands in my pockets and waited for Luke to blow.

"What the hell do you have going on that is better than working with your brothers? This is supposed to be a family business, Kurt. You're just going to jump off the train and run off to fuck around by yourself?" Luke ranted.

"This," I swung my arm toward the massive Skid Row Kings building, "is not mine, Luke. That isn't Mitch's either. It's fucking yours, and we were just your Goddamn workers who happened to have the same last name as you."

"If you believe that, you're fucking insane. I started this place so we would have a place to be together and make money. I paid you damn good, Kurt, let you make your own fucking schedule and have full reign of the fucking garage. I don't know what the hell I could have done differently." He ran his hands over his head, and he looked like he was about to bust a blood vessel in his forehead. "You're not going to get it any easier anywhere else."

I shook my head. "Easy? Is that what you think I want? Easy is the last fucking thing I want." I couldn't even believe Luke

197

thought that was what I wanted. "I want something that is mine. That I have to work hard for. Put my blood, sweat, and tears into something that is mine and that no one can take away from me because I fucking did it all. I don't want a premade fucking life that I'm just supposed to slip into and not say a fucking word against. I don't want what you are offering, Luke. I know there are millions of people who would take what you're offering and not bat an eyelash, but I'm not that person. I need to do this on my own."

"So, that's it. You're just gonna walk away from all of this? From this family?" Mitch asked.

"This business is not what makes us family, Mitch. We were brothers before we had Skid Row, and we're going to be brothers after Skid Row." I didn't want to lose my family, but I couldn't keep going the way I was.

"Skid Row isn't going anywhere, Kurt," Luke growled.

"And I don't want it to go anywhere, Luke. I know that this is *your* blood, sweat, and tears. I didn't build this place. I come in, punch the clock, work on some cars, and then I punch out. That's not building something that is mine. That's working on your dream to make it better."

"This is all of ours' dream. We got out of the fucking gutter, and I made a better life for all of us."

"You! You made a better life for us, Luke. I don't want what you're forcing down my throat anymore," I screamed. I didn't know how else to get it across to Luke. I wanted out of the shop, but I didn't want to lose him or Mitch. "Why can't you just accept the fact that I want to do something that doesn't involve you?"

"And why do you have to do something that doesn't involve us? You wanna start new; then I'll sell this fucking place, and we'll start over."

"Do you hear yourself?" I asked. "Why in the hell would you do that? Do you have to be a part of everything? This is yours, and you should be damn proud of it, Luke. Now, let me go make my own life to be proud of. You don't need me to run this place. I can give you a list as long as my arm of guys who can come in and do the exact same thing I had been doing." Hell, if I were honest, they would probably do better than I did and give Luke less attitude.

"I don't want anyone else," Luke bellowed.

"Well, you don't get a fucking choice in this, Luke. I'm out, and I'm not coming back."

Luke stalked off behind the garage, and I closed my eyes. Did he finally get it? Or was he just taking a break, trying to figure out his next plan of attack on what I wanted?

"You gonna yell at me next?" I asked Mitch who was standing in front of me with his arms crossed over his chest.

"No." Mitch shook his head and sighed. "I get what you're saying, Kurt. But don't shit on what Luke and I are doing. I don't feel that I'm just working for Luke with my thumb up my ass. A shop with my brothers was my dream too."

"But it's not my dream, Mitch. I need to give up everything I want because you and Luke want the same thing? This isn't something that majority wins, and I just get to be the odd man out who gives up what he wants. I'm out. I'm done. I can't do this anymore."

"So, what are you going to do?"

"I'm opening up my own shop."

Mitch shook his head. "So, you're going to open up your own shop and take work away from Skid Row."

"No. That's not what I want. This is a big fucking town, Mitch. You really think that there can't be two shops in town? Plus,

Luke does it all. I want to focus on the racing crowd. Mods and upgrades."

"And you think you're going to do this all on your own?"

"Yes, but I'm also going to have a partner, and Nos has agreed to take care of the front end."

"So, Nos is your partner?"

"No." I shook my head. "He's just going to work for me."

"So, who is your partner?" he asked.

"Someone that has no idea."

"Holy fuck," Mitch breathed out. "You're fucking taking Lee with you, aren't you?"

I ran my hand through my hair. "Yes, if she'll fucking come. I know she loves working at Skid Row, but I know she also wants something that is hers. She struggles with the assholes who come into the shop and treat her like she's just a girl who doesn't know anything about cars. Lee knows cars better than I do. Having her as an equal partner is one of the smartest things I could do."

"So, not only are you leaving Skid Row, you plan on taking our best mechanic with you." Mitch paced back and forth, mumbling under his breath.

I knew it was shitty to do this, but it wasn't my intention to piss off Luke and Mitch. Leelee and I were together, and I wanted her next to me on everything I did. "I'm sorry, Mitch, but I have to start thinking of myself. I'm almost thirty years old, and I don't have anything to show for it."

"Then go, Kurt. But just know that Luke and I will always be here for you." I glanced over Mitch's shoulder to behind the shop where you could hear Luke cussing me out. Mitch smirked. "Luke will be here for you once he cools down."

"I'm gonna have to take your word on that."

"Time. It's just going to take time." There was a loud bang of Luke throwing a rock at something and Mitch laughed. "Kind of like you might want to give Luke some time before you tell him that you're taking Leelee with you."

"That's only if she wants to come with me. She has no idea what I've been doing."

"So, what the hell have you been telling her?"

"That I've been working on my shit."

"Jesus," Mitch said with a laugh. "You might have your hands full with her when you tell her."

I shrugged. "I guess I'll cross that bridge when I get there."

"Might wanna bring a boat in case she decides to blow that bridge up, brother."

Wasn't that the fucking truth? I thought I was doing the right thing, but I really didn't know how Leelee was going to react when I told her. Either she would love it, or she would be like Luke and think I was out of my fucking mind.

Mitch leaned against the GTO and glanced up at the shop. "So, I take it things are going good between you?"

"As good as can be expected. We're married; it's about fucking time we start acting like it."

Mitch nodded. "You happier now?"

"I'm getting there. I know every day I have Leelee with me will be better than the last."

"Well, then I guess I can't really knock it, can I? I'm just glad you're figuring out what you want. Even though your new plan is knocking mine off course for a bit."

"That's not what I want, Mitch."

Mitch laughed and pulled his phone out of his pocket. "I know that. There is room for two shops in town; it's just going to take some getting used to. So," he mumbled, as he turned on his phone, "you planning on racing once you get that cast off? It looks like the next race is out of town on Thompson."

"I think I'm done racing for a bit. I need to focus on Lee and the shop."

Mitch grinned. "Well, hell, miracles really do come true. With you out and AZ out too, I'm golden to win the top this season."

"You never know, I might pop into some of the races just to keep you on your toes." Without AZ and me racing, Mitch wasn't going to have any competition.

"I'll be ready, brother."

I clapped Mitch on the shoulder and headed to the shop. Luke, Mitch, and I had come to somewhat of an understanding, and I was ready to go home.

Home with Leelee.

****

CHAPTER 24

Leelee

"So, what did you and Luke end up talking about?" I asked, as I washed my face and got ready for bed. Kurt was leaning against the frame of the bathroom door with his arms crossed over his chest.

"I let them know about my plans."

"Hmm, and what did they have to say?" I didn't even know what Kurt's plans were, but Mitch and Luke did.

"Luke is pissed, and Mitch said it'd take some adjustment."

"So, when do I find out what your plan is?"

Kurt pushed off the door frame and stood behind me while I piled my hair on top of my head. "When the time is right."

"So, do you get to decide when the time is right or do I?" I was really getting sick of hearing about Kurt's plan but not really knowing what the hell it was.

"Soon, gorgeous," he mumbled, as he wrapped his arm around my waist. "Did everything go okay with Violet and Scarlett when I left?"

"Yeah, they asked twenty questions, but you were right. They're my friends and were just making sure I was all right." I grabbed my toothbrush and squirted toothpaste on it. "They want us to have a wedding."

"We did have a wedding."

"No, they want us to have a *wedding*. I'm talking dress, tux, and the whole shebang."

"Is that something you want?" he asked as his hand lifted the hem of my shirt and he brushed his fingers over my stomach. His eyes watched his hand in the mirror, hypnotized.

"Um, maybe? I guess I never really thought about it. I wasn't one of those girls growing up that daydreamed about their wedding dress or anything like that."

"Is it something we need to decide right now?"

"No, but it's something we need to figure out sometime. I don't want Vi and Scar to make a bunch of plans and then we decide not to do it."

"It's all up to you, Lee. I'll give you whatever you want. I know we got married quickly. Hell, we don't even have a picture of our wedding day. Maybe having a little something wouldn't be a bad idea."

I set my toothbrush down on the sink and turned around in his arms. "I think it's a good idea, although I think I might need to rein in Vi and Scar, though. They're planning a pretty big shindig." I wrapped my arms around Kurt's neck and looked up into his eyes. "They also want to have a bachelorette party."

"Lee, you're not a bachelorette."

I couldn't help but laugh. "I know that, but I think it'll just be like a girl's night out."

"With booze and every guy hitting on you. I don't think I like that idea."

"Why Mr. Jensen, are you getting a little territorial over me?"

"You're mine, Lee. I don't like the idea of you going out on the town all dolled up trying to get guys to buy you drinks as some dare."

"You do know that if I get a bachelorette party, that means you get a bachelor party."

Kurt shook his head and pressed a kiss to my neck. "I'll pass, gorgeous. My bachelor days are long over."

"Well, you're going to have to tell Violet and Scarlett that. They've got the second wedding train rolling, and they seem to be the conductors."

"So, I'm going to need to either hop on the train or get run over, huh?"

"It would appear that way."

"How about we continue this in the—"

"Lee? Kurt? You guys home?"

"Son of a bitch," Kurt cursed. "Am I ever going to get my hands on you?"

"Not tonight, Mr. Jensen," I informed him with a laugh. "In the bathroom, Jay. There's leftovers in the fridge." I heard Jay go immediately to the kitchen.

'Hey, those were my leftovers," Kurt protested.

"You had to know with Jay in the house those weren't going to last long even if I hadn't told him they were in there."

Kurt grumbled under his breath and buried his head in my neck. "I'm going crazy not being with you, Lee. I feel like a damn sixteen-year-old with blue balls."

I ran my fingers through Kurt's hair and leaned against the sink. "Hmm, poor Mr. Jensen."

"Stop calling me that," he mumbled. "Those words go straight to my dick."

"Maybe you can sleep in my bed with me tonight."

Kurt's head sprung up. "Fuck yes."

"Sleeping, Kurt. Just sleeping," I warned.

"As long as I get to have you in my arms all night, Lee, I'll be golden."

I reached up, cupped his cheek and gently patted his face. "Stay golden, Ponyboy."

Kurt blinked slowly, and I saw it dawn on him what I said. He laughed. "You're a damn dork, Lee."

I shrugged and pulled out of his arms. "I maybe a dork, but you're the one who's wanting to sleep with my dorky ass tonight."

"Every fucking night, Lee. Your dorky ass and me in the same bed."

"I think that can be arranged, Mr. Jensen."

Kurt growled and crashed his lips down on mine. "Every Time, Lee. Every time you say those words, all I want to do is strip you naked and have you ride me 'til the sun comes up."

The image of Kurt laying naked below me while I rode his rock-hard cock filled my head and a full-on tremor rocked my body. "Now who's killing who?" I whispered against his lips.

"Turnabout is fair, Mrs. Jensen." I gasped at his words and our eyes connected. "You're mine, Lee. Everything. Your body, your heart, and your last name. Mine."

"Damn, I really wish Jay wouldn't have come home," I grumbled as I skimmed my hands down Kurt's back.

"Me too, gorgeous, me too." Kurt pulled away and stood back as his eyes traveled over my body. "I've waited over a year for you, Lee. I can wait a little bit longer."

He could, but I didn't know if I could.

****

CHAPTER 25

Kurt

"You're a free man, Mr. Jensen."

I couldn't help but laugh at the doctor's words. Mr. Jensen sounded completely different from when Leelee said it. I flexed my fingers and slowly rotated my arm. I winced under the pressure and tightening, knowing even though the damn cast was off, I still had a little bit 'til I was one hundred percent.

"Within a week or two, you should be back to normal range of motion. Your arm has been in the same position for two months. Just give it some time."

I nodded, knowing if the damn cast was off, I was already doing better.

I stood, testing my weight on my leg and was happy as hell when I didn't collapse. My leg was less sore than my arm was, partially due to the fact I had been walking on my leg more than I should have been.

Nos was waiting for me as I ambled out of the clinic and felt the sun shining down on my shoulders. The doctor had told me to come back in a month for a check-up to make sure everything was still good, and then, I would be done with damn doctors.

"Looking good, brah," Nos said as I slid into the car. "That was a hell of a lot quicker than I thought it would be."

"Once that nurse pulled the damn saw out, I was done within minutes. I definitely wouldn't mess with that chick," I said, laughing.

"Where you wanna go? I just talked to my uncle. He said the sign just got delivered to the shop."

"Shop." Hell yeah. The sign I had ordered a week ago to hang over the shop was there, and that meant it was time to tell Leelee what my plan was.

It had been twelve days since the dinner at Luke's, and although I have been sleeping in Leelee's bed, sleeping was all we were doing. Don't get me wrong, just being that close to her warm, soft body was Heaven, but I was ready to make her mine in every way possible.

Jay was always fucking around, and as much as I loved the kid, I was ready to fucking strangle him. I got where Leelee was coming from, not wanting to do anything with Jay around, but she was starting to fucking kill me.

"You think she's going to flip when she sees the name?" Nos asked as we pulled into the parking lot.

"More than likely, or she'll tell me I'm fucking crazy and leave me. It's really a toss-up of how this is going to go." I had been going back and forth, trying to decide if what I was doing was the right thing, and I never came up with an answer.

I pulled my phone out of my pocket and texted Lee a time and a place to meet me. I shoved my phone back in my pocket and looked up at the sign.

Lee's Speed Shop.

The words were bold and a neon green you could see from a mile away. This is what I had worked toward, and it was finally done.

"That sign looks killer, brah," Nos said as he stared up at the sign. "You know, if people don't know your girl, they're going to think Lee is a dude."

"That's why I put Lee. I want those fuckers to walk into the shop, thinking that I'm Lee and then I want to watch their jaws drop when I tell them the drop-dead gorgeous, sexy as fuck woman in the back covered in dirt and grease is Lee."

Nos laughed. "That is going to be a trip each and every time it happens."

"And now with you being locked to take care of the front, all we need is Lee."

Nos clapped me on the shoulder. "You got this, brah. Now, get the fuck out of my car. Thank God after today I'm done carting your ass around."

I laughed and opened the door. "You know I couldn't have done this shit without you, Nos. I'll see you Monday?"

"Bright and fucking early. I have a feeling we'll be putting in some long hours these next couple of weeks."

"Not too early, fucker. Let's not get too crazy." I stepped out of the car and slammed the door shut.

Nos took off, and I was standing in the parking lot of my very own shop. Well, it was half mine.

I pulled out my phone to see if Leelee had texted back. It was ten to five, and I knew she would be getting off work soon. She had replied she would be there in fifteen minutes and my nerves skyrocketed.

I had called Mitch last week and told him I would be opening the shop next Monday, and although I knew he was happy for me, I knew he was still a bit pissed off at me. Mitch had told Luke about Leelee hopefully coming to work for me, and all Luke had texted me was one word. *Dick.*

I had to admit, I had fully expected him to call me up, ranting and raving, so when all he did was text me that one word, I thought he was taking it better than expected.

I glanced at my phone again, wishing fifteen minutes had gone by but realized one minute had barely passed.

Lee needed to get here, and she needed to get here fast. I looked up at the sign and hoped like hell this was going to blow her mind like it did mine.

This was my dream, and I hoped Leelee wanted the same.

If she didn't, I was fucked.

****

Leelee

I pulled my phone out again, double checking the address. All Kurt had sent me was a time and an address, and my mind was racing with every possibility of what I could be driving up to.

I was familiar with the area and knew the address was either a bakery, body shop, or an old liquor store. It was a toss-up of which one it could be.

My question was answered when I pulled up in front of the body shop and saw Kurt standing on the sidewalk. I parked next to the curb, and Kurt opened my door before I could get my seatbelt off.

He reached his arm out, and I gasped when I saw he didn't have a cast on anymore. "Your cast is gone." I looked at his leg and saw they were both gone. "I thought you had a couple of days until they were able to take it off."

Kurt shook his head and smirked. "I called and asked if they could fit me in sooner. I was going crazy with those fucking things on."

"So, you sweet talked the receptionist into getting an appointment." Totally sounded like something Kurt would do. Hell, it sounded like something any of the Jensen boys would do.

Kurt shrugged and smiled down at me. "I do have a way with words." He winked and my heart skipped a beat. This man was going to be bad for my health. "That was the longest fifteen minutes of my life, Lee," he grumbled as he grabbed my hand and pulled me out of the car.

"I had to finish up a Toyota before I could clock out. Luke insisted I needed to get it done today." I had no idea why the hell Luke was so adamant about it, but I had gotten the damn thing done. Thankfully, tomorrow was Saturday, and it was my day off, so I didn't really stress over Luke's attitude.

Kurt wrapped his arms around me, and I breathed a sigh of relief to be back in his arms. I was getting addicted to being there, and I missed him like hell those nine to ten hours I was working.

"Miss me?" he whispered into my ear.

I closed my eyes and breathed him in. Miss him was an understatement. I was becoming one of those whiny girls who couldn't go an hour without their boyfriend. "Just a little. It was a long day."

"Well, hopefully, I can make it a little better. There's something I want to show you." Kurt stepped to the side and pointed up to the sign that was hanging over the body shop.

"Is this where you're working now?" I had never been to this shop before, but I had heard they were a reputable place to get your car worked on.

"I guess you could say that."

"What does that mean?" I turned to look at Kurt, wondering what the hell was going on. Was he just going to work here when they needed him?

"It means I work here, but I also own it, along with my partner."

His words hit me, and they were the last thing I thought he would say. "This is yours?" I asked, looking at the building. It was a long, brick building that stretched the length of the road and had four bay doors that each faced the street and also had a large office at one end.

"Yeah, at least, half of it." He crossed his arms over his chest and looked smugly at the building. "This is what I've been working on the past few weeks. Nos' uncle used to own it and retired. I got the building and everything in it for a steal."

"Really?" Walking into a key-turn shop was ideal, but it rarely ever happened. Typically, walking into a body shop meant you were getting bare bones because the previous owner had sold everything off except for the building. "So, Nos is your partner?"

"No, he's just going to take care of the front end for me."

"Oh." Then, who in hell was going to be his partner? I thought for sure it would be Nos since he had been spending so much time with him lately.

Kurt grabbed my hand and tugged me up the sidewalk and to the front door. "Come on; I'll show you around." Kurt pulled his keys out of his pocket and unlocked the front door. "You have no idea how weird it is to open this door and know that everything here is mine."

I could only imagine how amazing that would be. I loved working for Luke, but I think it was always every mechanic's dream to be able to open their own shop. I just knew that wasn't going to be a possibility for me for a long time, if that. "Wow, this is really nice, Kurt," I marveled as I looked around and took in the clean and tidy waiting area. "Are these made from actual car parts?" The benches lining both walls were made from tailgates from pickup trucks.

"Yeah, I thought they were pretty impressive. I found a guy online who made them." Kurt motioned behind the front counter. "The chair back there is also made of actual car seats. Nos flipped out when he saw those. They're comfy as shit."

The top half of the walls were painted dark gray with a chair rail in the middle with the bottom half of the wall covered in steel plating. Various car signs were hanging on the walls over the benches, and there was a big neon sign behind the counter that boasted "Lee's Speed Shop." "So, are you going to change the name?" I figured if Kurt was going to go after his dream, he sure as hell would name the place something with his name in it.

"Nah, I like the one I have." I guess that made sense if Kurt was trying to keep the old clients coming in. Although, it was really hard to believe. "Come check out the bays and workstations. They're really top of the line. Most of this stuff was left from the old owners, but I rearranged it to better suit what I want to do."

"And what exactly is it you want to do?" We walked through a door behind the counter, and I sucked in a breath when I saw all the space behind the office. I was in mechanic Heaven. The six work bays each had a car lift and every tool you could possibly ask for. Huge bright green tool boxes at each bay had huge Lee's Speed Shop stickers on the sides of them and my fingers itched to open the drawers to see what was all inside.

"I want to specialize in racing. Any and everything that has to do with racing, I want to be able to build and fix it here. American, foreign, drag cars, oval track cars, hell, even dirt track cars. I want to be known as the place you go to when you need anything for your race car." Kurt's eyes lit up as he talked and I knew this was what he had been wanting. His dream was coming true, and I couldn't have been happier for him.

"That sounds like a really good idea, Kurt. I know Luke works on drag cars, but that's about it. It looks like you're going to carve out your very own niche in this town."

Kurt grabbed my hand and pulled me into his arms. "Yeah, that is part of the plan. As long as my partner goes along with it."

He brushed my hair off my neck and pressed a kiss to the side of my head. His hands brushed down my back, and he pulled me close.

"You haven't run any of this by your partner yet?" Was Kurt crazy? How was he doing all of this and yet his partner had no idea?

"No, she hasn't really known anything."

She? Kurt's partner was a woman? "Oh." I gulped. I hated to admit it, but I was jealous as hell. "When do you plan on telling her?" I tried like hell to make my tone even, and not sound like a raging, jealous bitch.

"Today."

Jesus, was Kurt's partner about to walk through that door, and he was standing here groping the hell out of me. I tried to pull out of his arms, but he wouldn't let me go. "Kurt, knock it off," I scolded. "Your partner is going to walk through that door any minute, and I don't think this is the type of impression you want to give."

"It's exactly the impression I want to give, and she's already here, Lee." Kurt buried his face in my neck and nuzzled my ear.

"She's here?" I screeched. "Stop! Have you lost your mind? You can't make out with me in front of her." As much as I wanted to show this chick Kurt was with me, I didn't think making out in front of her was the best way to make my point.

"Lee," Kurt said firmly. "I haven't touched you all day, now stand still before I spread you out on that work bench and really show you how much I missed you."

"Kurt, you just said your partner is here. You're absolutely crazy to be even thinking about having sex with me right now."

Kurt's hands moved to my ass and gave me a firm squeeze. "I actually planned on doing this differently, but you're driving me insane."

"What? Do what differently?" What in the hell was Kurt talking about?

Kurt shook his head and laughed. "I was surprised you didn't get it when you got out of the car."

I smacked him on the shoulder. "Kurt, you're killing me here. What in the hell are you talking about?"

"You, Lee. I'm talking about you." Kurt closed his eyes and leaned his head back. "You are my partner. You are the one who is hopefully going to do this all with me."

"You want me to come work for you?" Huh?

"No, Lee. This," Kurt pulled away from me and swung his arm around, "is all yours. I want you to be my partner. Fifty-fifty. You and me."

"You...this...me..." I choked on my own words. I sputtered and coughed as I looked around. "I'm Lee?" I asked, as I pointed at the huge Lee's Speed Shop that was painted on the back wall.

"You're the only fucking Lee. I can't believe it took you this long to get it."

"I thought Lee was Nos' uncle and you weren't going to change the name because you wanted to carry over his customer base. Except that didn't make sense anymore when you said you were going to specialize in racing."

"Nos' uncle's name is Pedro and the shop used to be called Elm Street Garage."

Oh. Well, holy hell. To say I was a bit off was an understatement. "How did you do this, Kurt? This is huge, and now you want me to run it with you?" My chest tightened, and my breathing got short. Opening a shop was crazy and insane. Opening a shop with me was even more insane. "I can't be Lee!" I sputtered.

"Well, there isn't any other Lee I plan on doing this with. The signs have been bought and hung, Lee. I need you to do this with me," Kurt declared.

"This is pure insanity, Kurt. All that keeps running through my mind is the word insane."

"To start your own business, you need to be a bit crazy, Lee. This is us breaking out and doing what everyone is afraid of."

"They're afraid because they're smart."

"No, you're wrong, Lee. I have thought this over and played out every scenario in my mind. Admit it, before I told you that I wanted you in with me on this, you thought it was a good idea. Hell, you said I was going to carve out my own niche in this town, Lee. I want you there, right next to me, building this business with me. You know more about cars than any mechanic I have ever met. Hell, Luke is pissed as hell that we're doing this."

"Wait, Luke knew about this?" How in the hell did Luke know about this before I did? "Don't you think you should have run this by me before you told my boss that I was quitting?" I rubbed my chest and wondered if this was what a heart attack felt like. My chest was tight, and it felt like I couldn't suck in enough air. I tried running my fingers through my hair and ran into the messy ponytail I had thrown it into. I ripped the hair tie out and looked at Kurt who looked like I had kicked his puppy.

"I let him know what my plans were and he figured that you would come with me, but I told him you were going to be my partner. At least, I thought you would be my partner."

"I didn't expect this." I ran my fingers through my hair and paced a short length of the shop. "I came here thinking, hell, I don't know what I was thinking, but it sure as hell wasn't this. You bought a shop and are giving me half of it, Kurt. Do you know you are doing that?" I stopped pacing and tossed my arms in the air. "Who in the hell does that?"

"I do. This is something you want?"

Was it something I wanted? Hell yes. Was I expecting it? Fuck no. "Of course, I want this Kurt, but you're just giving it to me. I didn't do anything to earn it. You keep saying you don't want shit given to you and you're sick of Luke and the garage, but here you are, giving me a garage."

"I'm not giving you a garage. Well, I am, but you're going to have to work your ass off just as hard as I am, if not harder. We have this, Lee, but we need to make it something. Buying this is only a small step into having a successful business, and I know I can't do it without you." Kurt grabbed my hand and pulled me into his arms again. "I know we started off backward as hell, Lee, getting married and not just getting to know each other, but I know that I don't want anyone else in my life and that you are the only person I can do this with. If this is not what you want, I'll sell it, and we can find a place that you want. Hell, if you don't want this and would rather work for Luke the rest of your life, I'll be fine with that. I'll sell and go back to work for Luke, too. This is nothing without you."

"I can't wrap my head around this, Kurt." I looked up into his eyes and saw the man I had fallen in love with. "We're both insane for doing this."

"Does that mean you'll be my partner?" he asked, his eyes full of hope.

I looked around, now seeing this shop as my own. A place I would come every day, work on cars, build a customer base, and all the while, do it with the man who had stolen my heart when he stopped his life to help save me.

I believed in Kurt with everything I had and knew whatever he put his heart and soul into, it would be successful. "You do know that you're asking a smart-talking, half-Puerto Rican *woman* to be your partner. Not only will we be husband and wife, but we'll also be business partners. We are going to be with each other every hour of every day."

"See, you see that as a drawback. I just figured if I'm with you all of the time, there's going to be a time when Jay isn't around, and then I can have my way with you."

"So, this all goes back to naked woo, doesn't it?" I laughed.

"Did it ever stop being about naked woo?" he countered as he pressed a kiss to my lips. "Say you'll be my partner, Lee."

"What if I say no?"

"Don't say no. That sign out front was expensive as hell."

I threw my head back laughing and knew this was it. This is what Kurt and I were going to be. The smart-ass woman mechanic and the hot as hell gear head. "Well, I wouldn't want you to go to all of the trouble of getting a new sign, so I guess I'll say yes."

"Yes?" Kurt asked, sounding a little shocked.

I nodded and wrapped my arms around his neck. "Hell yes."

Kurt lifted me off the ground and twirled me around. "Fuck yes!" he shouted.

I wrapped my arms around his waist and kissed my way down his neck. "I feel like this was like you asking me to marry you, but that already happened." I giggled.

Kurt walked over to the nearest workbench and set me on the top. "This is the second best day of my life."

"And what was the first?" I asked, as I ran my hands down his arms.

"The day you agreed to marry me will always be the best day of my life, Lee."

"But we got married because you were helping me."

Kurt shrugged. "So, we did this a bit backward. That doesn't change the fact that we're married, does it?"

"It better not," I whispered. With each day that went by, the more I loved that Kurt and I were married. I had found the person I was meant to be with by accident, but I wasn't going to let him go.

"You know, this is the first time in over a week that I've had you all to myself. I swear Jay was never around that much before."

I couldn't help but laugh. Every morning we would wake up, and Kurt would try to get some action, but each time, he would be interrupted by Jay's alarm going off in his room. With Jay being back in school, he rarely stayed the night with his friends and was always home at night doing his homework. Kurt wasn't able to catch a break all week. "Hmm, my poor Mr. Jensen is feeling neglected?" I purred.

"Yeah, but I'm about to make up for the past year right here on this bench. I never realized what a perfect height these were for fucking my wife." Kurt threaded his fingers through my hair and tugged my head back. "I'm gonna make you mine in every way possible, Lee."

My heart leaped at his words. He slammed his lips down on my mouth, and it felt like I was finally home. Kurt was all I needed. Even if we were in a body shop with tools and cars surrounding us, he still felt like home to me.

"I gotta have you, Lee. I can't fucking wait any longer," he growled against my lips.

"Take me, Kurt. I've always been yours," I gasped as his lips traveled down my neck and his hands grabbed the hem of my shirt. He pulled it over my head and tossed it on the bench behind me.

"Thank fuck, Lee, because you've had me since day one." His hands roamed over my body, cupping my breasts through my bra and I arched into his touch. He roamed to my back, caressing my skin as he unhooked my bra and the straps fell down my arms.

Kurt shook his head and reached into his pocket. "I knew I was going to fuck this up. I swore I'd wait to get you naked until I gave you this." He pulled a ring box out of his pocket, and my breath caught. "I should have given you a better ring the day we got married, Lee, not some shit from Wal-Mart, but I was so in shock that you actually agreed to marry me, that everything just went out the window." He opened the box, and I swear, I felt my heart stop. "I know you're not into girly shit, but when I saw this ring, I knew it was made for you."

He took the ring out of the box and slid it onto my finger. "It's perfect," I sighed. The ring was a dark silver with a huge, round diamond in the center with tiny little diamonds surrounding it. The darkness of the silver toned down the femininity of a normal wedding ring, but it also helped to let the diamond sparkle. I laughed. "Except this wasn't how I pictured you slipping my wedding ring on my finger."

"You should have figured out by now, Lee. You and I are never going to do things the normal way." Kurt moved back in between my legs and grabbed my hand he had just slipped the ring onto and put it over his heart. "This will make for an interesting story to tell our grandkids one day." He smirked.

The light caught my ring and glistened. "I think this is a story I'll keep to myself. You ravishing me on a workbench topless isn't something anyone needs to know."

Kurt wound his arms around my waist and pulled me close. "You topless is enough for me to forget my name. I'm amazed I remembered to give you the ring."

My fingers delved into his hair, pulling his head down. Kurt's mouth devoured my lips, and my tongue explored his mouth, tasting and teasing with each swirl. My hands grabbed his shirt, tugging it up his body and I pulled it over his head. I sailed it over his head, and my hands began exploring every tight muscle and ridge of his hard chest. "I think both of us topless is even better."

"You getting your fucking pants off would be better." Kurt pulled me off the bench and knelt in front of me. "You work on the jeans; I'll get your boots off." My hands instantly went to the button of my jeans, unsnapped them and pulled down the fly. "You changed out of your damn work uniform, woman, but not your damn steel toes?" Kurt cursed as he worked the laces loose and pulled the first boot off.

"I was in a rush this morning because someone distracted me and forgot to grab an extra pair of shoes. This is your own fault for kissing me too much before I went to work."

Kurt untied the other boot and pulled it off. He grabbed the waist of my jeans and stripped them down my legs and tossed them over his shoulder. "I could never kiss you enough, Lee. Each one just makes me want to taste you even more." His finger traced my underwear, and he pressed a kiss to my stomach. He looked up and wiggled his eyebrows at me. "Now, I have even more places to taste."

"You're a perv, Mr., Jensen." I laughed. "But I wouldn't have it any other way."

"As much as I want to taste all of you, Lee, my dick has been begging to sink into your sweet pussy ever since I saw you bent over the fender of that car." Kurt stood, slipped out of his jeans and grabbed me around the waist. "Wrap your legs around me, gorgeous, and hold the fuck on."

"Underwear first, Mr. Jensen. This is one thing we can't do backward." I hooked my thumbs into the waistband of Kurt's boxers and pulled them down his legs, and his hard dick bobbed in my face.

Just as my hand reached for it, Kurt grabbed my arm and tugged me up.

"No time for that, Mrs. Jensen. My dick is so hard, I could pound nails with it, and I know just one touch from you is going to send me off like a rocket." Kurt pulled my underwear down, and I stepped out of them. I wrapped my arms around his neck, and he pulled me up into his arms again. He set me down on the bench, but I didn't move my legs from his waist.

"I pray to God you locked that door, Kurt, because I don't think meeting anyone with us naked would be the best start to our new shop."

Kurt laughed. "It's locked, Lee. No one gets to see you naked but me." He brushed my hair from my neck and his mouth assaulted me, nipping and nibbling.

I delved my fingers into his hair and tossed my head back. "You know just the right thing to do with your mouth, Mr. Jensen." I moaned as he sucked on my earlobe. His warm breath washed over my neck and my hand snaked in between us.

My fingertips grazed the tip of his cock and Kurt growled low. I stroked his long, hard shaft as Kurt's kisses traveled down my neck. "Kurt, please." My body was going crazy with need for Kurt, and all he was doing was driving me more insane.

"Are you ready for me, Lee?" He growled against my breast. His hand snaked between us, his fingers grazing my wet folds and I shuddered under his touch. "Fucking soaked for me." His finger parted my lips and grazed my clit. My hips rocked into his touch, begging for more. Kurt rested his forehead against mine and closed his eyes. "I've been waiting forever for this, Lee."

"The wait is over," I whispered against his lips. I threaded my fingers through his hair and kissed his lips as his fingers brought me to the edge, but never let me tip over into ecstasy.

"Keep those arms wrapped around me, gorgeous." Kurt grabbed his dick, stroking it from tip to root. "I'm taking what's mine."

I scooted forward on the bench, my ass hanging over the edge and wrapped my arms around Kurt's neck. "I'm ready," I whispered.

The tip of Kurt's dick nudged my clit, and a tremor rocked my body. "I'm gonna make you go off like a firecracker, Lee."

His hard dick slowly sunk into me, stretching and pulling me in the most delicious way. "Kurt," I moaned as I dug my fingernails into his shoulders and arched my back into him.

"I know, Lee." He buried his face in my neck, sucking and kissing all over my skin. "I don't want to move. I just want to stay here for the rest of my life."

I flexed the walls of my pussy around his dick, encouraging him to move. "If you don't move, Kurt, I'm going to scream."

Kurt tugged on my earlobe with his teeth and his hands traveled to my ass. "Patience, Mrs. Jensen."

I moaned and closed my eyes as he fingers dug into my ass and lifted me up. I sunk down even further on Kurt and I was seconds away from cumming all over him. "Just do that one more time, and I'll be good," Kurt grunted and strode halfway across the shop. With each step he took, his pelvis rubbed against my clit, making me clench my teeth and pray he was going to make me come soon. "Where the hell are we going?"

"Right here," Kurt growled as he pressed me against a bare wall. "I'm gonna fuck the hell out of you." He pulled out, leaving just the tip inside. "Hold the fuck on."

He slammed his dick into me, and stars exploded behind my eyes and he immediately pulled out and did the same thing, over and over.

I moaned Kurt's name, looking for my release but he never let me reach it. "Kurt, please," I begged, tossing my head back.

He pressed me firmly against the wall, while his hand snaked up my body and grabbed my hair. "You need me, Lee? How bad do you need me?"

"Yes…yes." I gasped out.

"Tell me," he growled. With each word he spoke, his body slammed into me, giving more but not enough.

"I need more. I need…" My words died in my throat as he tugged on my hair.

"More what?"

"You. I need more of you," I gasped.

Kurt slammed his lips down on mine, sucked my bottom lip into his mouth, and pounded into me. The hand holding my hair slinked down my body and found my clit.

My back dug into the hard brick wall behind with each thrust of Kurt's hips and the bite of pain from the wall mixed with the pleasure that Kurt was giving me.

"Fucking hell," Kurt growled into my mouth.

I clenched the walls of my pussy around him and felt the telltale pulse of his dick. Kurt was close and so was I. "I need you," I gasped.

Kurt's hand left my clit and grabbed my ass. "This is mine. Every day, mine," he swore. He plummeted into me one more time, finally reaching what I had been missing.

I slammed my eyes shut as my orgasm rode over me. I moaned Kurt's name as his hands traveled over me and he grunted low. He thrust fast and erratically as I wound my arms around Kurt's neck and held on.

"Mine. Mine!" he screamed. He thrust one last time, his cum filling me and I collapsed in his arms.

His breathing was heavy, and body heaved against mine. I ran my hands over his back and closed my eyes.

Finally, I was completely Kurt Jensen's, and I couldn't have been happier.

I was officially Leelee Jensen.

****

CHAPTER 26

Kurt

"Did you really tell Luke that I was quitting?" Leelee called from the bathroom in the office.

I grabbed a soda from the mini-fridge behind the front counter and popped the top. "I didn't tell him exactly you were quitting, but I told him that I was going to offer you the shop."

Leelee walked out of the bathroom and tied her hair up in a messy ponytail on the top of her head. "That would explain why he was acting all weird today. He was rushing me along, trying to get as many cars possible done."

"Yeah, he's going to be short-handed until he can find someone to replace you."

"Hell, he never found someone to replace you." She laughed. "I think short-handed is an understatement."

"He'll figure it out. Nos said he has a couple of friends that are good with cars and are looking for jobs."

"Yeah, but do you think they can work with Luke?"

Probably not, but that wasn't my problem. I shrugged and turned off the lights in the shop. "You want pizza for dinner?"

"Is that really all you have to say?"

I ran my hand through my hair and leaned against the counter. "Luke has always landed on his feet, Lee, and if it comes down to it, we can always help him out."

"You wouldn't mind if I worked over there until he finds someone to take my place?"

Did I want her to work at Skid Row any longer? Hell no. Was I going to screw Luke over completely? No. "He's got two weeks to find someone. I don't plan on opening for at least another week because we need to find at least one or two more guys, too."

"Well, I can honestly say I'm surprised, Kurt," she said with a laugh. "I thought for sure you would have said screw Luke."

I shrugged, rounded the counter, and grabbed Leelee. "He can have you for a little bit longer, but that's only because I know I've got you for the rest of my life."

"Well, Mr. Jensen, I do believe that is the most romantic thing you've ever said."

I pressed a quick kiss to her lips and tugged her out the door as I flipped off all the lights. I pulled my keys out of my pocket, handed them to Leelee, and motioned to the door. "You lock up; I'm driving home." I reached into her pocket, grabbed the keys to the GTO, and made my way over to the car.

"Hey," she protested, "you can't drive." She quickly locked the door and shoved the keys into her pocket. She sprinted over to the driver side, but I managed to close the door and hit the locks before she got her hand on the door handle. "Kurt, open the door," she insisted.

I shook my head and cranked up the car. "I can't hear you," I mouthed as I revved the engine.

She flipped me off, walked around the car and slid into the passenger side. "You just got your casts off a couple of hours ago. Do you really think driving is something you should be doing?"

"I just fucked you against the wall, Lee. I'm pretty sure I can drive a car five miles."

Leelee grabbed the seat belt as I shifted into first and pulled off the curb. She clicked the belt into place and swore under her breath.

My leg was sore, but it wasn't going to keep me from driving anymore. "You never said if you wanted pizza for dinner."

Leelee rolled her eyes and pulled her phone out of her bag. "I'll see what Jay wants for dinner. I know he mentioned that he had a school project coming up that he was going to have to spend some time at the library." Leelee pulled up Jay's number and put the phone to her ear.

"If he's eating, we need at least two pizzas." Leelee waved her hand at me to shut up, and I grabbed it and placed a kiss on the back of her hand. "Two, Lee. I'm not kidding."

She rolled her eyes, but I knew she heard me. "He didn't answer," she mumbled. She shoved her phone in her pocket and leaned her head against the seat. "He might be at the library."

"If he is, I'm sure he'll be there until they close. We'll just order two pizzas, and he can eat when he gets home." Leelee nodded, but I knew that she was still worried Jay hadn't answered.

We pulled up in front of the apartment and saw Jay standing outside with four other people and one of those people was Frankie. "I didn't know that Frank and Jay hung out," I mumbled to Leelee as I pulled the emergency brake.

"I didn't either," she mumbled. We both got out of the car, and it looked like Frankie was as surprised as we were.

"Kurt?" she asked.

"What's up, Frankie?"

Leelee grabbed my hand and threaded her fingers through mine. "Take it easy," she whispered.

"Oh, um, we were all hanging out, and Jay said we needed to come over and see his sister's husband's car. I guess it didn't click that it was you and Leelee." She fidgeted with the zipper on her sweatshirt, and I couldn't tell if she was lying or not.

"Since when did you get into cars?" I asked.

"Kurt," Leelee interrupted, "why don't we go inside and order pizza while Jay talks to his friends?" Leelee tugged on my arm and pulled me toward the house.

"Pizza?" Jay asked, oblivious to the fact that I was wanting to know what the hell Frankie was doing hanging out with him.

"Yeah," Leelee called. "I'll make sure to order extra." She opened the door, pulling me through, and closed the door. "What in the hell was that, Kurt? I swear you were ready to wring everyone's necks out there."

"Since when did Frankie start hanging out with Jay?"

Leelee shrugged and unlaced her boots. "I don't know. Maybe she likes him; I'm not sure." She kicked off her boots and moved into the kitchen.

I pulled back the curtains in the living room and saw Frankie was still outside talking to Jay and his friends. "Lee, Frankie reads and hangs out at the library, not with a bunch of boys at six o'clock at night."

"You say that like six is late, Kurt. I think you just need to calm down. They're probably just friends."

"I don't like it, Lee. Frankie is young, and I know exactly what each of those guys is thinking."

Leelee laughed and pulled two beers out of the fridge. "Frankie has a boyfriend, Kurt, and it is none of those boys that out there. Calm down and have a beer." She handed me the cold bottle, and I popped the top.

"She has a boyfriend?" Why in the hell didn't I know that?

"Yeah. She's been seeing him for a couple of weeks."

"Does Luke know this?" I knew if Luke knew, he was going crazy.

"Yeah. Violet is pulling her hair out trying to get him to lay off Frankie. Kind of like how I was with you. She's growing up,

Kurt. Her hanging out with a couple of guys is normal. Plus, one of those guys is Jay. You know he would never do anything to hurt her."

Leelee was right, but I was still fucking worried.

"Here," she said, handing me the phone. "You order pizza and take your mind off Frankie. She's got a good head on her shoulders, Kurt."

I grabbed the phone out of her hand and watched her walk down the hallway to her room. Well, it was actually our room now. She had moved all my stuff into two of her drawers last week, and I was no longer living out of a suitcase and laundry baskets. "How come I have to order pizza?" I hollered after her.

"Because I'm not the one freaking out and I need a shower."

"Hold that thought for two minutes, and I'll shower with you." I punched in the number to the pizza place.

"Nice try, Kurt," she called, "but it's not happening." I heard the bathroom door shut and the lock fall into place.

"Son of a bitch," I cursed. The busy tone sounded in my ear, and I hung the phone up.

"What's wrong?" Jay asked as he glided in the front door.

"Nothing that you going to college won't fix," I mumbled under my breath. I turned around and saw Jay standing just inside the door. "How do you know Frankie?"

"Uh, we have shop class together."

Frankie was in shop class? That was a fucking surprise. "Why the hell is Frankie in shop?"

"Probably for class credit. I don't know. I didn't ask her."

"You know her boyfriend?"

"Curtis? Yeah, he's a fucking prick."

"What? Is he fucking mean to her?"

"Not really mean, just too into himself to care about Frankie."

"What the hell is Frankie doing with a guy like that?"

Jay ran his hand through his hair and shrugged. "I don't know man. Probably the same reason most people are with a dick, they like the way they look."

"That doesn't sound like something Frankie would do." Frankie was the least into what someone looked like. Hell, ninety percent of the time, she had her nose so far in a book, she didn't even see what was going on around her.

"I don't know, dude. All I know is I'm hungry. You order pizza?"

I looked at the phone in my hand and shook my head. "Nah, they were busy." I looked Jay over. "You keep an eye on Frankie for me?"

"From what I see, Kurt, you really don't have anything to worry about. No one messes with her for the simple fact that her last name is Jensen and whoever fucks with her would have to deal with you, Luke, and Mitch."

Well, that relieved me a little bit. "Just keep an eye on her?"

Jay nodded and headed to his room. "Order pizza," he called.

I dialed the number to the pizza place again and put the phone to my ear. The call went through, and I ordered three large pizzas and an order of breadsticks. Leelee had said two pizzas, but I had worked up an appetite this afternoon, and I knew Jay was always hungry.

I chugged my beer, tossed the empty bottle in the garbage and saw I had half an hour before the pizza would be delivered.

I grabbed a screwdriver out of the drawer and headed down the hallway.

I had half an hour to break into the bathroom and have a little fun with Lee.

****

CHAPTER 27

Kurt

"Was that the last car for today?"

Nos spun around in his chair with a big ass smile on his face. "Sure as hell was, and tomorrow is jam-packed, too."

"Nice." We had only been open for a week, and things seemed to be going well. Although they would have been better if Leelee would have been there too, but thankfully, today was her last day at Skid Row.

"I'm gonna head out. Del has been bitching about me coming home after eight every night."

I clapped Nos on the back and nodded at the clock. "No problem, man. I know Lee will be here after work and she'll help with anything I need. This is the first time we've been done before five."

Nos bumped fists with me. "Thanks, brah." Nos walked out the door, and I grabbed a soda out of the mini fridge.

It was close to five, and I was ready to lock the door and call it a day. Not having Leelee here was killing me and I thanked God my days of taking care of the back were over.

The front door opened, knocking the little bell Leelee had hung and I couldn't hide the growl that came out of my mouth when AZ limped in through the door.

AZ was the last person I expected to see. He pushed his sunglasses on the top of his head and looked around. "Not bad, brah."

I leaned against the back wall and crossed my arms across my chest. I didn't give a fuck what he thought. "You need something?"

The front door opened again, and fucking Ginny poked her head in. Could this get any fucking weirder? "I'm going to com—" she started, but AZ cut her off.

"No. I told you to stay in the car. This had nothing to fucking do with you," AZ growled.

Ginny's face transformed into a scowl, but she slammed the door shut and stalked back to her car.

"Trouble in paradise?"

"There ain't fucking paradise with that chick around. She's fucking thirsty, and I'm done turning on the damn faucet to keep her around." AZ limped over to the stool in front of the counter and dropped into it. "I'm just fucking done all around."

AZ sounded and looked defeated. As much as I wanted to revel in that, I had to feel sorry for the guy. I knew how bad it was to want to win and succeed in everything and could only imagine how shitty it would be to fail at every turn. I watched him and waited. I felt bad for the guy, but I wasn't going to forget all the shit he pulled with my family.

"I'm leaving. Heading back to Arizona. I've exhausted every option I have here."

I nodded and thought it was about damn time that this fucker gave up. "I wish I could say I'm sorry to see ya go, but fuck that. See ya, brah." I laughed.

A smile spread across his face, and he shook his head. "We're more alike than I thought. I'd have said the same thing."

"So, that it, just came here to wave your flag of defeat?"

"That, and I wanted to say thank you. Without you and your brothers, I wouldn't be standing here right now. Even the people who I thought had my back fucking ran when I flipped that car."

234

I shrugged. "Just did what was right. I had been there months ago, and wouldn't be standing here if it hadn't of been for a couple of guys pulling me out."

"I just wanted to come and thank you before I left town tonight. I know I gave your family hell this past couple of months and did some shady shit I'm not really proud of."

It was nice to know AZ regretted the shit he did, but it didn't take any of it away. My fucking aunt had been in rehab, Luke's car had been wrecked, and he had fucked with both Scarlett and Leelee. Not to mention he kept bringing that scab, Ginny, around. "I'd love to say that I hate to see you go, brah, but I think it's past time."

"Yeah, almost dying can put some shit in perspective." AZ looked around and nodded. "Looks like you got yourself set up pretty good here."

"Yeah, Lee and I are hoping to kill it with this place."

"I figured that's who the Lee was on the sign. You're a crazy bastard for starting this with your girlfriend."

"Naw, I didn't start this with my girlfriend."

AZ laughed and shook his head. "So, you named your new shop after your girlfriend. Even riskier."

"You're wrong again. This isn't just my shop, and she's my wife."

"No shit." AZ raised his eyebrows. "That new? All I heard on the streets was you two were together."

I shrugged. "Not new, and I could care less what is being said."

AZ stood and held up his hands. "I didn't come here to cause any more problems, brah. I just wanted to thank you and let you know I'm done trying to beat you and your brothers. Y'all were some of the stiffest competition I've ever gone up against. Hell, I couldn't beat any of you."

I chuckled under my breath and couldn't help how good it felt to hear those words. "You're good, brah, but not good enough."

AZ shook his head and moved to the door. "As much as I'd love to tell you you're wrong, I can't argue with facts." AZ pushed open the door and looked back over his shoulder. "I did give you a run for the money, though."

"Sure, did that." I laughed.

AZ walked out the door and swore under his breath. "Son of a bitch. She fucking left me here." The door closed behind him as he grabbed his phone out of his pocket.

"Shit." The guy was banged and barely able to walk, and that raging bitch had just left him here. I grabbed my keys off the counter and turned off the lights of the shop.

AZ had been a complete dick, but I couldn't let him walk. I pulled my phone out of my pocket and sent a text to Lee letting her know I closed the shop and would be home in a little bit.

I had one more thing to take care of.

****

Leelee

I shoved my phone in my pocket and dropped my steel toes on the floor. "Well hell," I mumbled. I had just gotten off work from Skid Row and had planned on heading over to the Speed Shop when I had gotten Kurt's text that he had closed for the day.

Jay had been running out the door when I had gotten home, saying he was staying the night at one of his friends and then he was gone. With Kurt coming home early now, I had to figure out what the hell to make for dinner.

For the past two weeks, we had been eating takeout and Hot Pockets. The idea of an actual home cooked meal made my stomach growl, and I hoped we had something in the freezer I could make.

After I rummaged through the freezer and found a pound of hamburger meat, I decided to make a big pot of spaghetti and garlic bread.

I popped the frozen meat into the microwave to thaw it out and heard a knock on the front door.

"Jay, what in the hell did you forget now?" I asked, as I opened the door.

"Is that your cute brother?" My jaw dropped when I saw Ginny standing on my front step. What in the hell was this bitch doing here? She had a bottle of wine in one hand and had her other hand raised to knock on the door again.

"My brother is none of your business."

"I'm okay with that; I was here for Kurt anyway." She tried to push her way into the door, but I put a hand on her shoulder and pushed her back.

"You might want to take his name out of your mouth, *puta*. I know for a fact that Kurt does not want you here."

"That's not what he said before."

Before? What in the hell was she talking about? "Ginny, get the hell out of here."

Ginny rolled her eyes and shifted her weight. "I don't have to do nothing, bitch, and Kurt sure hasn't minded his name or anything in my mouth before."

I clenched my fists at her words and was ready to rip her hair out. "Well, if you were actually talking to him, you would know he's not here, Ginny." I crossed my arms over my chest. I knew this bitch was lying, but I didn't know why she had sunk to this new low.

"I had stopped by the shop earlier and saw he was busy so I figured I could talk to him here."

"Well, you were wrong. I think it's best you just turn around and forget about Kurt."

Ginny tried stepping into the house again and got in my face. "I don't know where you bitches get off thinking that these Jensen boys are actually going to stay with your asses. They need women, not little girls, and especially not a bitch that thinks she can play with the boys."

I put my hand in her face and smirked. "I'm pretty sure this ring on my finger means this bitch who plays with the boys has a Jensen boy that isn't going anywhere."

"That's fucking bullshit," she spit out.

"Give it the fuck up, Ginny. Move on and try to find a different guy who'll be blind to your gold digger ways. Violet, Scarlett, and I aren't going to put up with your skank ass thinking you can take any of our guys. Move. The. Fuck. On." I pushed back on her shoulder, grabbed the bottle of wine out of her hand, and slammed the door shut in her face.

I heard her scream and looked out the peephole to see her stomping down the sidewalk. "Dumb bitch," I mumbled. I looked at the bottle of wine she brought over and was pleased to see it was actually a decent one. "Thank you, Ginny," I gloated as I set the bottle on the table.

I had dinner to cook and a night all alone with Kurt to look forward to.

Ginny was done fucking with me. She wasn't worth my time, and I was moving onto the life I had been wanting.

Nothing was going to take it away from me.

****

238

CHAPTER 28

Kurt

"Lee, I'm home." I walked into the house, smelled dinner cooking and slipped off my boots. "Where are you?" I asked, as I headed into the kitchen and saw the table was set, pots were simmering on the stove, but Leelee was nowhere to be seen.

"Lee?" I called as I strode down the hallway.

"I'm in the bedroom. Can you stir the sauce on the stove and pull the bread out of the oven?"

"Is it burned?" I asked, as I headed back down the hall.

The bedroom door opened, and I heard Leelee pad down the hallway behind me. "I put it in three minutes ago. It better not be burned."

I pulled open the oven door and saw the butter wasn't even melted on the bread. "Well, it's definitely not burned." I laughed as I shut the door and turned on the oven.

"Aw hell. I really can't get garlic bread right, can I?"

I shrugged and leaned against the counter. "You've got the rest of our lives to figure it out."

Leelee dumped the bubbling pot of noodles in the colander she had in the sink and pulled the sauce off the stove. "Let's hope it doesn't take me that long." She grabbed two glasses out of the cabinet and set them on the counter. "Would you like some wine? It was dropped off by someone who was looking for you." Leelee popped open the bottle of wine she had sitting on the kitchen table and filled each glass.

"Really? Who?"

Leelee handed me a glass and cocked her head to the side. "Ginny."

I took a sip and almost spit it all over Leelee. "Ginny was here? That's where she fucking went."

"What? She actually came to the shop?"

"Yeah. She drove AZ to the shop and then left him there when he told her to go wait in the car."

"Wait, wait, wait." Leelee set her glass down and propped her hands on her hips. "Not only was Ginny at the shop but so was AZ? What in the hell were they doing there?"

"Well, AZ came to apologize for all of the shit he had done and thanked me for getting him out of the car when he wrecked."

"Well, that is damn surprising. Does that mean he's going to be less of a douche on race nights?"

"Yeah, since he won't be there. He's going back to Arizona."

Leelee shook her head and peeked into the oven. "Was I the only one who thought it was ridiculous that his nickname was a fucking state?"

I laughed and drained my glass. "I'm sure you weren't the only one, Lee." I sat down at the table and crossed my legs. "So, what in the hell did Ginny want?"

"I think she was trying to make me think that you and her had a thing going on, except her story was so weak, there was no way I was going to believe it. Plus, she got pissed when I shoved my ring in her face."

I threw my head back, laughing. "God damn, I love you, Lee." The instant the words came out of my mouth, Leelee's jaw dropped.

"You wanna take that back?" she whispered.

I shook my head no and crossed my arms over my chest. "Hell no. This isn't the way I imagined telling you but the hell with it. I love you, Lee. I can't fucking help it."

"As crazy as it sounds, I think this fits in perfectly with the way we do things. I love you, too." She dropped her hands to her sides and shrugged. "I fell in love with you when you asked me to marry you."

A smile spread across my lips as she walked across the kitchen and stood in front of me. I uncrossed my leg, and she eased into my lap, straddling my waist. I brushed her hair out of her face and brushed it over her shoulder. "You were made for me, Lee," I whispered in her ear.

"We do seem to fit well together." She grounded her hips into me and wrapped her arms around my neck. "Did I mention that Jay is spending the night at a friend's house tonight?"

I wrapped my arms tight around her and shot up from the chair. "We can eat later."

"No, wait," she screeched, laughing, as I stalked down the hallway. "The bread is in the oven."

"Son of a bitch," I cussed as I headed back into the kitchen, turned off the oven, and opened the oven door. "I like burned bread anyway," I said, smirking as the smell of burning bread wafted out.

"I think I'm hopeless," she sighed.

I headed back down the hallway to our bedroom and kicked open the door. "When it comes to bread, yeah, you are, Lee. But I'm willing to overlook it if you promise to be in my bed every night."

"I'm pretty sure the two have nothing to do with each other, but I think I can agree. I solemnly swear from this day forward to only make you burned bread and snore on your chest every night."

I fell back on the bed with Leelee still wrapped around me. "I don't think I asked for the always burned bread or the snoring, but I'll take it." I grabbed the hem of Lee's shirt and pulled it over her head. "I don't think I'll ever get used to this, Lee. I feel like the luckiest bastard in the world whenever you're in my arms."

Leelee braced her arms on the bed next to my head and brushed her lips against mine. "I never thought I would get you in my bed, Mr. Jensen, but I've come to realize that dreams do come true. Especially those of the naked variety that involve you."

I skimmed my hands down her sides and grabbed her ass. "You're gonna be the death of me, Lee."

"Oh, but Mr. Jensen, it's going to be the sweetest death," she purred.

I had it all now. A shop that was mine, a life that I made the decisions in, Leelee Jensen was in my bed, and she was damn sure in my heart.

Life was fucking good, and it was only going to get better.

****

EPILOGUE

Leelee

"Kurt, get in the damn car."

He slid in the passenger seat and shook his head. "I don't know why you think you need to torture me by driving all of the time."

"Because I love driving your car, and since Jay drives my car all the time, I need to drive something."

"I'll be glad as hell when we're done building your own damn car."

I backed out of the driveway and headed to Skid Row. "If the damn parts weren't on back-order, it would be done by now."

"Nos has been on their ass all week wanting to know where they are."

"I have to admit, he's damn good at his job. Who would have thought the street-smart thug would be the perfect fit for the Speed Shop?"

Kurt shook his head and laughed. "I had it all planned out, Lee."

"Well, you have any plans for this?" I asked, as I pulled up to Skid Row and saw all the cars in the parking lot.

Violet and Scarlett had gotten their way, and Kurt and I were going to renew our vows. It had been a crazy and hectic six months since we had opened the Speed Shop and all the while, I had been dealing with Vi and Scar who became my wedding planners.

Kurt looked up at the shop that was once his home and shook his head. "Marrying you again? Hell yeah, I'm ready. Dealing with

243

all of my family while all I want to do is find my old bedroom and have my way with you? No."

"Well, Mr. Jensen, try to keep it in your pants for the next three hours during the rehearsal dinner, and I promise your own personal dessert after."

Kurt leaned over the center console, grabbed me behind the neck and pulled me close. "And that right there is exactly why I'll remarry you every day, Mrs. Jensen. Hot as sin, knows the difference between a V8 and V6, and puts up with my ass."

"Those are some superb qualities, aren't they?" I laughed.

"Plus, we're both mechanics, and we both know that mechanics are really good with their hands."

"Oh, are they?"

Kurt nodded, and I wrapped my arms around his neck. "I guess we'll just have to test that later."

"We definitely will, Mr. Jensen."

My fingers delved into Kurt's hair, and he kissed the living hell out of me. With every kiss, touch, and caress, Kurt was taking more and more of my heart. Each day, he gave me more than I ever thought I would have and I couldn't wait to wake up each morning to see how life could get any better.

"I love you, Kurt Jensen," I whispered against his lips.

"I love you, too, Leelee Jensen."

Life was fucking good.

****

Violet

"Get away from the window, Luke, and help me zip up the back of my dress."

Luke was standing in the window, watching Frankie and Jay down in the parking lot. I swear, if you listened closely, you could hear the large vein in his neck throbbing. "I swear those two are dating," he growled.

I held together the back of my dress and walked over to Luke. I grabbed his hand and turned my back to him. "Zip it." Luke's rough hands tugged on the zipper, pulling it up, and then he turned right back to staring out the window. "Frankie swore up and down she's not dating Jay. After she had broken it off with Curtis, she said she's not interested in dating."

"Yeah, now she's into working on cars, just like Jay is. That shit is not a coincidence, Vi."

I nudged my way in front of Luke and wrapped my arms around his neck. "You should be jumping for joy that Frankie is taking an interest in the shop."

"I am, but I want to know what this sudden interest is. But if she keeps going the way she is, she'll be as good as Leelee one day." Luke scowled and shook his head.

"Still pissed that she left Skid Row?" I laughed. At least once a week, Luke ranted how he just didn't understand why Leelee and Kurt had to open their own shop when he had a perfectly good one of his own that they could have worked at.

"Nah, just wish things would have worked out differently back then."

"It's not like you don't see them anymore, Luke. Every Friday we see them at the race, and I know you go over to his shop when you tell me you're going on a parts run."

Luke shrugged and glanced out the window one last time. "They're dating, Vi."

I shrugged. "And what if they are? Just let her be, Luke. Frankie is a smart girl who isn't going to let some guy take advantage of her."

"Kind of like how I took advantage of you?" Luke reached down and cradled my growing belly.

"Exactly like that." I smiled as I watched his eyes soften. "Four more months to go," I sighed when the little guy kicked. "Did you feel that?"

"Yeah." Luke laughed. "He's playing soccer with your bladder probably." The baby kicked again, and Luke's hand rubbed my belly.

"Bladder soccer is a pretty good name for what he's doing in there."

"Uncle Luke! Stop touching Auntie Vi's tummy!" Levi ran to Luke, and I jumped out of the way just as Levi went airborne and Luke caught him.

"Levi, I told you to wait in your room," Scarlett scolded from the hallway.

"I wanted to see Uncle Luke. He was touching Auntie Vi again. Eww." Levi pursed his lips and looked like he was going to be sick. "Mitch touches mama all the time, but that's cool because he buys me stuff."

Luke laughed and hung Levi upside down by his feet. "I'm pretty sure I took you mini golfing and brought you pizza last week."

"Oh, yeah. I guess you did." Levi giggled as Luke tickled his tummy. "I remember Pokémon better," Levi declared.

"Thanks for clearing that up, big man. We'll have to convince Auntie Vi to take us to the store later and maybe we can stock up." Luke set Levi down on his feet, and he took off out of the room and down the hallway.

"I thought he was into Transformers?" Luke asked Scarlett.

"He's into anything he can collect. He's got all the Transformer toys and movies, so he had to move onto something else. Pokémon is going to be the death of me, though," Scarlett sighed. "Are you guys ready for dinner? The table in the shop looked really nice when I saw it earlier."

"Yeah, I just had to squeeze into my dress and find some shoes that still fit my feet. We're be good to go."

Scarlett laughed. "Just put on tennis shoes, no one will notice."

"Scarlett, get your sexy ass in the kitchen," Mitch called.

Scarlett sighed. "I better go before Levi starts repeating what Mitch says. I swear, Levi told me to 'Cool my tits,' the other day, although he said tator tots instead of tits, thankfully." Scarlett shook her head and disappeared down the hallway.

"How long is this party?" Luke asked as he wrapped his arms around me from behind and rubbed my tummy.

"Three, four hours. I'm not sure. You should be happy you have your whole family under one roof right now," I reminded him.

Not only were Mitch and Kurt here, so were his Aunt who was finally out of rehab and getting her life straight, and all of Luke's friends from the track. "I still don't know why we had to have the rehearsal dinner here. Kurt's shop is plenty big to have a party in."

I turned in Luke's arms and rested my head on his chest. "You love your family, Luke. Stop acting like a grumpy bear who doesn't want to see anyone."

"I don't mind seeing them," he gruffed. "I just wish I didn't have to entertain them when I'd rather be up here with you, naked."

Luke wrapped his arms tightly around me, and I sighed. "It won't be long until Frankie goes off to college and Mitch and Scarlett move out, Luke."

Luke huffed and shook his head. "You heard where Frankie is thinking of going to school now? Fucking Wisconsin. She doesn't even know anyone up there."

"She wants to go to a good school. She was telling me about a program they have for car stuff."

"Car stuff?" Luke laughed.

"Oh, shut up. I have baby brain. I can't remember what she called it, but it sounded like a good place for her to learn everything she wants to know."

Luke sighed and pressed a kiss to the top of my head. "I know Frankie is going to go off to school, and Mitch is going to get his own place, but at least I know I'll always have you and our baby to come home to every night."

I leaned my head back and looked into Luke's eyes that were beaming down at me. "Can I say it?" I whispered.

Luke shook his head and knew exactly what I wanted to say. I had started reading children's books at night to my tummy and each night I said the same thing. "Oh Jesus, woman. You and those damn books you read. Go ahead and say it."

"And they all lived happily ever after." I sighed.

"Cheesy as hell, woman," Luke grumbled.

It may have been cheesy, but it was the damn truth.

The Jensen boys had proven to be a rowdy bunch, but when they finally figured out what they wanted, there was no stopping them.

Happily ever after was the only option they settled for.

THE END

COMING EARLY 2018

NITRO CREW SERIES

HOLESHOT
Frankie & Brooks

REDLIGHT
Jay & Delaney

BURNDOWN
Remy & Harlyn

COMING SOON

UNRAVELING FAYTH, BOOK 8 IN THE DEVIL'S KNIGHTS SERIES.
JANUARY 29TH, 2017

COMING IN 2017

DROPKICK MY HEART
(POWERHOUSE MARTIAL ARTS SERIES) BOOK 1

TALK DERBY TO ME
(BRAWL DOLLS SERIES) BOOK 1

FALL IN LOVE WITH THE DEVIL'S KNIGHTS FROM THE BEGINNING.

DIVE INTO THE FIRST CHAPTER OF LOVING LO!

LOVING LO
DEVIL'S KNIGHTS SERIES
BOOK 1

Chapter 1
Meg

How did just stopping quickly to get dog food and shampoo turn into an overflowing basket and a surplus pack of paper towels?

"Put the paper towels down and back away slowly," I mumbled to myself as I walked past a display of air fresheners and wondered if I needed any.

"Oh dear. Oh, my. I… Ah… Oh, my."

I tore my thoughts away from air fresheners and looked down the aisle to an elderly woman who was leaning against the shelf, fanning herself. "Are you ok, ma'am?"

"Oh dear. I just… I just got a little… dizzy." I looked at the woman and saw her hands shaking as she brushed her white hair out of her face. The woman had on denim capris and a white button down short sleeve shirt and surprisingly three-inch wedge heels.

"Ok, well, why don't we try to find you a place to sit down until you get your bearings?" I shifted the basket and paper towels under one arm to help her to the bench that I had seen by the shoe rack two aisles over. "Are you here with anyone?" I asked, as I guided her down the aisle.

"Oh no. I'm here by myself. I just needed a few things."

"I only needed two things, and now my basket is overflowing, and I still haven't gotten the things I came in for."

The woman plopped down on the bench chuckling, shaking her head. "Tell me about it. Happens to me every time too."

"Is there something I can do for you? Has this happened to you before?" She really was looking rather pale.

"Unfortunately, yes. I ran out of the house today without eating breakfast. I'm diabetic. I should know by now that I can't do that." My mom was also diabetic, so I knew exactly what the woman was talking about. Luckily, I also knew what to do to help.

"Just sit right here, and I'll be right back. Is there someone you want to call to give you a ride home? Driving right now probably isn't the best idea." I set the basket and towels on the floor, keeping my wallet in my hand.

"I suppose I should call my son. He should be able to give me a ride," the woman said as she dug her phone out of her purse.

I left the woman to her phone call and headed to the candy aisle that I had been trying to ignore. I grabbed a bag of licorice, chips, and a diet soda and went to the checkout. The dollar store didn't offer a healthy selection, but this would do in a pinch. The woman just needed to get her blood sugars back up.

I grabbed my things after paying and headed back to the bench. I ripped open the bag and handed it to the woman. "Oh dear, you didn't have to buy that. I could have given you money."

"Don't worry about it. I hope if this happened to my mom there would be someone to help her if I wasn't around."

"Well, that's awfully sweet of you. My names Ethel Birch by the way."

"It's nice to meet you, Ethel. I'm Meg Grain. I also got you some chips and soda." I popped opened the soda and handed it to Ethel.

"Oh, thank you, honey. My son is on the way here, should be only five minutes. You can get going if you want to, you don't need to sit with an old woman," Ethel said as she ate a piece of candy and took a slug of soda.

"No problem. The only plans I had today was to take a nap before work tonight. Delaying my plans by ten minutes won't be a problem."

"Well, in that case, you can help me eat this licorice. It's my favorite, but I shouldn't eat this all by myself. Where do you work at?" Ethel asked as she offered the bag to me.

"The factory right outside of town. I work in the warehouse, second shift." I grabbed a piece and sat down on the floor. If I was going to wait for Ethel's son to show up, might as well be comfortable while I waited for him.

"Really? Never would have thought that. Figured you would have said a nurse or something like that. Seems like you would have to be tough to work in a warehouse, sounds like a man's job."

I laughed. "Honestly, Ethel that is not the first time I have heard that, and it probably won't be the last. You need a certain attitude to deal with those truckers walking through the door. I have an awesome co-worker, so he helps out when truckers have a problem with a woman loading their truck."

"Sounds like you give them hell. My Tim was a trucker before he passed. I know exactly what you are talking about." Ethel took another drink of her soda and set it on the bench next to her.

"Feeling better?"

"Surprisingly, yes. It's a wonder what a little candy can do. How much do I owe you?" Ethel asked as she reached for her purse by her feet.

"Don't worry about it. I'm just glad that I was here to help."

"Mom! Where are you?" Someone yelled from the front of the store.

"Oh good, Lo's here. You'll have to meet him." Ethel cupped her hands around her mouth and yelled to him she was in the back.

I started getting up off the floor and remembered I wasn't exactly as flexible as I use to be while struggling to get up.

"Ma, you ok?" I was halfway to standing with my butt in the air when his voice made me pause.

It sounded like the man was gurgling broken glass when he spoke. Raspy and *so* sexy. Those three words he spoke sent shocks to my core. Lord knows the last time I felt anything in my core.

"Yes, I'm fine. I forgot to eat breakfast this morning and started to get dizzy when Meg here was nice enough to help me out until you could get here." Ethel turned to me. "Lo, this is Meg, Meg this is Lo."

Oh lord.

I couldn't talk. The man standing in front of me was… oh, lord. I couldn't even think of a word to describe him.

I looked him up and down, and I'm sure my mouth was hanging wide open. I took in his scuffed up motorcycle boots and faded, stained ripped jeans that hugged his thighs and made me want to ask the man to spin so I could see what those jeans were doing for his ass. I moved my eyes up to his t-shirt that was tight around his shoulders and chest and showed he worked out.

I couldn't remember the last time I worked out. Did walking to the mailbox count as exercise? Of course, I only remembered to get the mail about twice a week, so that probably didn't count.

His arms were covered in tattoos. I could see them peeking out from the collar of his shirt and could only imagine what he looked like with his shirt off. Tattoos were my ultimate addiction on a man. Even one tattoo added at least 10 points to a man's hotness. This guy was off the fucking charts.

My eyes locked with his after my fantastic voyage up his body, and I stopped breathing.

"Hey, Meg. See something you like, darlin'?" Lo rumbled at me with a smirk on his face.

Busted. I sucked air back into my lungs and tried to remember how to breathe.

Lo's eyes were the color of fresh cut grass, bright green. His hair was jet black and cut close to his head with a pair of kick ass aviators sitting on top of his head. He was golden tan and gorgeous. The man was sex on a stick. Plain and simple.

"Uh, hey," I choked out.

Lo's lips curved up into a grin, and I looked down to see if my panties fell off. The man had a panty-dropping smile, and he wasn't even smiling that big. I would have to take cover or risk fainting if he smiled any bigger.

"Thanks for looking after my ma for me. I'm glad I was in town today and not out on a run," Lo said.

Ok. Get it together Meg. You are a 36-year-old woman, and this man has rendered you speechless like a sixteen-year-old girl. I needed to say something.

"Say something," I blurted out. Good Lord did I just say that. Lo quirked his eyebrow, and his smirk returned.

"Ugh, I mean no problem. I didn't really do that much. No problem." I looked at Ethel while Lo was smirking at me; Ethel had a full-blown smile on her face and was beaming at me.

"You were a life saver, Meg! I don't know what I would have done if you weren't here." Ethel looked at Lo and grinned even bigger. "You should have seen her, Lo. She knew just what to do to help me. I could have sworn she was a nurse the way she took charge. She's not, though, just has a good head on her shoulders and decided to help this old lady out."

"That's good, Ma. You got all your shit you need so we can get going? I got some stuff going on at the garage that I dropped to get over here fast."

I took that as my cue to leave and ripped my eyes off Lo and bent over to get my basket and paper towels.

"Yes son, that's my stuff right here. I just want to get Meg's number before she leaves."

"Why do you need my number?" I asked, as I juggled my basket and towels.

Ethel grabbed her purse off the ground and started digging through it again. "Well, you won't let me pay you back for the snacks you got for me so I figured I could pay you back by inviting you over for dinner sometime. So, what's your number, sweetheart?"

"I don't eat dinner," I blurted out. I was really going to have to have a talk with my brain and mouth when I got home. They needed to get their shit together and start working in unison so I wouldn't sound like such an idiot.

"You don't eat dinner? Please don't tell me you're on a diet." Lo said as he looked me up and down.

"No," I said. Lord knew I should be.

Lo and Ethel just stared at me.

"So, no, you don't eat dinner?" Lo asked again.

"Yes. I mean no, I'm not on a diet. Yes, I eat dinner. I just work at night, so I meant that I wouldn't be able to come to dinner." I looked at Lo and blushed about ten shades of red. "Why is this so hard?"

"What's hard, sweetheart? Can't remember your phone number? I can barely remember mine too. Don't worry about not being able to make it to dinner; I can have you over for lunch. You eat lunch right?" Ethel asked with a smirk on her face. Lo had a full-blown smile on his face, even his eyes were smiling at me. That smile ought to be illegal.

I could see where Lo got his looks from. With Lo and Ethel standing next to each other, I could totally see the resemblance. Especially when they were both smirking.

I had to get out of here. I'm normally the one with the one-liners and making everyone laugh, now I couldn't even put two words together.

"Lunch would be good." I rattled off my number, and Ethel jotted it down.

"Ok, sweetheart, I'll let you get your nap. I'll give you a call later, and we can figure out a day we can get together." Ethel shoved the pen and paper back in her bag and leaned into me for a hug.

I awkwardly hugged her back and patted her on the shoulder. "Sounds good. Have a good day, Ethel. Uh, it was nice meeting you, Lo," I mumbled, as my gaze wandered over Lo again.

"You too Meg. See you around," Lo replied.

I gave them both a jaunty wave and booked it to the checkout. Thankfully there wasn't a line, and I quickly made my escape to my car. I threw my things in the trunk and hopped in. I grabbed my phone out of my pocket and plugged it into the radio and turned on my chill playlist, as the soothing sounds of Fleetwood Mac filled the car.

Music was the one thing in my life that had gotten me through so much shit. Good or bad, there was always a song that I could play, and it would make everything better. Right now, I just needed to unscramble my brain and get my bearings. Fleetwood Mac singing "Landslide" was helping.

I pulled out of the parking lot and headed home. All I needed was to forget about today. If Ethel called for lunch, I would say yes because she did remind me so much of mom, but I wasn't going to let Lo enter my thoughts anymore. A woman like me did not register on his radar, he was better just forgotten.

When I was halfway home, I realized I forgot dog food and shampoo.

Shit.

=======

Lo

I helped mom finish her shopping and loaded all her crap into the truck. I looked around the parking lot for Meg, hoping she hadn't left yet so I could get another look at her. As soon as I saw her ass waving in the air as she struggled to stand up, I knew I had to be inside her.

It took all my willpower to not get a hard-on as her eyes ran over my body. Fucking chick was smoking' hot and didn't even know it.

"Thanks for coming to get me, Lo," Ma said as she interrupted my thoughts about Meg.

"No problem, Ma. I'll get one of the guys to bring your car to you later. Make sure it's locked." Ma dug her keys out of her huge ass purse and beeped the locks. We both got into the shop truck, and I started it up.

"Sure was nice of that Meg to help out. I don't know what I would have done without her."

"Yup, definitely nice of her." I shifted the truck into drive, keeping my foot on the brake, knowing exactly where mom was headed with this.

"You should ask her out." All I could do was shake my head and laugh.

"Straight to the point huh, Ma?"

"I'm old, I can say what I want. Meg is just the thing you need."

"I didn't know I needed anything." I pulled out of the parking lot and headed to Ma's house.

"You need someone in your life besides that club." My mom grabbed her phone out of her purse and started fiddling with it.

"We'll see, ma. Meg didn't seem too thrilled with me." She liked what she saw, but it was like she couldn't get away from me quick enough when she saw that Ma was going to be ok.

"Well, you are pretty intimidating, Lo. Thank goodness you didn't wear your cut."

My leather vest with my club rockers and patches was a part of me. "What the hell is wrong with my cut? If some bitch can't handle me in my cut, she sure as shit doesn't belong with me," I growled.

"Not what I meant Lo. That girl has been hurt, you can see it in her eyes. You'll have to be gentle with her."

My phone dinged. I dug it out of my pocket and saw my mom had texted me. "You texted me her number, ma?"

"Use it, Logan, fix her," she insisted.

I sighed and pulled into mom's driveway. "Maybe she doesn't want to be fixed, ma. Maybe she has a boyfriend."

"She doesn't. Call her, or I'll do it for you," she ordered.

I knew my mom's threat wasn't idle. She totally would call Meg and ask her out for me. Fuck. "I'll help you get your shit inside, ma."

"I'll make you lunch, and then you can call Meg," Ma said, as she jumped out of the truck and grabbed some bags.

I watched her walk into her house and looked at the message she had sent me. I saved Meg's number to my phone and grabbed the rest of Ma's shit and headed into the house.

Looked like I was calling Meg.

=======

Winter Travers is a devoted wife, mother, and aunt turned author. With stories always flowing around her, Loving Lo was the one story that had to get out (new ones are knocking on the door daily now).

Winter loves to bake and cook when she isn't at work, zipping around on her forklift. She also has an addiction to anything MC related, her dog Thunder, and Mexican food (Tamales!)

Winter has two new series planned for 2017, Powerhouse Martial Arts Series and the Brawl Doll Series, with about 10 other series floating around in her head.

Winter loves to stay connected with her readers.
Don't hesitate to reach out and contact her.
www.facebook.com/wintertravers
Twitter: @WinterTravers
Instagram: @WinterTravers
http://500145315.wix.com/wintertravers

Made in the USA
Middletown, DE
13 February 2025

71173009R00148